This poignant and deeply moving story of orphans ~~

to me. Their separation at an early age, and Alisha's determination and pursuit of music, paralleled with her brothers' struggles and triumphs will stay with you long after you've finished their story. Its authenticity will touch your heart as it takes you into the lives of the amazing people who enter their lives to nurture and to heal. I loved this book.

—*Mary Ball, Alexandria, VA*

Alice Heath-Gladden reinvented her actual life to the point that I learned she lived in an orphanage only when she fictionalized herself in this book. So it is no surprise that *What About the Children?* is filled with enduring characters born of her imagination, and reveals a strength I always knew she had.

—*Sue Lachnit-Plott, Cumming, GA*

In a time when fiction is repetitious and it seems there's nothing new, Ms. Heath-Gladden has created a story that feels fresh and original. The narrative is gripping, and Angeni's descent into a suicidal state is haunting.

—*Julia Wooster, Instructor of English*
Jacksonville State University, AL

What About the Children?

Alice Neash-Glodden

Alice Heath-Gladden

What About the *Children?*

Two left,
three were taken,
and one was left behind.

*Can siblings separated by
death and abandonment
find their way
back home again?*

TATE PUBLISHING *&* *Enterprises*

Published by Tate Publishing & Enterprises, LLC
127 E. Trade Center Terrace | Mustang, Oklahoma 73064 USA
1.888.361.9473 | www.tatepublishing.com

Tate Publishing is committed to excellence in the publishing industry. The company reflects the philosophy established by the founders, based on Psalm 68:11,
"The Lord gave the word and great was the company of those who published it."

Book design copyright © 2009 by Tate Publishing, LLC. All rights reserved.
Cover design by Chris Castor
Interior design by Cole Roberts

Published in the United States of America

ISBN: 978-1-60696-675-4
Fiction / Family Life
09.04.19

Acknowledgement

To my family, John David (JD) and Rhonda Heath, Jason and Jennifer Gladden, and granddaughters Emily and Natalie Heath for their love and devotion; to the Lydia and Mannie Tucker family for counting me as one of their own; in memoriam of Robert Lee and Buena Vista Angel, birth parents; to author Elizabeth Ridley for broadening my vision of the story; to readers Jean Duke, Rhonda Heath, Mary Ball, William Gladden, Sue Lochnit-Plott, and Julia Wooster for their candid suggestions and support; to Tate Publications editor, Kalyn McAlister for her professional touch and for making my first novel shine; to Tate graphics designer, Chris Castor for covering my book with creative style; to my enduring friends and colleagues for encouraging me, each in his or her own way, to go the distance; and to the Spirit for inspiration and tenacity—to all, I am forever grateful.

Prologue

The massive doors of Carnegie Hall swung open. A bronze phoenix, goddess of all winged creatures, was perched in the south pergola facing its magical partner, the dragon, poised to leap out of the north pergola. In 1891, a Chinese diplomat presented the symbols of the ultimate yin and yang of fame and fortune to the mayor of New York City in honor of the grand opening of Carnegie Hall's first auditorium, Carnegie Lyceum Recital Hall. For seventy years, theater patrons marveled at the detail in the symbols and persisted in rubbing the famous representation of rebirth, wearing away the bronze with their wishes for good luck. A June 22, 1961, New York *Tribune* commentary posted under glass on the lobby wall, speculated that the destiny of twenty-four-year-old pianist Alisha Copper depended on her performance that night.

When the program ended, a delighted audience, unaware of the drama awaiting Miss Copper, streamed out of Carnegie into a starlit evening, chatting and assuring one another that the performer had indeed met the challenge of *Tribune.*

Alisha stepped backward and stood absorbing

the stillness. She moved to the piano she had left only moments ago and softly caressed the keyboard, at last feeling release. When she turned to go, a voice called her name. She looked up and smiled, thinking it was the producer, a legend in the music business who had coached her for this performance with the passion of a lover. Alisha marveled at his patience but also at his ability to elicit that final sliver of flair they both knew she held back. Her smile faded though, when she saw that it was the *Tribune* reporter, whose legendary reviews made many musicians famous, but were also responsible for countless others receding into oblivion.

Alisha stood motionless, holding onto the piano to steady her trembling hands. The stage crew removed props and began turning off overhead lights, one by one. The footlights dimmed until Alisha could see only a silhouette of the reporter coming toward her. The curtain parted and a second silhouette joined the reporter. Engulfed in silent darkness for what seemed like an eternity, her only thought was, *this is it; he didn't like it.*

For an instant, Alisha was five years old again, sitting at the old, upright mahogany piano, daring herself to touch the keyboard just hard enough to hear how the notes sounded. She could feel the air against her legs swinging in time with the song in her head, hear herself arguing with an unseen witness who insisted she could play and demanded that she must.

In due course, she had played her songs, one note at a time at first, then all the notes until she played her melodies in an inimitable style, branding her music.

Since then, she practiced, studied, wept, and struggled—
at times even against the thought of success—to arrive
at this point in her life. She knew her inherited fortitude
triumphed over the fearless shadows born of her
beginnings and realized the direction of her life unfolded
during that first encounter with the piano and the unseen
witness. The journey had surely been long. Must she—
could she—turn away from the truest knight in shining
armor she had ever known: her music, her love.

Chapter 1

Angeni Millwater Copper eased out of bed, pulled the curtains aside, and raised the window shade. The rain that had pelted the tin roof for a week had finally stopped while she slept. *Just in time,* she thought, watching the clouds float away leaving a clear blue sky; *the moon will be full tonight.* Angeni smiled, remembering her older sister, Kate, begging the moon to shine on her for good luck. As a little girl, one of Angeni's favorite games was running between Kate and the moonlight to steal her sister's good fortune. When Angeni married, her husband, Asyah, indulged her fascination for the moon. He altered the bedroom window by hinging two window frames to swing outward and hook to the outside wall. Their village of Koasati Springs, Tennessee, was set on a western plateau of the Appalachian Mountains. Angeni could open her window, turn off the light, and feel like she *was* outside in the night, watching the moon float across the sky and over the horizon.

Angeni, awaiting the birth of her fourth child, paused at the calendar, checked off May 11, 1935, and slipped back into bed to read and wait out the day. As her head hit the pillow, the first pain stabbed her like a knife. She grabbed two rails on the iron headboard, clenched her teeth, and choked back an agonizing wail. When the pain subsided, Angeni slid deep into the featherbed, recalling her vow of six years ago never to become pregnant again. In an attempt to delay the next pain, she curled up and took slight delicate breaths, but the next pain came too fast and too brutal to suppress. She grasped the rails again and screamed—from the excruciating pain, but also from the hopelessness of the long hours that lay ahead.

After an early supper, Asyah sent his sons, Robert, Martin, and James, outside to play. The rain kept the boys confined to the house for a week, and they could no longer restrain their energy. Asyah began clearing the table and realized they would soon need more plates— one twin or the other seemed determined to break a dish every time they helped in the kitchen.

Jolted by Angeni's scream, the dish Asyah held slipped out of his hands and broke into pieces on the brick floor. "Now we're down to four," he mumbled, swiping the broken glass into the corner with his shoe. He grabbed a cloth, wet it with cold water, and rushed to the bedroom, folding the cloth on the way. Asyah pulled a chair close to the bed, ready to cool his wife's forehead, but the agony on her face wilted his fright into compassion. He laid the towel aside, stretched out beside Angeni and pulled her close to wait for the next pain. When it came, he offered his arms for her to grasp instead of the bed rails.

Between Angeni's pains, Asyah relaxed and uninvited memories came. He thought about growing up in this house with his twin brother, Daniel. Until Daniel, at age fifteen, contracted leukemia and died a year later, the boys were constant companions, exploring woods and caves, swimming in the creeks, fishing and hunting. Three years later, Asyah's sister, Sarah married and moved away, and within the next two years, both his parents died. With the aloneness unbearable, Asyah sought friendships at church and social gatherings, and by age twenty, he with his banjo found a comfortable way of life playing and singing in small bands.

Angeni grasped his arms again, shocking Asyah out of his reverie. When at last she relaxed her grip, he eased out of bed and looked out the window to make sure the boys were still in sight and then returned to Angeni's side.

Soon, Asyah's closest friends began marrying and having children, inspiring him with a desire to have a family of his own. In church one Sunday, he sat in the pew behind Kate Millwater, an "old maid," and her younger sister, Angeni, both descendants of the local Coushatta Indian tribe. Although he had no designs on Kate, he could count on the Millwater sisters to distract him from a boring sermon. He grinned, remembering the teenage Angeni twiddling with the rose that Kate insisted she wear. He would count to ten—the magic number—when Kate would elbow her sister and whisper angrily, "Leave it alone," and Angeni would scowl. Then almost overnight, Angeni matured into a beautiful young woman with black hair and dark, mysterious eyes.

When Angeni turned fifteen and began looking grown-up, it was evident that Kate had lost the last vestige of her authority. Asyah remembered the Sunday when after the ten-count jab, Angeni flung the rose under her pew and crossed her arms in defiance. He had retrieved the rose and placed it gently over her ear. When she turned to him and mouthed, "Thank you," he realized the *girl* was becoming a *woman*. Her spirit rushed over him like a tempest. A few Sundays later, Asyah boldly sat next to Angeni, and they stole glances at each other, much to Kate's annoyance. Asyah and Angeni had fallen in love, and the more Kate tried to protect her sister, the more impatient Asyah became. Then, at the spring picnic, he realized Kate was trying a new ploy: portraying herself as his prospective bride. Asyah knew he must act—and soon. As prearranged, before dawn on Angeni's sixteenth birthday, Asyah stopped the horse and buggy a safe distance from the Millwater home, tapped on Angeni's bedroom window, and took the suitcase she lifted out ahead of herself. They returned to Asyah's house, left the suitcase, picked up the marriage license Asyah had forgotten, and went to the preacher's house. They were married before noon that day, infuriating Kate for the rest of her life.

A knock on the door startled Asyah out of his daydream. Star, an Indian midwife who concealed a medicine bag under her shawl, was intermittently knocking on the door and shuffling back and forth across the porch. Star was as wide as she was tall, and her braids fell almost to her knees. Life had bent her, and weather had furrowed her once-handsome face—but those depending on her welcomed her calm presence and the relief she brought in her medicine bag. Star and Angeni were distant cousins, and Star made a habit of visiting

Angeni whenever she came near the Copper home. She had delivered Robert and the twins, and upon learning Angeni was with child again, Star became very protective of her cousin.

Asyah led Star to Angeni's bedside. She touched Angeni's brow and whispered to her in their native tongue. When she finally saw a hint of a smile, she hurried to the kitchen to brew a concoction she used to ease a long and painful birth. After giving Angeni the first sip of tonic, Star spoke to Asyah in a sign language they had worked out through the years, instructing him to force Angeni to sip tonic after each pain. She indicated she would return the following afternoon. When Asyah asked how she would know it was time to come back, Star gave him a patronizing smile, patted his arm, and left.

Asyah sent the boys to bed early and stayed near the bed to give Angeni tonic. For a while, he stood at the window and watched the full moon drift across the sky while Angeni drifted in and out of sleep. Late into the night, he eased into bed and slept as she slept, feeling her temperature rise and fall in the dampness of the cloth. Asyah suspected the tonic did more than ease pain.

The day Alisha Copper was born marked the end of the coldest winter ever seen in the foothills of the Appalachian Mountains. On May 12, blue skies and a bright sun announced the arrival of spring. A warm breeze blew away the morning chill and a creek pulled away from the river like a boisterous child, skittering over rocks into a meadow near the Copper home as it raced through the foothills to reunite with the mother river.

Generations of the Copper family had lived in Koasati Springs on their lush and unspoiled land, accepting the consequences and reaping the rewards of living in the mountains they loved. Asyah was clever enough to survive the harshest of climates, but the past winter had also tested his physical endurance. He shoveled snow and rushed through farm chores that he normally could stretch into hours while horsing around with his three sons. On the worst days, the little school house closed and the family stayed huddled near the fireplace. Asyah played banjo, and the boys made up silly songs. He began teaching James and Martin, the six-year-old twins, to weave baskets and under a watchful eye showed Robert, the nine-year-old, how to carve the handles with a pocketknife. After the twins went to bed, Asyah and Robert would burn the Copper name on the rim and stack the baskets in the hallway for market. The Copper family not only survived the long, harsh winter, they thrived.

The Copper boys inherited a curious mix of features from Asyah and Angeni. At birth, Robert looked like a miniature Asyah and had the serious look of his mother, which helped now when he tried to boss the twins around. As he grew, Robert began punctuating his mannerisms with Asyah's personality. The twins had brown hair and blue eyes like their father, and Angeni's high cheekbones and mellow complexion. They were identical except each had a quarter-inch birthmark on the side of their face opposite their twin. James had piercing eyes and a hint of clairvoyance, but with charm and charisma that melded the circle of brothers.

On the big day, the brothers were too excited to sit and play. They raced from the hallway outside their parents' bedroom to the yard, then back again to the hallway. They listened for the cry of a baby, their signal that a new brother or sister had arrived, but so far, they had only heard their mother screaming.

"Want to play baseball?" Robert asked, anxious to distance himself from his mother's screams.

"If I can pitch," James said.

"It's my time to hit," Martin said.

"Okay, come on. I'll catch first," Robert said.

By mid-afternoon, they had finished their baseball game, eaten lunch, and puzzled over how a baby was born.

"All I know is, I wish mama didn't have to hurt," Robert said.

At sunset, they ambled back to the hallway, and Robert stood with his ear pressed against the bedroom door. Martin sat on the floor with his ear over a crack in the door, and James lay flat peeking through a knothole he had punched out of the door. After having nothing to report but his father's feet going back and forth, James said, "Let's play marbles; I'm tired of waiting."

"Me too," Robert agreed and spread a quilt on the floor. He dumped a sack of marbles on the quilt, and the boys turned the hallway into a shooting gallery.

James let his brothers go first and watched for his father through the knothole. Finally, he whispered loudly, "Here he comes; get on the quilt." They scurried onto the quilt, and James grabbed a handful of marbles as his father came bursting out.

"James, keep the marbles on the quilt," Asyah said. "When your mother hears them rolling on the floor, she gets agitated. Martin, help put the marbles back on the quilt."

"The marbles won't roll on the quilt, Daddy," Robert said, crawling and tossing the remaining marbles one by one for Martin and James to trap on the quilt.

"Robert, settle down and read your book. If you boys will be quiet and listen to your brother read, you'll soon hear a baby cry, and you'll have a new brother or sister."

"They won't listen to me, Daddy."

"Then find something else to do. Go outside but stay in the yard; it'll be dark soon." Filled with nervous energy, Asyah straightened the family photograph hanging near the bedroom door and lined up the baskets against the wall on his way back to Angeni.

The boys ambled back to their listening posts.

"We'll have to get another picture made with the new baby," Martin said, looking through the door crevice with one eye.

"Robert, read something like Daddy said, so the baby will cry," James said.

"Ha, ha," Robert replied without moving.

"Let's go outside and wait for Miss Alma; she'll have food," James said.

Jesse and Alma Green, the Coppers' nearest neighbors, arrived with a basket of food early in the day and, based on history, more plates. The Greens appeared to have physically grown in opposite directions through their forty years of marriage. Jesse was stocky and hunched by age, with a shock of white hair that boldly contrasted with his ruddy complexion. Alma was tall and thin, fair skinned and dark haired. Even after struggling through the harsh Appalachian winters, the Greens retained their youthful vitality. Alma set the table with new plates and food and ironed shirts while she waited for the boys to finish supper and return to their listening post, and then she cleaned up the kitchen before she and Jesse went home for the evening.

At dusk, Asyah stood at the bedroom window, watching the full moon rise over the mountaintop, preparing to dominate the night sky. He heard a slight rustle in the woods and saw Star shuffling toward the house. As Asyah left the bedroom to admit her, he gently closed the bedroom door and tiptoed past the boys, whispering, "Shhh, be quiet. Put the marbles back on the quilt."

"They're on the quilt, Daddy," Robert said without looking up.

After Asyah and Star disappeared into the bedroom, the boys became more agitated and began knocking on the door.

"What's Mama doing in there?" James asked through the knothole.

Martin called out through his crevice, "When is she coming out?"

"Daddy, we just want to see her," Robert insisted.

Asyah came out and sat on the floor with his sons. "Please be patient," he said. "Your mother is sleeping off and on—when you're quiet. Try to remember, she's giving birth."

"Giving birth, what's that?" James asked.

"It means how you are getting a new brother or sister;

and it means how you were born. Star's a good midwife—sort of like a doctor—your mother's going to be fine," Asyah said tentatively.

"We just want to see her, Daddy," Robert repeated, deaf to his father's pleading.

Asyah surrendered. "Okay. *Okay.* Come in for *one* minute—no more—and walk," he said, too late, for as soon as he opened the door, the twins rushed in and jumped onto the bed near their mother.

Robert stood at the bedside and began straightening his mother's matted hair and looked angrily at Star and said, "You look awful, Mama; what's she doing to you?"

Angeni opened her mouth to speak just as a pain struck. Star moved closer to the bed, holding up a blanket, her eyes wide with fear. When the twins attempted to move out of the way, they bumped Angeni's leg, causing her to cry and groan louder.

"Get off the bed," Robert yelled, yanking his brothers to the floor.

The twins yelped and started onto the bed again, but this time, Asyah pulled them away. "That's enough!" he whispered loudly and ushered his sons out of the room.

Robert returned to his listening post, and the twins alternately played marbles and wallowed aimlessly on the quilt. An hour later, Robert yelled, "Listen! Hear that? The baby's crying!"

James scrambled for a marble rolling off the quilt, and before taking his place at the knothole, he jumped up and down, reporting, "It's a sister! It's a sister!"

Martin echoed James. "Yeah, it's a sister! Yeah! Yeah!"

"You don't know, James," Robert said, laughing, his ear still to the door.

"Yes, I do."

"He does too," Martin confirmed.

Asyah held his exhausted wife close while Star attended to the newborn baby. He listened to the boys argue, and when the noise escalated, he left his wife and daughter in Star's care, closed the door softly, and gathered up the twins under his arms. "Come out on the porch with me; you have a brand new sister."

"Told you, Robert," James said, sticking out his tongue.

"Let go; put us down, we want to see our sister," the twins pleaded, trying to wriggle out of their father's grasp.

"Shhh, your mother needs rest. Before you go to bed, I'll ask Star to bring your sister out so you can see her—I promise. Let's sit on the porch, and I'll tell you a story about your mother."

"Bring the banjo, Daddy, and sing us a song," James said.

"Okay. Robert, get the banjo," Asyah said, hurrying to the porch with the twins.

Robert stopped at the hallway table and carefully removed the banjo from its case. He liked the smell of the old worn leather. The red velvet lining was almost threadbare, but the banjo always reminded him of the story he'd heard so often from his father, he could now tell it himself. When Daddy was still a baby, Grandma Copper gave him a spoon and a cooking pot to keep him playing near her on the kitchen floor. Daddy surprised Grandma by tapping the spoon on the pot a certain way, resulting in unusual melodic sounds. When he started walking, Daddy followed Grandpa to the barnyard and became mesmerized by the jangle and tinkle of cowbells. Grandpa was scared when Daddy first walked close enough to the cows to remove their bells, but on and on Daddy went, playing with different bells, making new sounds. Grandpa Copper gave Daddy the banjo for his fourth birthday to keep him safe and to keep the cowbells in their proper places. As Grandma routinely declared, Daddy had an ear for music. His brother, Daniel, danced while Daddy played the banjo. After Daniel died, followed by Grandma and Grandpa, local musicians began inviting Daddy to play in their band. When he got older, he also developed a powerful baritone voice, and everyone wanted to hear Daddy sing. The end of the story made Robert feel especially good. Daddy would say, "Music was my life—that is, until you boys came along."

Asyah, relieved that the day's ordeal was over and that Angeni was now resting, moved his rocker so it faced the swing and took the banjo. Robert sat in the center of the swing, and James and Martin found their places on each side.

"Move back, Daddy; we can't swing," James said.

"I know," Asyah said, smiling and stretching his legs out on each side of Robert, immobilizing the swing. He leaned back, positioned the banjo on his chest, let his fingers find their home strings, and strummed in rhythm. "Sit still and listen for a while."

"But Daddy, I want to swi—" James began.

"Shut up, James, I want to hear a story," Robert said.

"Okay, okay, sons of mine, listen up, and I'll tell you the story about your mother and Star." Asyah began the story, interspersed by strums and bursts from the banjo. "One night, probably a night like tonight, it was springtime. The sky was clear. The moon was full. The stars twinkled. Star was there. August the fifteenth, 1908. That night was the night your mother was born. Soon after she was born, your grandparents moved off the reservation into Koasati Springs. They were among the first Indians in this area to move into a house."

Martin leaned forward. "Why did they move? It would be fun to camp out every day."

Robert elbowed his brother. "He said to be quiet."

"Ouch. No he didn't. He said to sit still and listen up. I'm listening."

"Well, Martin," Asyah strummed a short burst. "I suppose after the Indians began working outside the reservation and saw how much better it was to live in a house, they began to dislike camping so much and built houses for themselves. Your great-grandparents were *real* Indians, and they were real *old* Indians when your mother was born—sixty-five years old, in fact. Your mother's grandmother was a midwife, and Star learned to be a midwife from her. Star was your grandmother's sister's daughter—your cousin."

"You mean that weird old woman is kin to us?" Robert asked, frowning.

Asyah chuckled. "She sure is, son, a third cousin, but still a cousin."

"Daddy, there're some people I don't want to be kin to."

"Too bad; we don't get to choose our kinfolk, Robert. Most families around here are related to Indians in some way." Asyah leaned back in the rocker and strummed the banjo in barely audible sounds, slowly rocking in rhythm, the swing following. Elements of the day blended with the night—the swing, the rocker, the voices, the banjo— all moving and flowing in synchrony.

"Daddy, finish telling us about Mama," Robert said. "James and Martin, don't talk."

Asyah stopped the swing and rocker and continued his story. "Indians had ancient beliefs we find strange today. For example, they believed that children born to older parents, as your mother was, came to earth to ease their parents into their next life. That's how your mother got her name: Angeni, the '*Spirit Angel.*'" Asyah sat silently, playing softly, until the boys became restless. "Well anyway," he continued, "your mother lived up to the legend, however strange it now seems to give such a big job to a little girl. When your mother was six years old—the same age you are, James and Martin—she found her parents holding hands, lying side by side under a very old oak tree near the riverbank. Both were dead. There was no obvious reason for either of their deaths, but hardly anyone was surprised because everyone believed the story about the spirit angel and your mother's supposed purpose. Your mother said she remembers the sound of the Indians drumming that day, just like it was yesterday."

James leaned forward. "Did they live that close to her?"

"Not everyone left the reservation. Some of the

older Indians stayed with their tribe living by the beliefs and customs of their ancestors. Anyway, you can hear drumming without being real close. If you're downwind or on the same side of the mountain, you can easily hear the drums. Indians have a special way of drumming to show respect for a person who has died, and they drummed a funeral cadence for your grandparents. By all accounts, Grandpa and Grandma Stillwater eased into their next life, and your mother got the credit. That's why your mother and Star like each other—they're family. Star's also a good midwife. She delivers most of the babies in this area. She even delivered you boys."

"Ah, hah, Robert, she touched you, she touched you," James teased, as he jumped out of the swing and ran into the yard.

"You too, James," Martin said, running after his brother.

"Don't tell anybody she's kin to us, Daddy; she's weird," Robert pleaded before following his brothers, yelling, "Come back, James; let's play chase; you're *it*."

"She's just *different*," Asyah called out, explaining to a son no longer listening.

Asyah turned his rocker so he could watch his sons play, and he leaned forward strumming his banjo, this time in celebration. The banjo, harmonizing with Asyah's smooth, baritone voice, echoed through the mountains as he sang *Blue Moon of Kentucky* to a chorus of crickets, night frogs, and young boys squealing in the moonlight. Afterwards, he stretched his legs out, pushed back in the rocker, and gazed at the stars, certain they were winking at him. A silvery moon shone on the boys, now quieted by music and darkness, darting in and out of the night shadows. Asyah felt at one with the night sky, the moon and the stars, and made a secret pact of indebtedness with that exclusive world, savoring the sweet relief of the day's end and the arrival of his daughter.

Suddenly, Asyah laughed and called to his sons, "Hey, boys, listen to this. Star wants to name your sister *Songbird*."

Martin ran to the edge of the porch, winded from play. "Why?" he asked, but before his father could answer, he ran toward James. "We don't want to name our sister Songbird, do we, James?"

James fell on the grass, laughing and rolling his head from side to side, agreeing with Martin.

When the boys settled down, Asyah said, "Because that big old moon you see up there was shining through the window when your sister was born, and a songbird perched on the windowsill in the moonlight. I thought the moon was shining just for our new baby, but Star believes the songbird is her companion for life and foretells her future."

Robert hurried closer to the porch. "It's a pretty moon, Daddy, but our sister would be mad if she found out we named her *Songbird*—oh, I get it, another Indian rule, right?"

"As a matter of fact, it is."

"You didn't let Star name her *that* did you?"

"Oh, no, I know better than that, but actually, the songbird was a cardinal, and my mother used to say cardinals keep singing until they learn their true song. And, when they learn their song, they sing it again and again. That wouldn't be so bad, would it?"

James stopped laughing and ran to the porch. "No, Daddy, but you can't name her after a bird; I'll bet she looks like an angel."

"That means she looks like Mama," Robert declared. "Let's name her *Angel*."

"But, Robert, what if she looks like Daddy?" James asked, and everyone laughed.

Asyah was finally relaxed. "Hey, whatcha mean? You boys look like me. Anyway, we're handsome men. Maybe she *will* look like us ... wouldn't that be something?"

James looked at Robert and Martin in mock panic.

"Did you boys eat supper?" Asyah asked.

Martin nodded his head yes. "Robert made us eat Miss Alma's yucky green beans, but I'm hungry again."

"Me too," James said.

Asyah tousled Robert's hair. "Thanks, son ... you need a haircut." Asyah stood and slapped his forehead. "How could I forget? Let's go cut the chocolate cake and see if it's better than green beans."

"I knew it," James said. "Where'd you hide it? I looked everywhere. I knew Miss Alma would bring something better than all that stuff on the table."

"She brought new plates too," Robert said on the way to the kitchen, glancing up at his father, who looked straight ahead, grinning sheepishly.

After they had their fill of cake, Asyah sent the boys to get ready for bed. He built a small fire in the fireplace and then retrieved his banjo from the porch, carefully stowing it in the case for another time.

"Remember your promise, Daddy," Robert said from

the doorway then dashed back to help his brothers with their pajamas.

Star followed Asyah to the fireplace, with the new baby wrapped in a clean white blanket, belying the difficult birth by which she had entered the world. Asyah called to the boys, "Hurry up in there." Beaming, Asyah sat in his chair and held his arms out like a cradle to receive his daughter.

Robert tiptoed in first, arms outstretched to restrain Martin and James. This time, the twins, with shining faces and hair slicked back to conceal the length, yielded to Robert's guiding arms. The three boys crept delicately to the fireplace and gathered around their new sister.

James was shocked. "Why is she red and wrinkly? She sure don't look like *me!*"

"Don't let Mr. Green make a picture of her looking like *that!*" Martin demanded.

Asyah hugged his new daughter close. "Don't you listen to them," he said to her. "You're beautiful. Martin, look how sweet she is, cute little hands and fingers and tiny little fingernails." He pulled back the blanket. "Look, she has pinkies just like yours, and do you know the best thing about her?"

"What?" the twins asked anxiously.

"Why, she's ours," Asyah said.

"Can I hold her?" Robert asked.

"No!" James shouted, "That's stupid, you'll break her."

"Shhh," Asyah whispered. "We won't break her," he quietly assured his sons while gazing at his daughter, his eyes filling with tears.

"Sing her a song, Daddy," Robert said.

"Okay, if you'll sing with me, but softly now, and don't dance. Let her get to know us gradually."

Chapter 2

For three months, Angeni lingered in bed most of the time, feeling guilty because she was not well enough to help Asyah run the household or care for the children. After Star left, Angeni sent Asyah to get Doctor Ansley Russet, the only doctor in Koasati Springs. Dr. Russet reported she must never have another child but that with extended bed rest she could gradually recover. The prognosis was fine with Angeni. She was terrified at the thought of bearing another child and felt a pressing need for stillness. Angeni followed Doctor Russet's advice, and her body gradually began to heal. After Star's weekly visits, her spirit was rejuvenated, too.

After much discussion and argument, Asyah and the boys had settled on the Indian name Alisha, after the baby's grandmother. Alisha was three months old when Dr. Russet came by to check on Angeni's progress and to complete the birth certificate. Angeni argued with Asyah about the cardinal legend, insisting on adding Moon to Alisha's name on the birth certificate, and Asyah consented only when his wife promised to tell no one but Star. The following week, after listening to Star's low, soothing voice for a while, Angeni asked her to rock Alisha *Moon*. A rare smile filled Star's face as she rocked Alisha and whispered endearments.

Holding Alisha in one arm, Star brewed a fresh pot of tea, all the time pointing, grunting, and shaking her head, admonishing Asyah and the boys to watch over Angeni and to keep her in bed another month. With the tea brewed, Star laid Alisha next to Angeni and whispered a native Cherokee blessing, *"May the warm winds of Heaven blow softly on your home, and the Great Spirit bless all who enter there,"* and then she slipped out of the house. Alisha paused from nursing, stretched her spidery legs and arms, and made cooing sounds. Angeni watched and tried to imagine her own life beginning again. Soon, mother and daughter fell into a slumber, faces so near that their breath ebbed and flowed almost as one being.

On August the fifteenth, Angeni awoke to the sounds of the boys opening the door and sweet smells drifting into the room. She watched the cake appear first, as if it was suspended in midair, then arms followed by Robert grinning and walking gingerly through the door. *I almost forgot my own birthday,* she thought. Just as Robert cleared the door, James and Martin raced around him like the wind, bumping his arm, nearly causing him to drop the cake.

James yelled, "We want to see our sister!"

"Yeah, wake her up!" Martin said, racing James to the bed.

Asyah, close behind, rescued the lopsided cake he had helped the boys make to celebrate Angeni's twenty-seventh birthday. He had also cut the boys' hair, and they wore freshly ironed shirts. Asyah placed the cake on the trunk at the end of the bed, stacked pillows behind

Angeni, and presented her with a rosebud, the first one from a rosebush he had planted for Alisha the day she was born.

Robert held the cake steady while his father lit the candles. When Asyah presented the cake, Angeni tried unsuccessfully to blow out the candles.

"I'll blow them out for you, Mama," Robert said and rushed forward to help, the twins close behind.

Asyah served the cake and returned the dishes to the kitchen. He went back and slipped into bed next to his wife. James squeezed in between his mother and Alisha, and Martin crawled in on the other side. Robert sat cross-legged at Alisha's feet, pointing out to Martin that Sis was no longer red and wrinkly and declaring that she looked like him. "I think we should call her Sis," Robert said, caressing his sister's tiny feet.

Angeni smiled weakly at her eldest son. "I like that."

After the birthday celebration, Asyah planned something each day to keep the boys away from their mother, insisting that his wife would recover, given enough rest, trying to ignore an ever-present fear that she might not. Asyah had sold all the baskets he and the boys made that winter, so most days, they gathered river cane, sweet grass, oak and ash logs to make into splints for new baskets that they would make the following winter. During the noisy activities of the day, Asyah patiently taught his sons elementary skills of tending the garden, mending fences, chopping firewood, and caring for the farm animals. Following Asyah's lead, they jumped into the cool creek water and swam, ending their day with fun.

Wherever Asyah went, whatever he did, Robert, Martin, and James trailed close behind.

Asyah Copper loved his family and his life, and it never crossed his mind that death would enter without knocking. Even so, early on an August morning, with his sons following him out the back door, Asyah clutched his chest and mumbled, "Oh no, *not now…*" and tumbled down the porch steps, his heart surrendering its last beat before he ended the fall.

Angeni heard Robert scream, "Mama, come quick! Come help Daddy!"

Robert sat on the ground, lifted his father's head onto his lap, and brushed his hair off his forehead, screaming, "Daddy, Daddy, answer me!"

James and Martin cried and pulled on their father's arms, trying to lift him up. James said, "Get up, Daddy, get up. We have to find the baby deer today."

James gave up first. Martin followed his lead, slumping to the ground, sitting silent and rigid, and staring incredulously at Asyah's ashen face.

Angeni threw on a robe, ran to the porch, took one look at her husband, and realized he was dead. She fell to the ground with the boys, clutched her husband, and gently closed his eyes. Angeni found James' eyes and shivered, feeling a cold, dark nothingness seep through her, creating a void not even her children could fill. Without taking her eyes off James, Angeni said, "Robert, go get Jesse and Alma."

After the funeral, Angeni remembered few details of the week, and time became indecipherable. At daybreak, she sat on the porch and envisioned her husband alive. Like the morning mist dissipating in the sun, the strength Angeni had gained since Alisha's birth began to vanish, leaving her eyes dark and hollow and her skin pale.

When school started the first week of September, Jesse and Alma began driving the boys to and from school, leaving Angeni alone with Alisha during the weekdays. After school, the twins played, but Robert sat on the back porch steps watching his mother through the pink and yellow roses that surrounded the family cemetery. At dusk, he saw her kneel at his father's grave and watched darkness transform her into a shadow. He then walked to the cemetery, took his mother's hand, and led her back to the house. "Come on, Mama. Sis is crying for you."

After their parents died, Angeni and her sister Kate continued to live in their family home. Kate had objected to her marriage to Asyah, but still, Angeni could not understand why Kate had not attended his funeral or visited in such a long time. Later Angeni wrote her a letter, but Kate had not responded. Seemingly forgotten by the sister she loved, Angeni longed for Kate's companionship and help with the children. When help did not come, hopelessness did, and she began to imagine other ways to give her children a better life.

Robert slowly grew angry as he struggled to assume the man-of-the-house role. He did his best, but the tasks of play often called out more forcefully than work and shielded him from taking on adult responsibilities for which he was unprepared. Every now and then, he would become a child again, but when he tucked Alisha into bed and she turned her head toward her mother, Robert would watch his mother's hollow stare shift from the ceiling to his sister, and the compulsion to protect his siblings grew stronger.

Fall arrived. The days began to cool. With the harshness of winter coming soon, Angeni waited indifferently for each day to end and felt increasingly anxious as the gold and red autumn leaves fell, leaving the trees barren like the family resources. Her confidence had depended on her husband's presence, and her own unassuming nature would not allow her to ask for help.

By the first of November, Angeni had taken the last of the medicine Star left and felt transformed into a person she no longer knew—a stranger. Angeni was losing control and reality was slowly disappearing. One morning, she sat on the back porch steps and listened to the "stranger" make a decision from which it became impossible to go back. From then on, the stranger arose each morning, strong and healthy, knowing what she had to do.

Star stopped by to visit Angeni on her way across the mountain to deliver another child. She took one look at Angeni and knew the medicine was gone. When Star told Angeni she would bring more medicine on her return, the stranger asked "What medicine?"

Jesse and Alma Green came for their usual Sunday visit. Angeni watched the stranger entertain Alma as if everything was right with the world. She constantly heard the stranger's reassuring words: *You're all right now.* The Greens were so impressed with Angeni's energetic behavior and the cleanliness and orderliness of the house that they were certain she was recovering physically and that her mourning would run its due course.

The following week, the stranger was convinced that it was time to get everything in order. Angeni was amazed at the stranger's enthusiasm as she cleaned the house and mended, washed, and ironed the children's clothing. On Sunday morning, Angeni went about the house singing while getting ready for the day. When she finished packing the picnic basket and saw no food left in the cupboard, the stranger shrugged and slipped off to the cemetery. She clipped the roses and threw them as far as she could into the woods, saying "I hate roses" as she threw each stem. Around noon, Angeni buttoned the boys' sweaters to ward off the fall chill, and the stranger insisted it was time to leave for the picnic. As Angeni closed the front door, worn from decades of use, she saw dirt on the edge. The stranger hissed, *you missed a spot,* and tried to clean the smudge with her finger, but Angeni pushed her aside and caressed the door instead.

"Come on, Mama, let's go," Robert called, and they headed off to the meadow.

Angeni looked up at the sparkling blue sky and found she was enjoying the stroll on the familiar path. She laughed at her children running back and forth, giggling and crushing leaves to amplify the sound. Angeni leisurely followed, swinging the picnic basket and carrying her baby, but without warning, the stranger rushed to catch up with the boys.

When they arrived at the edge of the meadow, a short distance from the river, Angeni was struck by the beauty and stillness. She stopped in awe of the sweet smell of fallen leaves and the cool breeze on her face. "Wait," she said. "Your father and I called this path our special place on earth. We took a walk here on the day we married. Asyah loved the woods, especially this meadow."

The boys had their own stories. "This is where we've been looking for a baby deer," James said.

"Doe," Robert corrected.

"Daddy taught us how to swim in that creek, Mama, right over there," Martin added.

Robert pointed to where the creek left the river to jut out toward the meadow. "Mama, remember that fish we had for supper the night before Daddy di—? Well, anyway, that's where we caught it."

James jumped up and down. "Robert, help me catch a fish!"

Martin jumped and echoed James, "Me too, Robert, me too!"

Angeni became rigid, and the stranger said curtly, "No, not today. You can fish later. Come on, we're on a picnic."

James, shocked by his mother's sudden change in mood, moved away and looked toward Robert for a response.

Robert wanted to show his brothers how to bait a hook, but to indulge his mother, he said, "Come on, let's go play in the leaves," and he ran into the meadow ahead of the twins.

When James looked back, his mother had turned her head away. The stranger spread a blanket for the baby, and began arranging the food. Six-month-old Alisha sat up and kept her eyes on the activity and sounds of her brothers. They raked up a pile of leaves with their hands, jumped in, wallowed around, raked up the leaves, and then jumped in again. Alisha followed the activity with her eyes, as her brothers chased each other around the meadow, then raised herself up to a crawling position and rocked back and forth, watching the action. When they came close, she sat up and held up her arms to be picked up, but when the boys laughed and streaked by, she returned to her crawling position and rocked toward them and their pile of leaves.

Angeni smiled and pulled Alisha to the blanket, wiggling her feet in the leaves, but the stranger quickly diverted the baby's attention with a cookie and returned to arranging the picnic.

The scene appeared picture perfect. The day was cool, the sky blue and glorious. The creek whooshed by, and a limb broke away from its mother tree in the distance. If the angels watching from above had not known the stranger's intention, they would have been singing with joy. Instead, they hovered close, watching over the picnic scene.

After devouring all the cookies, the brothers patted their full bellies. "Umm, umm, good," they said and hurried back to play in the leaves. The picnic was over.

The stranger stared at the boys with their endless energy, feeling relief from worry about their next meal. "Come here now," she called to them when the baby fell asleep. The day was passing quickly. The stranger stiffened when the twins flopped down on the blanket and the older boy sat protectively near, looking at her with confusion. "It's time for your nap," the stranger said sharply, moving the sleeping baby, still holding an empty bottle, next to the oldest boy. "Stay here; I'm going for a walk."

Angeni left the children. She enjoyed the feel of the warm sun on her face and began gathering wildflowers until she had a small, bouquet. She stopped, smelled the fragrance of her bouquet, and turned to walk back to the meadow. Then she remembered Asyah, stopped suddenly, and flung her flowers on the ground.

Alone in her sorrow, Angeni had silently and completely surrendered to the stranger, barring everyone from her world, even her children. The stranger began repeating, *you'll see Asyah soon,* and ordered Angeni to walk a steady pace around the bend in the river and did not allow her to look back or to respond to Robert's angry sob. Out of view of the children, the stranger ran for more than a mile, forcing Angeni closer and closer to the riverbank and into the deepest part of the river. As she sank into the water, her words, "Asyah, help me," bubbled to the surface, in view of only the guardian angels.

Late that Sunday afternoon, Jesse and Alma arrived for their Sunday visit and were puzzled to find an empty house. Searching the house and barnyard, they found no activity except hungry cows and a horse standing by an empty trough. Two doe lingered at the edge of the woods. Alarmed, the Greens walked toward the meadow and soon heard noisy play.

Martin was sailing paper-plate spaceships over the meadow. James caught the plates, wadded them up for baseballs, and threw them back to Martin. Robert had given Alisha the last bottle of milk and was picking up the spaceships and baseballs. Afraid and upset, he knew it was time to stop waiting for his mother and had everything ready to go home when the Greens arrived. Robert's relieved expression sent a welcome message to the Greens, but when Alma bent to pick up Alisha, he took her instead, saying, "No! I'll take her."

"Where's your mother, boys?" Jesse asked.

Robert pointed toward the river. "She went that way for a walk, but she should've come back by now, it's getting cold."

"She's not coming back," James said.

"Shut up, James; she is too coming back. Let's go home. We can wait for her there."

In silence, Robert walked to the house beside Alma, holding Alisha closely, lulling her to sleep. At home, he gently covered her in their mother's bed and went to the porch to wait with Martin. James went directly to the living room, a room the family seldom used.

Alma walked through the house and noticed the extreme cleanliness, but she was shocked to find no food in the pantry. She followed a noise coming from the living room and joined James looking through cardboard boxes, each labeled for one of the children. The clothing inside was washed, ironed, and neatly folded.

On Robert's box, James found a sealed letter addressed to Kate. He felt a new bolt of fear. "She's really not coming back," he whispered, leaving Alma and running to the front porch. He sat close to Robert and Martin and tried once more to talk to Robert. "Robert, when I was asleep, Mama said it was too beautiful and she couldn't come back."

Robert said, "What's too beautiful...that's a lie. She couldn't have talked to you. She wasn't even there. Don't say that again, stupid," and shoved his brother off the porch to silence words too scary to hear.

"Stop, Robert, look what you did!" Martin said and jumped off the porch to help James.

"I didn't hurt him. Get up, James and, don't say that again. I don't know where she is but she is too coming back. As soon as they leave, we'll go back to the river and look for her. She probably just got lost...shhh," Robert said, nodding toward Jesse returning from the search.

Jesse had searched the woods along the river, calling for Angeni. When darkness fell, he returned to the house. A thin fog was gathering on the meadow and a moon illuminated a family tragedy seemingly with no end.

"Did you find her?" Martin asked.

"No, son," Jesse said. Fearing the worst and overhearing Robert talking about going back to the river, he added, "I'll get more neighbors to help, and we'll find your mother. You boys go put out feed for the cows and horses—and those two deer—while we put your things in the car. You can stay with Alma while we search."

"We'll put the feed out, but you can leave our things here. We're not going. We're staying here to wait for Mama."

Alma walked to the front porch holding Alisha and

saw the frustration on her husband's face. She turned to the boys. "Robert, there's no food here for you and your brothers and no milk for the baby. Come to our house; we'll eat supper and wait for Jesse to find your mother."

"She's not com—," James began.

"Don't say that again, James," Robert interrupted but softened his tone when he saw Martin's glare. "Okay, we'll go. Go feed the deer, James, and get in the car. I'll take Sis, Miss Alma."

Alma said, "No, Robert, I'll take your sister to the car while you help James. You can hold her on the way to our house. Martin, please turn off the lights and close the front door."

Robert was silent and angry as he threw feed in the troughs. James imitated Robert, throwing feed and stomping through the task, unconsciously trying to fill a desperate need to reconnect with his brother.

Martin turned off the inside lights and in the light of a full moon, left the front porch light on and closed the door. He stopped briefly to touch the worn spot, as he had seen his mother do earlier in the day, and then he slumped in the back seat of the car with his brothers.

As the night turned cold, Jesse drove away from the Copper home. He looked in the rear view mirror and saw the lone eerie glow from the porch recede in the distance. He hoped the boys would not look back. Robert sat between the twins, holding Alisha close. James and Martin sat on each side, resting a hand on their sister and their heads on Robert's shoulders.

High above the riverbank, a grand mountain shielded the river. The sun made its western descent, and an eerie glow bubbled from the entrance of a mountainside cave, illuminating the shimmering branches of an ancient oak tree façade. In the beginning, the People lived in a great underground cavern beneath the bubbling cave. One day, the shimmering tree led the People to the cavern entrance. Some exited the cavern to the left of the tree and became the Alabamas Indians. Others exited to the right side and became the Coushatta. Those who refused to choose returned to the cavern.

Tonight, on the mountainside above the river, the oak tree was ghostly still, guarding the cave and standing watch over the river. The tree offered no clue about the scene that brought it to life earlier in the night or the presence of the guardian angels watching over the meadow and waiting alongside the Copper children for the return of the Spirit Angel.

Star had walked back over the mountain during the night and found Angeni floating in the shallow current near the river crossing. Near dawn, the searchers found Angeni, her hands securely entwined in protruding roots, anchoring her body on the surface of the water, saving her from disappearing forever in the rushing river. Star stood by the oak tree, weeping and watching the men remove Angeni from the river, and then walked far into the cavern and sat down among the bones of her ancestors to die.

Jesse returned home and told Alma about the strange events of the night.

"What about the children?" she asked.

"We'll talk about it tomorrow."

James listened from the door and crept back into the dark room, mouthing silently in anguish, "Why did you do it, Mama?" He returned to bed and told Robert and Martin, "Mama's not coming home."

"I heard," Robert said, beating his pillow and crying until he had no more tears. Martin moved close to James, feigning sleep, unable to comprehend what had happened to his family.

Chapter 3

The day after the search ended, Jesse drove to Bremington, Tennessee, to bring Angeni's sister, Kate, back to Koasati Springs for the funeral. Her husband, Dr. Hank Parker, remained at Bremington City Hospital repairing a child who had broken both legs in a fall.

Angeni was laid to rest next to Asyah in the family cemetery. Immediately after the funeral, Jesse insisted on separating the children from the crushing sadness that pervaded their home. He loaded the car with the boxes Angeni had prepared for the children and a small trunk holding her personal belongings. He and Alma took Kate and the children to wait at home for Hank.

Asyah's sister, Sarah Copper Devinwood, and her husband, John, stayed behind to close down the house. Before sorting Asyah's belongings, they wandered back to the cemetery once more, dismayed at the broken rosebushes that Asyah and Angeni had always tended together. They gathered cards from the flowers surrounding Angeni's grave and made their way back to the house to pack away Asyah's belongings.

Sarah had always loved going back to the farm where she and Asyah grew up; now the joy had been replaced by gloom. She opened the trunk she knew well. Its contents held remembrances of generations of Copper men, all felled by young, defective hearts. Silently, she gathered items representing her brother's life—his watch and chain, the shirt Asyah wore on the day he died, and a frayed handkerchief in which she wrapped a pocketknife she knew he carried every day since their father gave it to him.

John left Sarah alone with her sorrowful task and walked through the house searching for some way to help. He looked through the wardrobe and bureau drawers to make sure he and Sarah had not missed anything of importance. In the bottom bureau drawer, he found a small wooden picture frame. He turned the frame over and saw Angeni and Kate sitting on the grass by their house when Angeni was still a young girl. John tucked the picture in his jacket pocket, went to the hallway, and removed the family portrait from the wall. He wrapped each picture in a paper bag, secured them in a pillowcase with a string, and took the package to the car.

After Sarah finished packing away the collection of memories, she went to the hallway table, opened Asyah's banjo case, and wept. The memory she loved most was of Asyah playing his banjo and singing with all his heart. She left the banjo on the table where it had always lain, waiting for Asyah.

John returned to the house as Sarah closed the banjo case. When he saw her tears, he said, "Let's go, Sarah, Jesse can take the animals. We don't need to do anything else right now. Go on to the car; I'll lock up the house."

On the drive home, Sarah was at last able to talk

without crying. "At least the children will have a home. I hope when they grow up they'll come back and reclaim the family home their father loved so much."

"You think they'll have a home, Sarah?" John said. "Don't be so sure. Hank is peculiar; I never know what that man is thinking. You did notice he didn't come to Asyah or Angeni's funeral."

"He's a surgeon, John. Surgeons often can't get away."

"Not even for a funeral? I don't believe that for a minute, and I don't understand how he can operate on children either. It's obvious that he doesn't even like children."

"John, ease up; Hank's been good to Kate. Now with a family, maybe he'll change his mind about children, too."

"Don't count on it. I wish we could bring those kids to live with us."

"We could take one or two of them," Sarah said, "but remember Angeni's last request in her letter to Kate was to keep her children together."

Sarah and John had eight children. Married at the age of fifteen, like most other girls, Sarah gave birth every year for seven years, bearing ten children, including two sets of twins. One of the twins and her third child were stillborn, still leaving them with a large family.

"Let's try to visit them next week," John said. "We have to keep in close contact with Kate until they're settled and Hank gets used to the idea of having kids around. If he's not good to them, I swear we'll bring them home with us and somehow make the best of it."

"I think they'll be fine," Sarah said. "I know Kate has always wanted children."

As instructed in Angeni's letter, Kate debated the children's care with relatives. After the discussions, Kate found none with the financial means or the living space to add four children to their already large families. Kate was now in charge of her nephews and niece, but she realized she was not the only one in control of their fates.

Before Hank turned into Jesse and Alma's driveway, he saw Kate rushing toward the car and the anticipation on her face. He stopped, lowered the car window, and said, "No, Kate, we agreed, the children cannot live at our house."

"Hank, you agreed, I didn't. We can take care of these children; you know we can. It's the right thing to do."

"No," Hank replied. "We're not the only family they have."

"But Hank, without us they'll be separated and might never see each oth—" Kate stopped when she sensed the boys behind her.

Robert disliked his Uncle Hank at first sight. He and his brothers peered at their uncle from behind Kate. Robert barely remembered Hank from the last visit to their house, and from his tone of voice, he did not want to remember.

Hank's eyes were narrow, and he wore a twisted scowl on his face, giving him a mean and distant look. He looked straight at Kate, never greeting the children, as if daring them to care for him. Then Jesse came out the front door with a box, and Hank realized he had no choice but to help move the family belongings to the car.

On the ride to what he presumed would be their new

home, Robert propped his elbows on the back of the car seat, watching Alisha looking up at him from Kate's lap. When they arrived home though, Robert crossed his arms and slumped back into the seat with his brothers.

Hank got out of the car and stood leaning against a porch column with his hands in his pockets, indifferent to Kate's efforts to coax the boys out of the back seat. Kate stood at the open car door holding Alisha. "Come on in the house, boys; you're safe with us. James, Martin, did you know that I took care of your mother when she was a baby?"

"Daddy told us," James said.

"Both of you look just like your mother when she was your age."

"Really?" James said, smiling, causing Martin to brighten up.

"Yes, you do. Come on inside; Alisha needs changing. We'll take care of you," Kate said, glaring at Hank.

"Get out," Robert said. The twins obeyed, and the Copper brothers followed their Aunt Kate to the porch.

The afternoon had turned to twilight. Across the street in the park, people were already gathering on the midway, looking festive in their coats and scarves. A few stood around cooking fires to stay warm; others lingered near the vendors displaying homemade Christmas candies, cookies, and gifts.

"Hank, take the boys over to the park to see the Christmas trees while I give Alisha her bottle," Kate said.

Glaring at Kate, he replied, "Come on, we'll just have hotdogs for supper."

Robert turned toward the midway and started walking without answering. The twins followed and Hank lagged behind. Robert stopped at the merry-go-round and waited for Hank and his brothers.

"Get on; take a ride. I'll meet you over there with hotdogs," Hank said as he pointed toward a nearby table and held out three nickels.

Robert shook his head. "We don't want to ride, Uncle Hank. Let's just go home."

"Ah, go on, take a ride; it might do you good," Hank said and offered the nickels again.

Robert ignored the money and shoved his brothers toward the table. "We'll wait over there."

Hank put the coins back in his pocket, shrugged, and walked away. He soon returned with the food, but instead of sitting with his nephews, he turned away while they ate their hotdogs and drank hot chocolate. Hank had not thought about his childhood in a long time. His nephews suddenly reminded him of years of pain at the hands of his cruel parents. They spent much of their time in church and reading their Bibles. They felt obligated to beat Hank and his brother. Instead of protecting children, the court system expected parents to beat their errant children. After Hank's parents stood before a judge several times falsely accusing their sons of serious infractions and received instructions to punish them more severely, Hank and his brother learned to hang their heads and let well enough alone.

Hank's brother ran away from home at the age of thirteen. A devious uncle traded a promise of a college education in return for Hank, then fifteen, to work long hours on his farm. Hank thought he was free of the cruelty, but lived three more years in constant fear of his uncle, who kept his promise of college, but only after bargaining for another young nephew.

Hank immersed himself in his newfound freedom at college, excelling in medical school, conquering the rigors of becoming a surgeon, and widening the gap that separated him from his life in bondage. Long ago, Hank stopped trying to understand why the cruelty of his youth left him with such contempt for children and accepted the compulsion to repair their broken bodies as payback for the contempt.

"Let's go back to the house," he said quietly and walked away. James and Martin trailed behind Robert, following Hank home.

Kate had bathed Alisha and dressed her in a new, soft pink gown, a gift from Angeni's sister-in-law, Sarah. *I'm so close to having children—a real family—I have to change Hank's mind.*

Hank walked inside and left the door open behind him, feeling the intrusion of his nephews running around him, into the house—his house. He grimaced as the boys surrounded the rocker and jabbered to their sister. He had to admit, the baby, totally insulated by her infant world, was delighted with her brothers. *The baby certainly knows them. No, no, if we kept one, we would have to keep them all—this is going to be a long night.* "Kate, you might as well stop playing mother," he said sarcastically and headed to the kitchen to make coffee, asking over his shoulder, "Where's the paper?"

"It's still outside," Kate said sweetly. "James will you get the paper from the porch, please?"

"I'll get it; I'll get it," James and Martin said in unison while running to the front porch, unaware that their Uncle Hank was gripping the countertop and cringing.

Finally in his easy chair drinking coffee, Hank hid behind the newspaper, annoyed by the grating sounds of the boys entertaining their sister. He looked around the paper to frown at Kate from time to time, reminding her how displeased he was and was careful to show no interest in the children. Hank was well aware this could be the last time the baby would be with their brothers; he was satisfied knowing that tomorrow would be the last time he would see them, too.

Kate tucked the children into bed, and when they were asleep, Hank agreed to talk. At first he listened, although impatiently, while Kate repeated most of what she already said. "They have no one else. We have the money and the space. The twins can share a room for a few more years. Robert and Alisha would have their own rooms, and we would still have two bedrooms left, Hank. Anyway, it's the one chance we'll have for a family."

Hank cut her off. "That's what this is about, isn't it Kate? You don't really care about your sister's children; you care about *you* having children. Get this straight. They're not yours and never will be."

Hank offered his wife two choices, knowing she would not be receptive to either. "I will never agree to keep the children here, and you know you can't care for them; you have to be cared for yourself at times. Although I can't stop you legally, if you keep the children, I'll leave you, and you'll have no financial support. On the other hand, if you place the children in an orphanage, your life—our life—will go on unchanged."

"Can't we at least keep Alisha?" Kate pleaded, "She's only an infant; how can we give her away?"

Hank laid his head back on the chair, closed his eyes, and sighed. "No, Kate, we cannot keep her. It would be unfair to keep one and not the others, and I'm not spending the rest of my life taking care of four bratty kids."

"They're not bratty, Hank. They're good children; they're our family."

Hank slowly and methodically folded the paper, placed his glasses on the table, turned off the reading lamp, and left the room. Kate followed Hank to bed and continued her pleas, first struggling to find convincing words, then, accepting that Hank would not give in, resorting to anger. "It's hard to believe you dislike children so much, Hank. Just remember, I'm holding you responsible for this decision." When Kate got no response, she reverted to pleading, "Hank, they're such sweet children, how can you do this?"

Hank lay awake long after Kate had stopped berating him, thinking back over their marriage. He had saved her from a fate much worse than being childless. He and Kate had married soon after they met, and Kate made it clear from the beginning that she wanted to have a child. He would not give in, and then early in the marriage the matter resolved itself. After Kate began talking to herself as if she were still caring for her sister and staying in bed for days at a time with no apparent physical ailment, Hank sought help from his former roommate from medical school, Harry Philpot, now a psychiatrist. Harry hospitalized Kate and diagnosed her with dementia praecox. Hank suggested to Harry that while Kate was in the hospital, he needed to make sure she never became pregnant. The discussion about children ended.

After the surgery, Kate's condition degenerated. Her depression turn into a frenetic state almost overnight, and Hank admitted her to a residential care facility. She had been in and out of the facility three or four times a year since. Now he realized that Kate and Angeni inherited the same genetic makeup that doomed them to a life sustained only by medication. Angeni's depression surfaced after her husband died and because she had no medical intervention, the consequences had been tragic. Kate needed no such trauma. Her manic-depressive state was permanent and would come on at unpredictable times. Because Kate was in the care facility when Asyah died, Hank kept the news from her, but Angeni's suicide had unwittingly renewed Kate's hope of having a family.

Kate tossed and turned, then slipped out of bed to check on the children. Earlier James and Martin had argued over the twin beds, and now they were empty. The sheets on Robert's bed were rumpled, pillows and blankets lay in bundles on the floor, and the three boys were sleeping peacefully. Kate retrieved the covers, gently covered her nephews, and kissed their foreheads. Alisha slept between the two pillows on another bed. When Kate removed a pillow and slipped in the bed, Alisha rolled her head toward Kate without waking up.

Before dawn the following morning, Hank moved Angeni's trunk into the hallway and took the boxes she had carefully packed into a guest bedroom. He dug around in the clothing, until he found their birth certificates. After inking out their location of birth and names of the parents and attending physician, there was no legible vital information to identify where the boys came from. He replaced the birth certificates under the clothing and slipped the boxes back in the trunk of the car before anyone in the house awoke. By mid-afternoon, he had rescheduled a surgery for the following morning, and on an impulse, stopped at a nearby clothier to purchase three winter jackets and wool caps. He made one final stop at a gas station to fill up the car and get three bottles of Coca Cola. Before driving away, Hank opened each bottle, dropped in a sleeping pill, and forced the caps back in place.

Kate busied herself with Alisha's needs and paid little attention to Hank until she heard him call the boys to come with him for a ride. She hugged each nephew, then held Alisha near so her brothers could say goodbye. She stood on the front porch to see them off, pleased to see Hank in a better mood than he had been in yesterday. Watching the boys walk toward the car with Hank, Kate prayed that by some miracle, they could cause Hank to rethink his attitude about having children.

"Where're we going, Uncle Hank?" James asked, moving to the other side of his uncle to walk next to him.

"Oh, I don't know; maybe we'll go see something new. Get in the car."

"It's almost dark, we won't see much," James said.

Robert, suspicious of the trip, shoved his fists in his pockets, weaving more than walking toward the car.

Hank looked back at Robert. "Lights…you'll see a lot of lights."

"That don't sound like much fun," Martin said, shoving his hands in his pockets like Robert. Uncertain about imitating his brother, he jerked his hands out and crossed his arms, but when he saw James' hands in his pockets, Martin slid his hands safely back in.

Kate thought her three nephews made a mournful sight—walking away, heads down, hiding their hands away while slowly weaving toward the car.

"Just get in the car," Hank thundered, handing each boy a bottle of Coca Cola.

Kate drew Alisha to her chest with one arm, waved awkwardly with the other and called, "Hurry back; supper will be ready soon." She watched until she could no longer see the taillights of the car zigzagging down the curving street and went inside the house. She rocked Alisha to sleep and went to the kitchen to prepare dinner.

It was barely dark when Hank noticed the boys nodding off. He drove two hundred, three hundred, then four hundred miles, stopping only when the boys woke up enough to ask for water and restroom breaks and again ask when they would be home. "Soon," he replied.

Near daybreak, he was in West Virginia, driving through the Shenandoah Valley. The Holy Cross Boys Home was just ahead. Hank stopped on a side road that looked uninhabited to remove the car tag, breathing a sigh of relief. According to his directions, they were almost there.

The orphanage, well known in its own state, was far away enough so that Kate would not find her nephews, even if she dared search. Hank drove too fast around a curve to see the sign, *Holy Cross Boys Home* and missed the driveway. He ignored a small *Keep off the Grass* sign, swerved across the front lawn to the back yard, and stopped at a porch that ran the entire width of the large farmhouse.

In the distance, Lester Green had started up the tractor and lowered the rake when he saw the headlights of a car. He turned just as it screeched to a stop a few steps from the porch. When he saw a man open the car door and three boys slowly getting out, he shook his head in disgust. He knew what was happening. As a World War I veteran, he had seen orphanages in war-torn cities in Europe where children were taken for food and shelter— for survival. Although orphanages were now available in America, and for good reason, he could not understand how families could abandon their children, sometimes under the cloak of darkness.

Hank called to his nephews, "Wake up, sleepyheads; we're here. Hustle up, get out."

The boys stretched and looked out. "We're hungry. Where are we? Are we home?"

"I figured you'd be hungry, so guess what; we're here just in time for breakfast," Hank said. "Wake up and get out."

Outside the car in the cold, crisp air, the boys shivered and their chatter changed. "It's cold out here, Uncle Hank. Where are we anyway? What are we doing here?"

"I thought we were going home," Robert said.

Hank opened the trunk to get the new jackets and caps and jerked off the price tags. "As a matter of fact, Robert, you *are* home; this is your *new* home. Hurry up, put these on, and go up there on the porch. I have to go."

Robert frowned at the color of their coats and hats, but he was too cold to complain. He motioned to his brothers to put them on and cautiously trudged up five wooden steps. The three brothers lined up on the edge of the long gray porch. Hank retrieved their boxes from the car, unceremoniously set them on the porch, and turned to go.

Robert noticed fog rising from the fields and the sun peeking over the mountain. He was angry and felt defeated. "What about us, Uncle Hank? Why did you bring us here?"

"Because you're going to live here, Robert; have a seat on that bench over there and wait," Hank sang out, keeping an eye on the man in the field.

Robert followed Hank's eyes. "Who's that man out there?"

"I don't know who he is," Hank said, anxious to leave.

"They don't even know we're here, do they?"

Hank glanced at Robert but stayed alert to the approaching man. "They'll know you're here soon enough."

Robert, shaken and scared, moved closer to James and Martin, partly to feel safe himself, but also to protect his younger brothers.

James felt brave beside his brothers and protested loudly, "We don't want to stay here, Uncle Hank. What if they don't want us either?"

"Yeah, where would we go? Nobody even lives out here," Martin chimed in.

"Shut up," Robert ordered, watching his uncle ease further from the porch.

Before Hank opened his car door, he turned toward Robert. "Don't worry, they'll take good care of you."

Robert squinted in anger. "How do you know that; what if they don't? You didn't."

"They have to. I don't!" Hank said in a panic as he saw the man come closer and take something from his shirt pocket. Hank jerked open the car door. He jumped in, slammed the door, started the engine, and kicked up dust as he sped away. The last image Robert had of his uncle was of him leaning over the steering wheel to start the car engine. Then he saw taillights and dust.

James and Martin sat on the bench "Come on, Robert, sit over here with us. Let him go; you'll figure out something," James said.

The Copper brothers huddled and shivered in their bright red jackets and caps, watching the taillights fade in a cloud of dust.

"You know what I hate, James?" Martin asked. "I hate this jacket."

"Me too, I wanted a blue one."

"Not funny," Martin said.

Robert crossed his arms and recoiled into the corner of the bench. "You know what I hate? I hate Uncle Hank."

"Robert," Martin asked, "what do you think they'll do with Sis?"

"Keep her."

"No, they won't," James said. "If they didn't keep us, they won't keep her either."

Robert scuffed his shoes on the porch and sighed. "Yeah, I know. I wish we could've brought her with us."

"Me too," James and Martin said together.

Robert was scared, cold, and hungry. He had no idea who lived here, but neither did he know where else to take his brothers.

Chapter 4

Lester walked to the edge of the porch, breathing hard and pushing back his cap and thick ear flaps. "Morning," he said, "I'm Lester. Are you boys all right?"

The three brothers looked down, their caps almost hiding their frightened faces. When the boys did not answer, Lester eased onto the porch, squatted down in front of the bench, and looked from one boy to another, focusing on the one who looked the oldest. "Where did you guys come from?" he asked gently, breathing easier now.

They drew close together, still not looking up. Lester saw one of the smaller boys shiver and asked, "Are you cold, son?"

After their experience with Hank the previous two days, the brothers were suspicious of any man, even this man with a kind voice. Lester persisted. "Have you had anything to eat this morning?"

"A cookie," James said, looking back and forth from Martin to Robert.

Robert raised his head enough to see Lester's face. "I'm Robert," he said with more confidence than he felt and nodded toward his brothers. "They're my brothers, Martin and James. Uncle Hank said we have to live here, but we don't know anybody here—anyway, I think the door's locked." Nodding to a lighted window, he said, "We'll just wait here for somebody in there to come out and let us in."

"I think I can get us inside," Lester said. He opened the door, and an irresistible aroma of bacon drifted out of the kitchen. He walked back to where the brothers sat. "Wouldn't you rather go inside where it's warm and have breakfast with some other boys? I'm hungry, and I'd bet you are too. Come inside with me." Lester helped Martin and James, already getting off the bench, and reached for Robert's hand. Robert glared at Lester, shoving both hands in his pockets.

"I know, Robert," Lester said quietly. "Come on in for now and meet Father O'Kelly."

Lester closed the door behind them just as the feisty Father O'Kelly came through the kitchen door, pushing a cart filled with breakfast food.

"Wow! Look at all that food," James shouted and headed toward the table.

"Yeah, Robert, look at that food," Martin said. "Can we eat?"

Robert looked toward Lester, who nodded. Giving in to hunger, Robert said, "I guess it'll be all right," and he hurried to find three seats at the noisy breakfast table where extra plates were set.

"Top 'o the morning to you, lads," Father O'Kelly said to everyone, maintaining his rhythm around the table, serving each plate with bacon, eggs, gravy, hot biscuits, and fruit. When he reached the new boys, he stopped at Robert's chair. "Welcome," he said lavishly. "I don't believe I know ya lads." He leaned around Robert to get a good look at the twins. "Am I seeing double this morning?"

Robert looked toward Lester for help. Lester smiled at the exchange and moved closer to the table. He introduced Robert to Father O'Kelly and pointed to the twins, guessing at matching a name with each boy. "That's Martin and that's James."

"I'm James." "I'm Martin." The twins corrected Lester, each twisting a forefinger on his identifying birthmark.

Father O'Kelly laughed at their ingenuity and served the Copper brothers and Lester with a nod. "Enjoy your breakfast," he said and moved on to greet and serve the rest of the table.

Lester had eaten breakfast at home earlier, but sat next to Robert, nibbling at his food and drinking coffee. After their curiosity about Father O'Kelly waned, Lester watched the Copper brothers with the other boys. Right away, James began joking with the boy next to him ... *good, a comedian.* Martin repeated everything James said. *Aha, a follower,* Lester observed and noticed Robert watching his brothers. *He's their protector; big job, son, for such a young boy.*

After breakfast, Lester helped Father O'Kelly set up three beds in one room for the Copper brothers so they could better claim a part of Holy Cross Boys Home as their own. He said goodbye, finished his work in the field, and returned to the Bing Cafe in Huntington Ridge to tell his friend, George Elliott, about the new boys.

After Jenny died, Lester fell into a routine of starting

his day at the Bing Cafe drinking coffee, reading the morning paper, and then fishing with George. Around noon, he returned home to wait out the day with little reason to look forward to the next. Early in 1913, when talk began about the United States entering the war in Europe, Lester had seen a chance to earn a regular income. At the age of seventeen, Jenny was his steady girlfriend, but he was among the first in Huntington Ridge to sign up for military duty. The odd jobs were over, but the following year World War I began. Lester spent two years in Europe before he saw Jenny again, and they waited three more years to marry.

After the war, Lester planned to continue his military career close to home, but his plans changed abruptly. Just before the war ended in 1918, Lester led his squad in a fierce battle in France. He had never been injured and felt excitement and exhilaration during battle, but this battle was different. The fighting subsided and Lester thought the enemy was defeated. Briefly distracted by the scene before him, he unconsciously lowered his rifle. Seeing dead and wounded men for whom he was responsible turned his exhilaration to distress. When renewed gunfire alerted him back to the battlefield, it was too late, for when he raised his rifle to fire at the approaching soldiers, a bullet struck him above his knee and knocked him to the edge of a cliff. Before falling over the cliff, Lester shot into the oncoming squad, killing the enemy soldiers and saving the lives of his remaining men. He lay at the bottom of the cliff for almost a week with no medical help. When help finally came, Lester was near death, and medics could provide minimal care, at best. He spent a year in the hospital fighting his physical pain and more so, the nightmares of his men laying dead on the battlefield. He spent another three years in and out of surgery to repair the damage to his leg.

Lester fought the increasing nightmares and was never sure who gave up first, the Army or him, but at age twenty-eight, he moved back to Huntington Ridge, a decorated hero. He walked with a limp and had difficulty adjusting to civilian life. To make matters worse, Jenny was ill. Looking back, Lester shuddered when he thought about what a terrible mistake waiting to have children had been. Lester and Jenny were almost thirty and alone, and soon they would not have each other. Two years later, Jenny died. They had let time steal too much of their happiness.

Most mornings after finishing their coffee and reading the morning newspaper, Lester and George went fishing, except a few days a month when they worked at the Boys Home. George was called Mean Old George by most people because of his crafty ways, which helped him survive the war uninjured. On fishing days, Lester and George climbed into a battered rowboat at the pier behind the Bing Cafe, paddled to the center of the lake, and fished a while. That's how they got to know each other. One day when Mean Old George brought a fish to the surface, some unknown force brought the real George to the surface too. "Look at that baby!" Mean Old George exclaimed, laughing uproariously. He unhooked the fish, held it up with both hands, kissed the fish right on the mouth, and then gently placed it back in the water.

That day, Lester discovered how caring Mean Old George could be underneath that gruff exterior, which he showed off like a prize trophy. Lester concluded that nobody who kissed a fish like that ought to be called mean, so from then on Lester just called his friend "George." When other people called him Mean Old George, Lester just laughed and said, "You ought to go fishing with him."

Chapter 5

Kate walked the floor and waited. After Hank drove away with the boys and the house was quiet, she felt a doom descending and instinctively knew her nephews would not be back. Midnight drew near, and she became increasingly horrified at what was happening. Kate was physically and mentally exhausted, and the night mocked her attempts to sleep. Since she and Hank moved into this house, she had listened with pleasure as the grandfather clock chimed, but tonight its musical toll seemed louder and more startling. When daylight came, Kate dragged herself to the kitchen and warmed a bottle for Alisha. The normalcy of a baby smiling, cooing, and making suckling sounds gave Kate an unfamiliar comfort, but she feared that comfort would be short-lived.

Around noon, she heard the wheels of Hank's car roll to a stop on the gravel driveway, and the car engine shut down. A single car door closing with a thump screamed what she already knew.

Hank walked through the door and saw Kate standing rigid and the message of desperation written on her face. "Kate, they're in a good home. I made sure of that."

Through tears and disgust, Kate cried, "You despicable, heartless man. We could have given them a good home, too. Where did you take them? I will not let this happen."

"It's already happened. I'll never tell you where they are, so don't ask again."

Powerless to change her husband's mind, two days later Kate, holding Alisha on her lap, accompanied Hank to the Newberry Home for Girls in the coastal town of Kinship, South Carolina.

Kate, an "old maid" according to social mores, cared for Angeni from birth. Five years later their parents died, and Kate assumed complete responsibility for her sister and their home. She enjoyed their mother-child relationship and often had to remind herself that she and Angeni were sisters, not parent and child. Kate was happy and content until that life-changing Saturday when she peeked in on Angeni, as she did every day, and found a note on the pillow saying that by noon she would be Mrs. Asyah Copper. Kate was stunned. Through the years, Kate had grown fond of Asyah and assumed he felt the same way; in fact, she recently began believing their fondness would lead to marriage. When Asyah chose Angeni, Kate was furious and felt betrayed.

On Sunday, instead of going to church, Kate went to Asyah's house, so upset that she walked into the house without knocking, demanding answers. "Angeni, how could you marry a man twice your age? He's over forty years old."

"So what? Now I won't be an old maid like you," Angeni retorted.

Kate knew Angeni had no idea she had married the man whom Kate also hoped to marry, but unable to face the loss and rejection, from that day forward, Kate alienated herself from the person she cared for the most, her beloved Angeni. Kate read Angeni's letters, but she could not let go of her hatred for Asyah and limited visits with Angeni to after the birth of Robert and the twins.

Kate thought their relationship had improved slightly by the time Angeni committed suicide. She knew her own life changed when her sister died, but she also knew that if she kept the children under the circumstances Hank laid out, her life would go into a downward spiral and end no differently than Angeni's. The decision had been clear. She remembered thinking, *I'm sure I'll hate myself for either choice, but God help me, I choose to live.*

Miles away, outside Kinship, Beatrice Newberry braided and pinned her graying hair across the top of her head. She slipped on a long-sleeved blue dress with a gleaming white collar, selected an apron covered in tiny yellow flowers, and placed a small gift box in her apron pocket. She laced and tied the strings on her high-top shoes and rolled and anchored thick stockings just below her knee. Beatrice was getting ready for another day at the Newberry Home for Girls. A hearty woman with blue eyes that were warming with age, Beatrice had the inviting look of a grandmother—a look that children are drawn to—and a face that radiated compassion for the children for whom she cared. She pushed back curtains to let the sunlight into the girls' sleeping room. She began this workday the same as every other day since assuming responsibility for the orphanage, formerly known as the Cumberland County Girls Orphanage.

"Good morning, little ones, time to wake up," Beatrice chirped.

As if the beds were coming alive, covers rippled, fluttered, and fell away from an array of flower-garden gowns and pajamas that Beatrice had sewn for the girls. With sleepy eyes and innocent faces framed by tangled hair, nine girls, ages one to five, began waking up in four large beds and one single bed. They sat up, yawned, and stretched. Some snuggled with dolls, some hugged their pillows, and others drifted in and out of sleep. The girls, abandoned for a variety of reasons, were in the legal custody of Cumberland County, with little or no chance of reuniting with their families.

"My bed's dwy, Miss Beatwis," Dolly said, standing on the single bed showing off dry pajamas. This was the first time Dolly had not wet the bed since her grandmother rescued her from an abusive aunt and uncle six months earlier and brought her to Beatrice.

Beatrice went to the tiny four-year-old, beaming at Dolly's success, and straightened her mass of tangled curls. She said, "Good, Dolly, very, very good," and took the box from her apron pocket where she had placed it every morning for weeks. The box held a delicate chain necklace with a gold heart that Dolly had spotted on her first Saturday morning outing to the town of Kinship.

"Here's your present, Dolly. I've been saving it for you." Beatrice hugged Dolly and gave her the box.

"Oh, tink you, Miss Beatwis. Now, can I swepp wiff somebody?" Dolly asked, jumping up and down on the bed.

"Yes, you can. Hold your hair away from your neck, and I'll fasten your necklace," Beatrice said and then watched as Dolly ran to the other girls, showing off her necklace, knowing that Dolly's true reward would be the other children accepting her at bedtime. *My reward will be to change sheets once a week instead of daily,* Beatrice reminded herself.

Walking by the front window, Beatrice glanced out and saw what looked like her first problem of the day. A woman in a long gray, unbuttoned coat, carrying a baby wrapped in a heavy pink blanket, was hurrying up the front walkway. A car parked on the circular driveway, its engine running and passenger door open, waited for the woman to return. The driver, the woman's husband Beatrice supposed, got out of the car, slammed the passenger door, and returned to his seat without making any effort to help the distressed woman.

Beatrice took her well-worn shawl from the coat rack by the door and rushed outside. "Good morning, I'm Beatrice Newberry. May I help you?"

Kate watched her feet as she walked precariously up the porch steps. She placed the baby in Beatrice's arms and in a broken voice and rapid speech said, "Here, you take her. I can't take care of her."

"Why not? What's wrong with her?" Beatrice asked and took the baby being forced into her arms. While Beatrice looked over the sleeping baby, the woman pulled the gray coat close around her, rushed back down the steps and to the car, retrieved a cardboard box, rushed back, and dropped the box on the brick walkway near the steps.

With a furrowed brow, Kate looked at Beatrice holding the baby, clutched her coat to her chest, and began walking back to the waiting car. The woman drew loud and deep groaning breaths, as if groaning fueled her forward movement. Beatrice followed her to the car. "Are you all right? Is your baby sick? Wait. Don't leave, at least tell me your name. Why are you doing this?"

Kate stopped abruptly, eyes glowing with tears, and replied in a defeated voice, "No, the baby is not sick, and no, she's not mine. Her parents are deceased. I'm Kate Parker, and she's my niece. Her brothers are in a boys home in … well … ah … I don't know where it is." Kate made a dismissive gesture and walked on.

Beatrice kept pace with Kate. "Mrs. Parker, wouldn't this child be better off with your family than in an orphanage? Why can't you take care of her? Help me to understand this."

Kate turned and dropped her shoulders. Without looking at Beatrice, she said, "I agree with you, but my husband does not. I have no family, and I just hope I'm doing the right thing." She turned back and walked faster toward the car.

Since Kate Parker appeared to have the resources to

care for the child and was clearly disturbed at giving her up, Beatrice tried once more. "This child is your niece, and you have no other children? Why, you sound like the perfect person to take care of her. Are you sure you want to do this?"

Kate paused and faced Beatrice. Anger began to replace her misery. "No, I'm not sure, but it's not just my decision. Can't you understand that? I'm asking you to take care of her for the time being." She added in a quieter, more confidential tone, "This might be temporary."

Kate got in the car, slammed the door, and immediately rolled down the window. "Her name is Alisha Copper, and her birth certificate is in the box."

Beatrice stopped, realizing there was no point in pursuing the matter further. *Ah well, this is a part of my job I will never understand.*

Hank mumbled, "Doesn't she ever give up?"

"Just shut up, Hank," Kate said.

Beatrice watched the car drive away. *What a tragedy. Temporary… that's what most of them say, but she seemed so upset, and she seemed to want her niece—not enough though, not nearly enough. Let it go, Beatrice, just let it go.*

Inside the house, Beatrice turned the blanket back and looked at her newest charge. The tiny baby awoke and looked around with searching brown eyes.

"Humm, ten toes, lots of brown hair… you're a cute thing, Alisha Copper. Looks like you have a new home and a whole bunch of sisters. Let's go find a place for you with the other girls. They're older than you are, but they'll like playing with you. You'll like them, too."

Beatrice now had ten girls in her care, all under the age of five. She sat in the room with the other children, rocked Alisha, and gave her a bottle. Curious about the new baby, the girls crowded around the rocker and looked on with fascination as Alisha looked from one girl to another, then fell asleep.

The following day, without fanfare, Beatrice processed the paperwork and integrated the newest child into her circle of abandoned children. When she saw Alicia Moon Copper on Alisha's birth certificate, she made a note to find out someday why this child had such a name. *Indian legend, no doubt.*

Once they had arrived home, Hank Parker checked his wife into the residential care facility for another thirty-day stay.

Chapter 6

The first time Father O'Kelly saw the Copper brothers rub their bellies and heard them say, "Umm, umm good," he was not surprised to hear they had favorite stories to tell. When Father O'Kelly asked about the routine, Robert told him the secret after the priest promised never to tell. "Daddy said for me to lay my fork across the plate and that would be the signal for us to count to three—just in our heads, not out loud—and when we say three we stand up, rub our bellies and say, 'Umm, umm good,' to thank Mama for the food she cooked. When Mama was sick and Daddy cooked, we did it to thank him."

"Not when he broke a plate," James said.

"Well, we broke some too," Martin said.

"Now we just thank whoever cooks," Robert concluded.

It turned out the boys were good storytellers, and Father O'Kelly imagined the Copper brothers had once had an enviable family life. Their recollections of fishing, hunting, and exploring woods and caves were stories about a rich home life filled with love. James and Martin remembered most of what had happened for the past year and did the most talking. Robert's grief was evident, and he punctuated his stories with abandonment and loss, which told Father O'Kelly he would be angry for a very long time.

James told about their father making them go to the woods before daylight to hunt deer.

Staring into space, Robert said, "His name was Asyah."

Martin chimed in, "We trapped a baby deer and fed it…remember James…and late in the afternoon, after we did our chores, he showed us how to swim, didn't he, James?"

"Yeah, I remember…the creek was close to our favorite place…where we played in the leaves. That was the last place we saw Mama before she—."

Robert interrupted, "Her name is—was Angeni. She was a spirit angel. Don't talk about that, James."

"Okay. Anyway, that's where Robert caught a fish, but I didn't."

"Me neither," Martin said.

Father O'Kelly laughed at how the twins told stories as one being, almost unconsciously. "Who taught you to twist your forefingers on your birthmarks to identify yourself?"

"Mama taught them to do that," Robert said. He softened up and talked about how in the evenings their father would play the banjo and they would sing and dance for their sister. He made his brothers laugh when he said, "At bedtime, Daddy carried James and Martin under his arms and threw them in bed."

Father O'Kelly knew he could never replace what these boys had lost, but he would try.

Joe Miller, smoking a pipe and tugging on a neatly trimmed beard, and his wife Bess, a petite, sparkling woman with curly hair, stood at the front window watching the rain and saw Lester Green hurrying toward the house. A tip from George had brought Lester to the Miller's front door.

"Come in, Mr. Green; come on in out of the rain," Joe said as he opened the door.

Lester removed his cap. "I hear you're looking for somebody to look after your farm."

"That's right, I am—you interested?"

"Yes, sir!"

"Good. Let's go sit by the fire and talk." Lester followed Joe to the living room, and they drew chairs closer to the fireplace. Joe said, "Mr. Green, if you can manage the work, hire workers, and get supplies for the household, you've got the job. For the most part, you'll be responsible. If you can do that, I can continue to work in peace, travel, and spend more time in my garden." Bess returned and sat two cups of steaming coffee on the table as Joe was saying, "I need someone to maintain the farm so it looks … well, good."

"I can do all of that, professor, if you'll call me 'Lester.'"

They shook hands and became Lester and the professor. Lester got along famously with the professor but not quite so well with Bess. When he mentioned he would begin work on the rose garden, she said, "Oh no you won't. No one touches my roses but me."

For weeks, Lester watched the garden deteriorate but kept his distance from the roses—and Bess. They were cordial but had no common ground from which to launch a friendship. Summer turned to fall. Lester knew he must act soon or the roses were doomed. He began working quietly at daybreak, tending one rose bush at a time. The plants began to stabilize. Bess did not mention the garden but arose each morning to watch the transformation from her bedroom window.

One morning, Joe swung his feet over the side of the bed and into slippers. "All right," he said irritably, "I'll talk to Lester today and explain again that the rose garden is off limits."

Holding her gaze on the work below, Bess said, "Don't you dare say a word."

Lester enlarged the garden, creating an oval maze and left a clear, grassy rise in the center. He painted two old Adirondack chairs and a small table, favorites of his deceased wife, and placed them on the grassy rise, side-by-side in opposite directions. On the day Lester finished the garden, he found a set of hand tools in his truck. An attached card read, *Thank you, Lester* and was signed *Bess Miller.*

One sunny fall morning, Bess brought two cups of coffee to the garden, walked through the trellis Lester had installed as a last thought, and picked out the chair facing the west, as Lester guessed she would. He sat in the chair that had fit him best for years, and both sat silently, enjoying a perfect view of the garden. Without predetermined intention, Lester and Bess had nurtured the rose garden to full bloom and unwittingly forged an equally promising friendship.

As the weather turned cold and the rose garden faded, Bess began planning for Thanksgiving and Christmas. She prepared invitations to their annual Thanksgiving open house; this year she suggested to Joe that they include Father O'Kelly, Director of the Holy Cross Boys Home.

Joe was skeptical. "I don't know about that, Bess. The church is responsible for the existence of Holy Cross and it has a rule that the director must stay close to the Boys Home. He's not supposed to venture out in the community."

"What a silly rule. Ask him anyway. What could it possibly hurt for him to come to our house on Thanksgiving?"

Joe personally delivered the invitation to the Boys Home, and to Joe's surprise, Father O'Kelly brightened up. "You know, Joe, the older I get, the more I want my freedom. This Thanksgiving, the order be damned. I'll be there."

The week after Thanksgiving, Bess followed Lester on the trail to the backwoods to select a Christmas tree. Bess finally pointed to an eight-foot blue spruce, which Lester cut and wrapped in burlap, and they dragged it to the house on a makeshift slide. Lester set the tree in a bucket of wet, sandy soil and untangled and tested strings of multicolored lights, while Bess sorted the decorations.

Lester stood on the top rung of a ladder securing the tree to a hook in the ceiling. He glanced down and noticed Bess studying a lone ornament with a look of yearning on her face.

Bess looked up. "This is my favorite Santa Claus, Lester. I've had him since I was a child. I always hang him up first."

Lester recognized the pensive look. "It's nice, but do you know what this tree is *really* missing?"

Bess walked to the window without responding.

Lester came down the ladder. "Well, I do, Mrs. Miller. What this tree is missing is a little red wagon sitting close to the fireplace waiting for a little boy."

Bess turned to leave but stopped abruptly. "Lester, you're not right about everything, you know. And stop calling me Mrs. Miller. My name is *Bess*."

The intensity of her response surprised Lester, and he stood open-mouthed watching *Bess* march out of the room.

$$\text{♩}$$

Because George was grumpy and rarely had a kind word for anyone, no one suspected he was responsible for some of the altruistic activities going on in Huntington Ridge. When spinster-Jane came home from the hospital in a wheelchair, she found a ramp attached to her back porch. She continued to feed her ducks by the lake and never knew where the ramp came from. A father learned his teenage son had stolen a Coca Cola only when the proprietor reported to him that the boy was in his store on Saturday morning cleaning shelves to pay for a Coke. George never contributed to the assorted theories batted around over morning coffee. Lester knew. He remembered George kissing the fish.

Lester arrived at the Bing Cafe just as George finished his first cup of coffee. "How's it going, George?" Lester asked, dragging up a red-cushioned bar stool.

"Humph," George mumbled.

"Christmas will be here soon, George."

"So what," George said, pushing back his cap. He filled two cups from a fresh pot of coffee and shoved one in Lester's direction.

"Have you bought my present yet?" Lester asked with a grin.

"You don't need a present," George muttered.

"Yes, I do, and you'd better get me a good one," Lester said and looked toward the door at the latest arrival, Father O'Kelly.

"What does *he* want?" George asked and quickly removed his cap. Unable to decide on the proper place for his cap, he gave up and laid it on the bar.

"I don't know, but he looks serious," Lester said and stood to greet Father O'Kelly.

"He'd better be serious. He's old, and he's gonna die soon," George mumbled and stood.

When Lester worked on the grounds at Holy Cross, he very seldom spoke to anyone. He saw Father O'Kelly watching him at times, but Lester had not been inside the house since the morning the Copper boys arrived. What Father O'Kelly was doing in the Bing Cafe was a mystery to him, but Lester knew he was almost certainly there for a specific reason.

Father O'Kelly stopped at the coat rack, hung up his hat, scarf, and long cloak and headed toward a table in the back. "Hello, Lester. George. Lester, come on to the back, and let's talk. I need your help," Father O'Kelly said as he walked.

Lester pushed the stool under the bar, grabbed the coffee pot, and followed Father O'Kelly, trying to guess what was on his mind. He filled two cups and set the pot on the table. "I'll do what I can," Lester said, sitting down.

As he poured four spoons of sugar in his coffee, Father O'Kelly said, "Actually, it's the boys who need help. I'm retiring in a couple of years, and I want to clear out that boys' home. Those boys—all of them—need families, permanent homes, not just on weekends and holiday vacations. Six of them have been there since soon after their birth, and they're growing up with only a hint about how families are supposed to function. If they don't learn that now, how can they ever live in society and sustain families of their own?"

"Father, I—" Lester mumbled.

"The answer is they can't. They'll be troubled for the rest of their lives. Take those three Copper brothers who arrived last month. If we could find a good home for them before they get too used to living there, we might save them from growing up marked for life. Who knows, maybe we could start a chain reaction in Huntington Ridge that would change the lives of the other boys too. I'm not sure where to begin, Lester, but I am determined to try this idea before I retire. Help me find the family I'm looking for—the first link in the chain."

Lester was deep in thought trying to absorb Father O'Kelly's request. He suddenly stood up and reached for Father O'Kelly's hand. "Father, maybe I can help, maybe I can't. But I know where I'm going to start trying."

Lester walked away, leaving Father O'Kelly to finish his coffee, but not fast enough to miss his mumbled words, "I knew it." On his way past the bar, Lester tapped George on the shoulder and nodded toward the door.

Outside, George listened in silence as Lester repeated Father O'Kelly's appeal.

Lester swung his truck into the Miller driveway to help Bess finish decorating the front porch. He screeched to a stop, jumped out, gathered his tools from the truck, and rushed toward the porch.

Bess laid down her hammer and stood on the porch steps. "Lester, why are you in such a hurry?"

"I'm here to put up the hooks for the lights."
"You're too late. I'm almost through ... uh-oh, Joe's home too. Joe, why are *you* home in the middle of the day?"

Joe walked up behind Lester. "I started thinking about Christmas and thought I'd come home while I had a break and help you and Lester. Is that hot chocolate I smell?"

"Not yet, but you will soon ... water's boiling, I hear

the whistle now. Finish the hooks on that last window," she instructed and hurried into the house. "I'll be right back. You and Lester know when to show up, don't you?"

Joe worked on the hooks while Lester relayed Bess's reaction to their conversation about the red wagon and the Christmas tree. He omitted Father O'Kelly's request, but he told the professor the circumstances of the Copper brothers' arrival at Holy Cross and suggested that he and Bess might want to bring them to the farm for a trial visit at Christmas.

The professor rubbed his chin thoughtfully. "I'll have to think about that, Lester. I stopped considering that possibility years ago."

Bess came through the door with steaming cups of chocolate. "What possibility? On second thought, don't tell me. You know how I love surprises, especially at Christmastime."

The two men looked at each other and grinned, drinking the cups of rich chocolate and enjoying the cold, clear winter day.

"Okay guys, I'm ready to work again," Bess said and began snaking the lights around hooks on the last window.

Joe asked, "Where's Mean Old George today, Lester?"

"He went down to Holy Cross to check on their supply of firewood."

Bess was absorbed in placing each light in the marked position, and the next sound she heard was Lester thumping down the steps.

"Going down to see if George needs any help," he said.

"Hold on. I'll ride down there with you. Bess can

finish here," Joe said as he gathered his hat and coat from his car. Joe hugged and kissed his wife. "You don't really mind, do you?"

"Go on, get out of here, both of you," Bess said with a shy smile.

Lester glanced in his rear-view mirror and saw Bess standing where Joe had left her. "There's that look, professor. I tell you, she's lonely."

Joe looked over his shoulder in time to see his wife pull her coat around her and turn back to her work. He said, "I think you're right."

Lester did not press Joe. He had an unsuspecting partner in his commitment to Father O'Kelly, and he did not want to push him away.

The following week, Joe and Bess thought they were paying a surprise visit to the Holy Cross Boys Home, but Father O'Kelly knew from Lester to expect the Millers, and he could hardly contain his excitement. He served coffee, sat in his easy chair, and listened to Bess Miller explain that she wanted a child to stay with them during the Christmas holidays, and she had specific requirements. She wanted a baby, and she wanted it to be a boy.

As if on a shopping expedition, Bess asked, "Where do you keep the baby boys?"

Father O'Kelly thought he might be pursuing a lost cause, but since he had solicited Lester's help, he encouraged Bess Miller for the sake of his plan. "To be sure, we have boys, but none younger than four."

"Oh, we wanted a little baby," Bess said, clearly disappointed. "You don't have babies?"

Father O'Kelly took a deep breath. "Would you consider giving a home to three boys, if they were brothers?"

Bess Miller looked at the priest in shock. "No. Absolutely not. I'm not sure what we would do with one child but three boys—that's out of the question. I'm sure you will get a baby boy soon; we'll come—"

"Maybe," Joe interrupted with his first word since hello.

"—back to see you again..." Bess said, trailing off, her eyes fixed on her husband.

The Millers looked at one another so intently that Father O'Kelly could almost see dialogue dancing above their heads. He settled back in his chair, crossed his legs, lit his pipe, and waited. Their conversation started up again, and this time Father O'Kelly was encouraged. *Maybe Lester was right,* he thought.

Bess Miller enumerated reason after reason why they could take only one child and listened as her husband countered each objection.

"We don't have enough room for three children," she said.

Without flinching, Joe replied, "Yes, we do; we have four bedrooms, and Lester can build a guest house for company."

Bess stood, placed her hands on her hips, and said to her husband, "It would cost a fortune to feed..." turning to Father O'Kelly, she asked, "How many boys did you say?"

"Three."

Turning back to her husband, she said, "... such a large family, and you're telling me I would have to cook and clean for five people?"

"You know money's not a problem. We'll find someone to help you."

"They'll wear me out and drive us crazy," Bess said, pacing back and forth in front of her husband and Father O'Kelly.

Joe said, "Of course they will…at times, but not all the time."

"We *cannot* fit five people in that car of yours," Bess pointed out.

"But we could easily fit everyone into one of those new station wagons coming out this year."

Stopping in front of her husband, she asked, "What new station wagon? Have you bought one of those strange looking *things?* They look like a box-car from a railroad track."

"They don't look so strange once you get used to them."

Father O'Kelly sensed that Bess Miller was overwhelmed with the new possibility and broke into their tête-à-tête. "Let me make a suggestion. Come next Sunday, have Christmas dinner with us, and meet the children. You'll see firsthand what it's like to have a large family—you might even like what you see." Father O'Kelly was feeling more optimistic. As the Millers were going out the door, he added, "By the way, Christmas dinner at Holy Cross begins at noon sharp."

When they left Holy Cross, Joe listened to Bess talk incessantly about the potential problems of having three boys in the house. He knew she was right. He remembered spending his own childhood without a father and knew there would be problems, but at least the boys would have a *family.* Joe's mother had died during childbirth and a woman who had no interest in children, especially a stepchild, drew his father into a marriage. Joe was lucky that he had been sent to live with his cousin's family who relished having a large family and hardly noticed they had a tenth boy to feed and clothe. But he seldom saw his father and grew up feeling different from other children.

Joe tried to steer Bess away from her imaginary problems with the boys and toward the fun of having a family with children. When their discussions evolved to planning the transition, they were struck with the reality of being responsible for children they did not know. Both agreed that if they accepted the boys, the commitment would be for a lifetime and they would make the children their own in every way.

Bess struggled to get Lester to express his opinion, but he remained aloof, making her think he was skeptical and disinterested. She expressed her apprehension to Joe. "What if Lester doesn't even like children? What'll we do then?"

"Let him think about it, Bess. He doesn't want to contribute to the decision, nor would we want him to."

"I'd be happy with *any* reaction from him," Bess said.

On the Sunday before Christmas, Bess had not openly shared her decision with her husband. When Joe insisted that *she* inform Father O'Kelly of their decision, Bess knew her husband was giving her a chance to back out of this lifetime commitment and admitted to herself that she was having second thoughts about changing their near-perfect lives.

Before leaving home to go to the Boys Home, Bess

and Lester walked through the winterized rose garden, which Bess now considered her year-round refuge. She wanted to discuss the changes the boys would bring to their home and Lester's relationship with the boys. After all, he would play a major role in their day-to-day lives. As they walked through the garden, Bess talked about the changes and watched Lester closely for a reaction. Lester walked with his armed crossed, saying nothing, and her anxiety increased.

As they neared the end of their walk, Bess stopped, stomped her foot, and crossed her arms. "Look at me, Lester. Tell me now and tell me straight! What about these children? Is this going to work with you or not?"

Lester stopped and turned slowly to face Bess. He placed both hands on the shoulders of this woman to whom he had become devoted. He looked into her eyes and slowly nodded. "I've kept out of this because I've been—and continue to be—reluctant to be a part of this decision. If I'd shown you how excited I really am, I would have taken the decision from its proper place. Having those boys here is exactly what I want."

Bess relaxed, let her arms fall, and rested her head on Lester's chest. "Thank you, Lester. That's what I needed to hear. Let's go get them."

Bess and Lester joined Joe in the new station wagon, where he was pulling and pushing the knobs on the dashboard, turning the lights on and off, choking a silent engine, then turning the windshield wipers on and off.

"New toy, professor?" Lester teased, getting into the new station wagon behind Bess.

Inside the dining room at the Boys Home, a two-part banner made from butcher paper fluttered from the ceiling on each side of the Christmas tree. Half the banner depicted reindeer sailing through the air pulling Santa Claus and a sleigh overflowing with an odd assortment of toys. The other half announced the *Annual Christmas Dinner and Basketball Game.* Each letter and drawing looked as if it had been sketched by a different hand.

Families from the community brought home-cooked dishes and dined as invited guests of the Holy Cross Boys Home. The food filled long tables that lined the wall on each side of the Christmas tree. Father O'Kelly walked around the dining room, observing the boys arranging place settings for the guests. He saw the pride in the eyes of the young boys as they checked and rearranged the tabletops, doing their best to please their mentor. Father O'Kelly assigned two boys to escort arriving guests to their seats and positioned two of the oldest with towels at strategic locations to serve as busboys, an inevitable necessity.

As soon as Bess entered the dining room, she knew with unmistakable clarity what she wanted—and needed.

After the boys had seated everyone, Father O'Kelly welcomed the guests, quietly blessed the food, and then proudly announced, "Christmas dinner is served!"

The Copper brothers had pulled their chairs close,

as if defending themselves against the world. Lester watched Robert try to take care of his brothers, but they were asserting their independence. James jerked his arm free of Robert to reach for his milk and tipped over the glass. Lester went to help just as Robert reached for a napkin, but a busboy beat Lester and Robert to the cleanup and soaked up the milk with a towel in one hand while patting James's shoulder with the other. Lester looked back at Bess, who was inhaling deeply. He also noticed that the professor and Bess were watching the Copper boys with curiosity.

After dessert, Father O'Kelly made an announcement. "For your entertainment, for the first time the Holy Cross Basketball Team will play the Huntington Ridge Methodist Church Basketball Team." Then he shouted, "Game time! Follow me!"

Walking across the courtyard to a small gymnasium, Lester advised Bess, "If you haven't guessed already, those boys—the three sticking together—are the brothers Father O'Kelly told you about. The taller one is Robert, and the twins are James and Martin. They're identical except for birthmarks."

Bess asked, "How are we ever going to tell them apart?"

"By their birthmarks. It's the right side for James, left for Martin; but don't worry, they have a way to help you," Lester said reassuringly.

Joe lagged behind Lester and Bess, mumbling to himself, "Yes, yes, those are the boys going home with us. Let's see, James has a birthmark on the left and Martin on the right … or did Lester say, it's James, right, Martin, left …"

The basketball game was over—finally. After two hours of play and each team with twenty points, the referees declared a tie. With a nod from Bess, Father O'Kelly left to help the Copper brothers pack. Someone had placed three suitcases in their room during the game. Once packed and ready to leave, Lester and Joe came for the suitcases. Father O'Kelly went with the Copper brothers to say goodbye to the other boys. Then James and Martin led the way to the station wagon, with Father O'Kelly and Robert following. About halfway there, Father O'Kelly saw Robert lingering further and further behind.

Joe, Bess, and Lester leaned against the station wagon, watching.

"Robert doesn't want to go, Lester," Bess said.

"He's taken on a huge load, Bess. He feels responsible for his brothers and he's scared," Lester explained.

James and Martin walked a short distance and stopped to wait for Robert and Father O'Kelly. Robert held his head low and shuffled toward Father O'Kelly. The walk seemed painful, and Robert looked like a boy much older than his nine years. He caught up with Father O'Kelly, stopped, and glared at Lester and the Millers waiting at the station wagon.

"We don't want to go," Robert said.

"What's wrong, Robert? Don't you think the Millers and Lester will take good care of you?"

"We just don't want to go. We like it here, okay?"

"Robert, there's more to it than that. Look at me and tell me the real reason."

Robert kicked a rock. "They think they're gonna be

our parents, Father, and they're not. I'd rather live here forever than let them think they're our mama and daddy. At least here, we don't have to pretend."

"Robert, I know you boys miss your parents. If I could bring them back, I surely would. You're feeling mighty alone right now; I know you are. I remember loneliness and confusion on the faces of children I've seen in orphanages all over the world, desperately wanting families. You don't know it yet, but you really are very fortunate to get into a good home."

"Did their parents die?"

"Who?"

"The kids all over the world."

"Not all. Some had no money for food. In the countries where they're fighting wars, some parents were injured or sick and could no longer care for their children. Of course, now a few parents take their children to orphanages simply because they can, but then you know about that, don't you, Robert?"

"I hate my uncle. He's not sick, and he has plenty of food. Our Aunt Kate wanted us, but he didn't."

Father O'Kelly placed an arm around Robert's shoulder. "I'm sorry for the terrible losses you've had in your life, Robert, but try to give yourself a break from thinking about it now and then. No one can replace your parents, and no one can make you forget them—you shouldn't even if you could. I know the Millers—and Lester—and I know they're good people and they want you in their home. Won't you just *try* to let them love you, and won't you *try* to love them? That's all I ask."

Robert looked up at Father O'Kelly and nodded, quickly brushing a tear away.

The three boys now ran toward the station wagon and stopped short in front of their new family.

"Let's go home, boys," Joe said.

The Copper brothers woke early on Christmas morning and slipped quietly down the stairs as Lester had conspired with them to do. Robert sat on the bottom stair step, watching his brothers exploring through presents that had magically appeared overnight. He wanted to join in the fun, but something held him back—he remembered Alisha and thought *fun* would mean having his baby sister with them for Christmas.

James crawled around the Christmas tree, loudly whispering the name on each present. He looked at Martin, "Where'd all this stuff come from?"

Martin crawled close behind and whispered, "Santa Claus, who else?"

"How'd he find us here?" Martin whispered.

"Who cares!" James said.

"Robert, look!" Martin shouted, unable to contain his excitement. "Red wagons, three of them!"

Robert sat on the stairs until Robert mentioned the red wagons. He could no longer watch from the sidelines; he was drawn into the magic of the celebration. The boys' excitement grew, and so did the noise. Soon Joe and Bess were awake and standing at the top of the stairs watching their new family.

Joe yawned and said, "How did you guys wake up so early? It's four o'clock in the morning."

Robert looked up. "Uh-oh, are we in trouble?"

"On Christmas morning? No way," Bess said, handing Joe his Christmas present before she headed for the kitchen. Bess had taken the hint from a magazine article conspicuously left on the kitchen table about the new Kodak Bantam pocket camera.

Joe opened his present and glanced toward the kitchen, just as Bess peered around the door, both smiling about her *surprise.* Joe joined the boys, started a fire in the fireplace, and began snapping pictures of the Christmas scene he had looked forward to for a long time. Just as the fire warmed the room, Lester came to the front door loaded with presents, reigniting the boys' excitement.

James ran to open the door for Lester, saw the snow that fell overnight, and said, "Hey, look everybody! It snowed last night. Come on, let's go outside."

Lester stopped him. "Hold up a second. George is driving up right behind . . . look, there he is."

"Wow!" James shouted with glee. "Mean Old George looks like Santa Claus!"

George came in with a bag thrown over his shoulder and wearing a red Santa hat. He handed out boots, hats, scarves, and jackets to the boys. "Merry Christmas, everybody."

Robert said, "Thanks, Mean Old . . . I mean . . . Mr. George. I'm sure glad our jackets aren't red." *Mean* or *old* didn't seem to fit anymore.

Chapter 7

With her family stripped from her, Alisha responded as if she had no protective skin—afraid and retreating. She lost three of her ten pounds and receded into an embryo of silence. Beatrice Newberry kept Alisha with her night and day, feeding her milk and soft food, rocking, cuddling, talking, playing music, and singing. At night, she lay in bed with Alisha on her chest and breathed with her as she slept, stubbornly and consciously willing the new baby to live.

Beatrice recorded Alisha's progress each day for one month, noting the smallest weight gain and the faintest interest in her eyes. One morning, Beatrice woke up, and Alisha lay beside her instead of on her chest, sucking an empty bottle left from a midnight feeding. It was at that moment that Beatrice knew the tiny child would survive.

Alisha steadily progressed, one activity after the other. She rocked on her hands and knees, crawled, stood, and held on to furniture to walk at a pace more than matching her age. The following spring, just after Alisha's first birthday, Beatrice looked out the window to see the child laughing and squealing with the other girls swishing across the yard. Alisha seemed propelled by a single force of energy and determination.

Beatrice had also gone through a major life change,

becoming a widow and a full-time surrogate mother of nine girls—in the same month. For years, she volunteered at the county-operated girls orphanage to fill her lonely days while her husband was away at sea, as the captain of a commercial fishing boat. A few weeks before a storm at sea claimed her husband, Beatrice accepted a full-time job at the girls orphanage.

When Beatrice assumed the responsibilities of managing the orphanage, one of the first things she did was to change the name. The Cumberland County Girls Orphanage, located on the outskirts of Kinship, was bleak, and the name or the sign did little to help the atmosphere where little girls lived amid each other's aloneness. Beatrice painted and erected a sign bearing a new name at the entrance: *Residence of Beatrice Newberry and Little Girls Only.* Besides serving as a way for deliverymen to locate the house, she hoped the new name would give the children a better sense of home. She sought help from neighbors to repair and paint the house and replace furnishings to make the aging house warm and more inviting.

Most mornings, Beatrice worked in her small office until the children awoke. For the rest of the day, she helped watch over her flock. The cook arrived early to prepare breakfast, followed by the primary caretaker, Elfie Fader. At fifteen years old, Elfie was the eldest daughter in a farming family. After her mother died three years earlier, she had been taken out of school to help care for her six younger sisters and had only returned to school the past fall. Elfie was pretty and talented, had parenting experience, and knew all the games children loved to play. A volunteer housekeeper cleaned house and kept the laundry moving from washing machine to clothesline to ironing board and back to the wardrobes and chests. A nearby neighbor slept on a cot outside the children's bedroom, giving Beatrice some much-needed rest. Before leaving the following morning, the neighbor built fires in the cook stove and, in the winter, the first and second floor fireplaces.

Alisha remained mute, but followed the other girls and smiled when they talked to her. Except for her animated response to music and her interaction with the other girls, Beatrice thought she also might be deaf. She cared for Alisha carefully—the bath, the bottle, the diaper, the hug—but soon realized this baby girl was noticeably different from the other children.

On rainy afternoons, Beatrice played lullabies for the girls on the Victrola in her second floor living room. A rug her husband had bought in the Orient covered most of the floor, and Beatrice threw pillows and blankets around so the girls could nap near the music. When the music started, Alisha sat up and scanned the room for the source, relieving Beatrice of the fear that the child might be deaf. With the corner of her blanket clenched between her teeth, she crawled around the other girls to get closer to the Victrola, where she sat, her eyes searching for something or someone.

Long after the other children were asleep, Alisha sat on her blanket and moved her arms and hands up and down in rhythm to the music. When the music stopped, she covered her eyes with her blanket until Beatrice picked her up. Beatrice turned the music back on, turned the volume on low, and said, "What am I going to do with you, little girl? I'll bet your brothers miss you too."

Swaying to the music, Beatrice gazed into space. *I wish I knew where those boys were taken.* When Alisha was sleepy, Beatrice laid her on the quilt near the other girls and watched her stir, then crawl back near the music to sleep on her own blanket. Beatrice covered the girls and left Alisha to sleep near the Victrola.

After a few afternoons of listening to music, Beatrice knew. "Somebody's been singing to you, haven't they, Alisha?"

Beatrice danced around, holding Alisha's hand high and singing. Alisha energetically moved her arms and hands up and down in synchrony with Beatrice. "Good, Alisha, very, very good."

When Alisha was almost two, she began to explore the house alone. When Beatrice scolded her along with the other children, Alisha began hiding. At first, she hid by sitting on the first step of the second floor stairway and covering her eyes with her blanket.

"We can see you, Alisha," Beatrice teased. "Come back down with us."

Nearing three years of age, Alisha moved up step after step until she had worked her way up to the third floor. She discovered rooms and closets where Beatrice stored furniture and boxes of possessions, and at last found the perfect hiding place where no one could hear her. Alisha played and whispered nursery rhymes until Beatrice came to the foot of the stairway and called her name. Then she returned to the first floor and her muteness.

The day she fell asleep in the back of a third floor closet, Beatrice declared the third floor off limits to "all little girls," looking at Alisha, "unless I'm with you." "There," Beatrice said as she secured a large board across the third floor landing. "Now, you can't play that little game anymore."

As far as Beatrice could tell, Alisha was healthy and normal. The County Health Department sent a doctor to the orphanage two or three times a year, but the exams were primarily to vaccinate children and make sure they were healthy enough to go to school. Beatrice routinely insisted the doctor examine Alisha, but each doctor reported that the child was healthy and verified that she could hear. Otherwise, Alisha seemed normal, and no one could find a reason that would keep her from talking.

Beatrice was frustrated with the child's inability—or refusal—to talk. Alisha would soon be three years old, and no matter what gimmicks the other children used to try to get her to talk and sing with them, she was fiercely independent and would not make a sound. The other children were accustomed to Alisha's behavior and called her Miss Noisy, imitating Beatrice. They developed their own sign language to accommodate Miss Noisy and continued to function as a typical group of children.

Beatrice refused to accept Alisha's behavior as

normal. There was something just too off-kilter—a hint that Alisha was in control. "We'll see about that, Miss Noisy," Beatrice said, devising a plan.

Beatrice had dealt with unique behaviors in the children she cared for, most resulting from parental deprivation or abuse. But refusing to talk was a new one for her. If parental deprivation caused Alisha's muteness, Beatrice was convinced that in time she could help. If Alisha had a mental deficiency, *well that,* she thought, *is another matter.* Beatrice was determined to test her theory; otherwise, she knew Alisha would be doomed to a life more isolated from mainstream society than she had already skirted by living in an orphanage.

Chapter 8

Once the Christmas holiday excitement had ended and a new year had begun, the Miller family found themselves discovering new routines for their day. One cold day in January, Lester installed an extra clothesline in the basement to accommodate additional laundry. Joe washed and hung clothes while Bess attended to Martin's cold. The following day, Joe asked Lester to find a housekeeper and cook—soon.

Martin lay in bed, enduring a hot, damp cloth slathered with foul-smelling Watkins Salve that Bess insisted on pressing to his chest. He refused the hot lemonade until Lester added extra sugar and honey and promised he would be out of the bed before the day was over.

"Poor old Martin," James said. "Mrs. Miller put that stinky stuff on him and made him drink hot lemonade. Who ever heard of *hot* lemonade?"

"Don't you remember when Daddy heated it for us before we went out to hunt deer?"

"Oh, yeah … but we didn't drink it though, did we?"

"You and Martin didn't, but it didn't taste that bad with a lot of sugar in it."

Bess packed away the Christmas decorations and instructed Robert and James to take the barren tree out to the burn pile. They tied it to Robert's red wagon and dumped it on top of the heap at the edge of the woods. Robert looked around from atop the heap and spotted a trail.

"Look over there, James. Let's see where that trail goes. We can get the wagon on the way back." Robert took off toward the opening.

"Shouldn't we tell Lester we're going?" James asked, hurrying to keep up.

"He's too busy. We'll tell him when we get back."

Deep in the woods, Robert said, "Daddy was a good hunter."

"Do you think there are any deer around here?" James asked.

"With all these woods, yeah, but we don't have a trap or anywhere to keep a deer if we caught one. I'll bet Mr. Miller wouldn't even know how to kill a deer, much less smoke it the way Daddy did."

"Lester would, but don't mention it. If we catch one, I don't want him to kill it."

They came across a snow bank at the edge of a small meadow, and James tugged on Robert's coat sleeve. "Stop, Robert, he's here," James said softly.

Robert looked around. "Who's here?"

"Shhh... Daddy's here."

"James, you're seeing ghosts again. If Daddy could come back down here, he'd walk around in his own woods, looking for caves and that stupid dividing tree. He wouldn't go in somebody else's woods."

"Yes, he would. If he could see us, he'd be right here."

"Well, if you can see him, show him to me too."

James moved close to Robert and whispered, "I don't see him... I feel him."

They stood still, listened for a few minutes, then silently walked on through a grove of small trees and across a frozen stream before entering the tall hardwoods.

When the afternoon wore on and Robert and James had not returned, Lester became concerned. He found the abandoned wagon and followed the same trail looking for them, afraid they would lose their way in the woods. When he heard their excited voices, Lester realized they were as much at home among the hills and streams as he was. He caught up, and they explored deep into the uncleared woods until they heard a bell clang in the distance.

"That sounds like the new dinner bell," Lester said. "Come on, let's head back home."

The Miller home became a beehive of activity from early morning until Joe sent the boys to bed at night. Although each had his own room, the twins found their way to Robert's bed during the night. Bess was frustrated because she had taken such care to plan each of their rooms, but Joe cautioned her, "Give them time, Bess. They've been through a lot."

"I know … how much time?"

"Oh, five or ten years ought to be enough."

Bess prepared breakfast while Joe and the boys made their beds and dressed. As if keeping the memory of their father alive, with the secret prompt from Robert, the brothers rubbed their bellies after breakfast and said in unison, "Umm, umm good."

Bess listened carefully to their breakfast conversations trying to detect their state of well-being and satisfaction with their new home. A few days after the New Year started, Robert and Joe discussed how the boys should address their new parents. Robert refused to consider "Mom and Dad." Joe, not wanting to impose a parental title, suggested they talk to Lester. "And," he said, "let us know what you're comfortable with."

"You're not like Uncle Hank," James declared.

"Aunt Kate either," Martin added, looking at Bess.

"Shut up," Robert said, just as Lester walked in and clasped Robert's shoulders from behind. "It's okay, son. I'll take that muffin if you're not going to finish it."

The twins bombarded Lester to ride in the back of his truck.

"Okay, but finish your breakfast first. We'll go see what's going on at the Bing Cafe."

Joe stood behind Bess's chair. "Bess and I are going to a dinner party tonight, so we're going to shop for a new dress today. Lester, guess you and the boys are on your own."

On the way to the truck, Robert pushed James out of his way to walk next to Lester. "I didn't know we'd have to call them something," he said angrily. "What would *you* call them if you were us? We're not calling them Mom and Dad."

"Oh, I don't know. The professor looks like a Papa Bear and I have no idea what to call Bess, other than Bess. Let's think about it today."

Lester took the long route to the Bing Café. He drove by the new Huntington Ridge School, where Robert would attend the fourth grade in the fall, pointed out the college where Joe worked, and finally parked at the Bing café. George walked out as they arrived.

"You missed coffee again," George said, dragging his dead Christmas tree to his truck.

"It was cold, so I slept in and then picked up the boys," Lester said to George's back.

"Doesn't matter, you still missed it. They need coffee too," George grumbled and tied the tree, stripped of all decorations and most of its foliage, to the top of the truck.

"All right, George, see you later. Oh, by the way, do you really need a housekeeper every day?" Lester asked. George got in the car, barely acknowledging Lester's question.

Lester turned to the boys. "We need to get here earlier next time."

"I don't like coffee anyway," Martin said. "Why's he so mean?"

"He has to be mean 'cause people call him Mean Old George," James explained.

"He sounds like Uncle Hank," Martin said sharply.

"Trust me, boys, George is not like Uncle Hank," Lester said. "Let's go inside where it's warm and see if they have hot chocolate."

When they had finished their coffee and hot chocolate, Lester drove them by the creek where they would fish in the spring. The boys walked on the creek bank while Lester tightened the rope around the tree that anchored the fishing boat to its makeshift slip.

"I thought you and Mr. George fished in the lake behind the Café," Robert said.

"We do most of the time, but sometimes we like to

go out in the river, and we can get out to the best fishing spot in the river from here."

Throughout the day, the boys kept trying out various names for the Millers, but none seemed to fit. The following day at supper, James announced to Joe with arms outstretched and with great flair, "Ta da! We named you Papa Bear."

"Oh, yeah? I kind of like that. How did you think of that name?" Joe asked and glanced knowingly at Lester's poker face.

Robert's mood had improved and he held up his new pocketknife. "Look what I found in Lester's truck."

"Wow!" Bess exclaimed, "Where did that come from?"

Joe looked at Lester and asked, "Mean old George?"

"Probably."

"What about Mrs. Miller? What did you name her?" Joe asked.

The brothers looked at Lester and then one another. "Robert, couldn't we call her Mama?" Martin asked.

"I told you, she's not our mama," Robert said.

"Well, Miss Bess, what do you think?" Joe asked in a tone he would address an ordinary dinner topic with, but reached under the table to touch his wife's knee.

Bess straightened her shoulders and smiled. "What I think is that Bess would be just fine, Robert; in fact, I like that even better," she said.

Chapter 9

In the spring of 1938, Beatrice announced, "Okay, Alisha, it's time for you to talk; you'll soon be three years old." She kept Alisha with her throughout the day, talking and urging her to repeat words. Alisha sat in her highchair near the kitchen table while Beatrice helped prepare meals and told stories and nursery rhymes, leaving off the ending word or phrase.

Alisha liked Beatrice's stories. She colored pictures while she listened, looking up eagerly when Beatrice paused. Beatrice gave Alisha the same expectant look. Motioning with her hand, she said, "Finish the line for me, Alisha."

Alisha shook her head. Beatrice repeated the same routine day after day. Beatrice's patience wore thin. Alisha clung to silence. Two weeks before Alisha's third birthday, Beatrice was making her favorite vegetable soup and bread. She chopped onions and carrots and opened canned vegetables and tomatoes that she had put up the previous summer. Alisha sat in the highchair, opening a new box of colors while Beatrice made the soup and repeated nursery rhymes.

"Jack and Jill ran up the hill to fetch a pail of water," Beatrice said and pleaded, "Alisha, please talk to me. I want you to talk before your birthday. If you don't talk soon…well, I know you will. Let's see, now for the bread," Beatrice said and went to the hallway to gather ingredients from the pantry.

Alisha opened her new coloring book and just as she selected a page to color, the soup pot lid paddled up and down. Alisha whispered, "Pot make noise," and looked back and forth from the stove to the hallway door. The soup bubbled higher, and when a red stream oozed over the side, Alisha became frightened. She threw her box of crayons on the floor, hoping Beatrice would rush back in. But when more soup streamed over the side of the pot and Beatrice still had not returned, Alisha screamed out loud, "Mama! Mama! Mama!"

Beatrice heard the scream and the soup pot lid clacking. She gasped aloud, rushed back to the kitchen, mumbling, "Oh no, not again. Wait a minute," she said, looking at Alisha while bumping the lid aside and shifting the soup pot off the firebox, "that was you screaming, wasn't it? Everyone else is outside. Alisha, you're talking! I knew you could!"

Alisha slid down in her chair, feeling shy and tongue-tied, but also proud of herself. Without moving, she pointed to the stove, smiled, and clearly reported to Beatrice, "Soup fall out, soup fall out." Then she sat straight up in her chair and with a loud recitation, finished the nursery rhyme Beatrice began earlier, "Jack fall down, break his crown, Jill tumble after."

"Good, Alisha; very, very good!"

Beatrice stirred the pot and replaced the lid, then

reached for Alisha and hugged her. "You little rascal, I knew you could talk."

"I whisper," Alisha said, barely audible, and pointed to herself.

"Well, that little game is over. Now you can tell me rhymes," Beatrice said, both relieved and excited that her efforts had been successful.

In the following months, Alisha made up stories and told rhymes at full volume, reversing roles and gesturing for Beatrice to finish lines for her.

On most nights, Beatrice lulled the children to sleep, taking turns holding each girl in her front porch rocker. She endeared herself to them with a nighttime ritual, especially her *Man in the Moon* story. Alisha was so enchanted with the moon and the story that one night when Beatrice was about halfway through, Alisha interrupted with a new ending. From then on, whenever the girls became bored with a story, Alisha surprised them with a different ending, soon becoming their favorite storyteller.

At mealtime, Alisha sang songs about imaginary effects of food, convincing the other children that spinach would turn them green and peas would pop out of their ears and nose. Beatrice laughed along with her, but at times, she did not think the food songs were funny. "Alisha, stop that. I have to get food down these girls so they will grow," she would say much to the delighted giggles of the children.

Beatrice welcomed the changing times. In 1938, the Cumberland County Adoption Board agreed to replace her wood cook stove with an electric one and within a year,

Beatrice added plumbing and indoor toilet fixtures to the first and second floors, cutting her workload in half. With ten girls to care for and a limited staff, Beatrice had little time to spend on organized play. Instead, she continued to employ Elfie to work on Saturdays and after school to teach the girls to read. Elfie taught the girls to play hopscotch and blind man's bluff and encouraged them to make up their own games and plays. She was alert to Alisha's hiding and was a co-conspirator in converting her stories into plays for the girls to perform.

Beatrice kept in touch with parents, aunts, uncles—whoever left children at the orphanage—trying with little success to reunite estranged relatives. Often the families were too ill or impoverished and could no longer feed or care for their children. For reasons Beatrice could not fathom, some families simply found orphanages a convenient place for absolving themselves of responsibility for their children, as in Alisha's case. Other families took children for visits on holidays and weekends and then returned them as if they were dolls to play with for a while and then lay aside—not real people at all. Beatrice watched these seemingly heartless parents creating heartless children that she knew would grow into heartless adults.

With few exceptions, Beatrice judged most prospective parents referred by the Cumberland County Adoption Agency as unworthy, rejecting their applications and sidetracking the county and state adoption and guardianship process. She researched and communicated through letters with a few parents long before she granted them an interview. The over-burdened adoption agency made little effort to overrule Beatrice; consequently, she allowed no family to adopt a child until she personally determined that they would be worthy parents. As a result, Beatrice successfully protected her girls from the risk and danger of unscrupulous families.

Sitting in her rocker one evening, Beatrice held Alisha and listened to her tell a new man-in-the-moon story, describing the man as her father who was absent because he was in the silver moon. Beatrice knew the connection too well. There were no men in these girls' lives to replace their fathers, and the way orphanages were organized, there never would be. Homes for boys were dealing with the same problem—no mothers.

When Beatrice was unable to find a home for girls turning five years old, she agonized over their futures. Alisha would soon be four and showed such promise at doing something special with her life, but Beatrice knew she had a challenge. "Alisha," she said, "I promise to find a family for you. You're strong, and if you'll hold on, you'll be just fine," but Beatrice was not all that sure.

Since adding an imaginary piano to accompany her stories and songs, Alisha found hiding to be more interesting and entertaining, and less of an escape. Any corner or alcove, in the many closets and storage rooms on the first floor, belonged to Alisha, but her favorite hiding place became the large storage room and pantry off the kitchen where Beatrice kept pots and pans, canned goods, spices, and a large collection of serving dishes. Alisha asked Elfie to help her make a *Stay Out* sign to keep the other girls from coming into the storage room, except Nancy, the newest girl. The shelves on the back wall had open-down doors where Beatrice hid her homemade cookies. She was aware that fresh-baked cookies did not hide very well, especially when Alisha hid long enough to get hungry and helped herself and Nancy to cookies.

Nancy sucked her thumb and stuttered when she tried to talk, which wasn't very often or very well. She learned to form a solid word when Alisha began allowing her into her hiding place and holding her thumb and making her whisper her words. "One word," Alisha said repeatedly, holding up both forefingers.

She pulled Nancy's thumb out of her mouth, and Nancy repeated the last word she heard. When Alisha turned away, Nancy reinserted her thumb. Alisha eventually tired of the process and left Nancy's thumb planted firmly in her mouth and busied herself singing. Alisha heard Beatrice and Elfie's voices coming closer to the pantry door. "They find us again," she whispered to Nancy and pulled her thumb out.

Beatrice and Elfie stood at the door, talking in low voices, but did not interrupt. Alisha poked Nancy's thumb back in her mouth and continued singing. Nancy scrunched down closer to Alisha to hide from Elfie. Alisha whispered, "It's okay, stop shucking thumb," and pulled her thumb out again.

Nancy whispered, "Tum, tum."

Alisha heard Elfie say, "I know Alisha likes being alone, but why does she have to hide, since she obviously has fun with the other children?"

"I don't know, Elfie. Maybe she has a good reason. She does let Nancy sit with her now," Beatrice replied, opening the door. She and Elfie stepped inside the storage room.

"There you are. What are you doing in here all by yourself?" Elfie asked.

"Hi, Miss Effie. I'm singing. Not by self, Nancy here. You hear singing don't you, Miss Beatrice?" Alisha teased and looked up.

"Bea, bea," Nancy whispered, peeking around Alisha's shoulder.

"Yes, we heard you. We were wondering if you'd rather sing with the other girls," Beatrice suggested.

"No, I sing to me."

Elfie said, "Come here, Nancy, it's time for your medicine."

"Why Nancy take medicine?" Alisha asked.

Ignoring Alisha's question, Beatrice asked, "Alisha, can't you teach your songs to the other girls?"

"Not today, maybe morrow," Alisha said, "I sing to me first."

Chapter 10

On Sunday mornings, Lester took the boys to Sunday school at the Huntington Ridge All Saints Episcopal Church. The Copper brothers met new friends, and Lester began feeling more and more like the father he had always wanted to be.

When spring approached and the vegetation began to grow, Lester hired two men to work on the farm and joined in the work a few hours each day. He showed no signs of slowing down and never talked about his war-wounded knee bothering him. Lester admitted he was happy again when George began to tease him about a gleam in his eye and a quickness in his step.

Robert discovered new interests in the fall when he began fourth grade. Unfettered by self-assumed responsibilities for his brothers, he found independence in a world of learning and socializing on his own. Riding to school with Joe gave them an opportunity to strengthen their relationship—not necessarily as a father and son, but as eager advisor and student of life. During class, Robert sailed through his schoolwork, but two new boys who had transferred to his school opened his eyes in a different way. During recess and on the school bus in the afternoon, he made friends easily. But at the bus stop near home, Robert was forced to defend himself. For reasons he did not understand, two older boys ridiculed him for being adopted.

One cold February afternoon, on the way from class to the bus, one of the boys pushed Robert and said, "Outta my way, *orphan boy;* you can't walk with us."

"I can walk anywhere I want to," Robert replied.

"No you can't, *orphan boy.* If you ever did have parents, betcha they throwed you in the woods—how'd you get yourself outta the woods afore the buzzards found you?" the second boy taunted.

"I have parents. It's none of your business anyway," Robert said.

"You mean the Millers? Ha ha, they're not your parents."

"Leave me alone."

"So what're you gonna do, tell your *par—ents?*" the first boy mocked.

"Don't have to tell anybody. I can take care of myself," Robert said.

"We'll see about that," the boy said, and both boys ran around Robert to get on the bus before him.

Robert lagged behind the boys at their bus stop, but the two boys waited for him behind some bushes. As he passed by, the boys threw rocks at Robert and continued their taunting. Robert dodged the rocks and walked on, but the boys followed close behind, laughing and singing, "Mama don't want him, mama don't want him, mama don't want her little orphan boy."

Robert listened for a few steps, then abruptly turned

and started swinging. He didn't stop until both boys had fought him off and wrestled him to the ground.

Lester saw Robert walking toward the house more slowly than usual and came out to meet him. Growing up, Lester had fought too often not to know the meaning of scrapes and bruises and recognize the "do not ask" message in Robert's eyes. The Millers were due home from a business trip later that day, so Lester left a note and took the boys to his house for the weekend. He patched up Robert's bloody scrapes and placed an icepack on a swollen shoulder. Over the next two days, he cooked nourishing stews and taught Robert to defend himself with simple boxing and wrestling maneuvers. The twins watched and, as Lester knew they would, mimicked the moves he taught Robert.

On Monday morning while driving to school, Joe asked, "Robert, what happened to your forehead? Have you been fighting?"

"No, sir," Robert lied. "When Lester was cooking supper on Saturday, James and Martin wanted me to teach them to wrestle. Guess I lost."

"Uh-huh," Joe said, "guess you did."

Robert had two more fights during the fifth grade, which he confided to Lester, never mentioning his tormentors to Joe. Lester later informed Joe of the fights, and Joe talked to the principal to make sure the other boys were not badly hurt.

When Robert began sixth grade, the fighting was over. He returned from school almost every day with a folded paper and showed Lester what he had drawn that day. At first, Lester saw crude drawings of a barn, but with a unique, uncluttered, and functional design. Robert had drawn doors on the floor of the loft above each stable to make feeding the horses more convenient. Although an impractical design, Lester saw the potential and gave suggestions to Robert, which he incorporated into the drawings.

"When do you draw these pictures, Robert?" Lester asked.

"Sometimes in Papa Bear's car or on the bus coming home, but mostly while everyone else is reading."

"Does your teacher know you're doing all this drawing in her reading class?"

"I think so. She walked up behind me one day and asked me what Susan had read. I thought I was in trouble for sure, but when I told her what Susan had read, she just walked away. She still walks by and looks at my pictures, but she doesn't bother me very much."

"What about you? Don't you read too?"

"Yeah, she makes me read first."

"Does she still ask you what Susan has read?"

"Nope, she asks me what David read," Robert replied with a laugh.

"Does she ask the other kids to explain what *you* read? By the way, I don't like *yeah* and *nope* very much. It's the soldier thing I guess."

"Yes, sir, she asked all of us. She switches around to see if we're listening."

"Think I need to give her a call to make sure it's okay?"

"No, Lester, don't—please—she might make me stop drawing."

Lester, working with a building crew, incorporated Robert's designs into the new barn that would replace one that burned down years before. He suggested Robert draw hooks, shelves, and feeding troughs for the horses. Lester traced the items onto boards, cut them out with a small saw, and taught the twins to sand and paint. When the structure was finished, the carpenter used Robert's drawings to cut matching fence posts and rails for the circular trotting pasture where the boys would learn to ride.

The following spring, Joe and Bess bought horses for the boys and Lester to celebrate completion of the barn and Robert's twelfth and the twins' ninth birthdays. Bess set up a picnic near the entrance to the barn, and Joe took photographs of Lester and the boys showing off their completed work. Lester taught the boys to ride and soon they were running the horses throughout the one hundred acres of the Miller land. With his life firmly centered on the Copper brothers, Lester had little reason to go home at night and was happy when Bess routinely began to ask him to stay for dinner. He had also spotted an ideal location to build a house for himself, but was waiting for the right time to approach the professor.

One night after dinner, James made a suggestion that led to solving the problem. When Robert complained because Lester was going home, James exuberantly said, "Lester, I've got it! Bring your house over here."

Robert chastised his brother. "Dummy, he can't do that; you can't move houses."

Everyone laughed, but Lester also noticed that the professor winked at Bess and she smiled and nodded.

"Lester, Bess and I've been talking about this anyway.

We're already dominating your life, but you know we need you here. In fact, I don't know what we'd do without you. It might be unfair to you to ask you to live here, but if you agree, why don't you select a location somewhere on the property and build yourself a house so you can live closer to us?"

The boys howled with delight as Lester's grin grew wider.

In the fall, construction began. George appeared each day to help, and one month before Christmas, the crew finished building the house, an exact replica of the home Lester had once shared with his beloved Jenny. Lester placed each piece of furniture exactly where it had been in the old house and felt Jenny's sweetness slowly infuse his new home like a soft mist. In the evening, he and the boys sat on the front porch that Robert had struggled so hard to replicate in his design. The porch ran the width of the house and on one end, George installed an oak swing in which the twins were now swinging as high as they could go. Robert and Lester sat in oak rocking chairs, a gift from Bess and Joe. The broad sky twinkled with stars and a bright new moon drifted across the sky between the rooftop of the barn and the mountains. Lester was at peace with his move.

James brought the swing to a standstill and in the quiet of the night said, "Robert, remember the night Sis was born and Daddy played the banjo on our front porch?"

"I can't play a banjo and don't have one anyway," Robert replied and quietly slipped inside the house and went to bed in the guest room.

Chapter 11

"My four birthday!" Alisha said to Nancy, holding up all her fingers. "It's May."

"Mae, mae," Nancy replied, sucking her thumb with more force than usual. Alisha already wore her new pink dress she had watched Beatrice sew, filling the bodice with ruffles and lace and embroidering a row of pink flowers on the skirt. Just before the party, Alisha stood in front of Beatrice to get her hair tied in a ponytail with a pink ribbon. She had practiced her new song for weeks and was ready to sing.

Elfie dressed the girls in their special birthday dresses and warned them several times to stay clean and, "Walk, don't run," she said. They vigorously agreed, and when she finished tying ribbons in their hair, they all ran to the kitchen as fast as they could. Beatrice had set the table with their customary birthday dishes and placed the lavishly decorated cake in front of Alisha.

After blowing out the candles, Alisha scrunched her eyes closed, and leaned closer to the cake to make a wish. For good measure, she covered her eyes with both hands: *I wish for a piano, one of my very own and maybe a family.*

After the girls sang "Happy Birthday" and finished

the cake and ice cream, Beatrice said, "Alisha, it's time to stand on the chair and sing your new song for us."

Alisha was surprised. "You don't let us stand on the chairs, Miss Beatrice."

Beatrice smiled. "I will, but just this time, Alisha."

Alisha's song was her version of *The Three Little Bears.* Since she started singing instead of telling stories, she'd had Beatrice's full attention—and now she had an audience.

"Once upon a time, there were eleven little bears," Alisha began her song. "A mama bear, and..." she pointed to Beatrice.

"A papa bear," Beatrice sung, in what she imagined would be the next line, and pointed back to Alisha.

"No. No Papa Bear," Alisha said, and finished the first line, "Ten ba-bee bears," naming each girl as she randomly enumerated the bears, pointing to herself last. "Mama Bear take very good care of baby bears all by herself. Mama Bear cooked bread and..."

Alisha pointed to Beatrice, who thought for an instant, smiled, and said, "Soup!"

"Good, Miss Beatrice, vewy, vewy good," Alisha said, imitating Beatrice's earlier words to her. Alisha stopped singing, looked at all the girls, and dramatized her next line, "Before supper, Mama Bear took baby bears for walk in woods and, uh oh, she forget soup—again. They run back to the house to eat supper, but baby bears go to bed hungry cause..." and she pointed to Beatrice.

"All the soup..." Beatrice knew the rest and pointed to Alisha.

"Fall out of pot, while they were gone," Alisha said,

finishing the last line in the tune of "Twinkle, Twinkle Little Star." She threw up her arms and twirled around, showing off her new dress and ending the performance.

During the next year, Alisha began singing incessantly whether or not she was playing her imaginary piano.

At the beginning of spring, Beatrice had purchased a small white bus large enough for the girls to accompany her on weekly shopping trips to the village of Kinship. Elfie would stand in the front and watch the girls as they rode around the small town looking at the local people, sights, and sounds. For these outings, Beatrice always assigned the same seats, which meant that Alisha always sat next to Nancy. When Alisha asked if they could sit elsewhere, Beatrice reminded her, "I'm the boss," and that was the end of that conversation

Beatrice would drive from merchant to merchant, picking up supplies and placing new orders. When the girls' anticipation peaked, she would park the bus in the heart of downtown for their walk down Main Street, which was always filled with shoppers. The oldest girls held the hands of the younger ones. Beatrice walked in front of the group to keep them from running ahead, and Elfie walked behind to keep the group intact.

The bright red calliope that played in the Radical Brothers Candy Store held the greatest fascination and always brought the girls to a stop. One of the Radical brothers would play all the forty-three gleaming brass whistles of the calliope, and the other brother kept Beatrice, Elfie, and the girls laughing with his jokes and magic tricks.

"I feel like I'm at the circus," Elfie said one Saturday.

"You are, at least at a small piece of what used to be the circus," Beatrice said.

On these outings, the children always looked forward to one of the Radical brothers playing the red calliope in the open window. The younger brother, Tobias Hurley, was a natural comedian, but a birth defect left him with an over-sized body, an oddly shaped face, and a head out of proportion to his body, giving him a strange appearance indeed. At the age of twelve, he ran away from home to escape a life of ridicule. After hitchhiking on a freight train for two days, he left his boxcar to resupply his knapsack with food and happened upon a crew raising a circus tent. One of the men, distracted by the odd-looking giant of a boy, let the tent pole slip. Tobias's quick reaction and great strength were sufficient to save the tent from collapsing. When the boss came by to recheck the stability of the poles, Tobias was leaning against his tent pole making the crew laugh at his antics.

"What are *you* still doing here kid?" the boss had asked.

"Looking for a job, sir."

"Come with me," the boss barked and turned to go.

"Can't, sir," Tobias said.

"Why not? I thought you wanted a job."

"I do, but if I move, the tent will fall."

The circus workers were accustomed to odd-looking people, and they adopted Toby into their curious family. When his sixteen-year-old brother, Axel, found him a month later, Tobias was the performer most in demand. He had found the perfect home and, more importantly, a purpose for living. Axel was relieved to see his brother safe and happy and wrote home that he would stay a while and watch over Toby, an explanation he thought more acceptable to his mother than both of her sons had run away to join the circus. The brothers eventually changed their name from *Hurley* to *Radical,* added a bright red calliope to create a double act, and permanently joined the Ringling Brothers Circus. After years of traveling, they retired and moved back to Kinship. Realizing they missed the excitement of the circus, they opened a candy store, placed their calliope in the front window, and again became famous for their Saturday morning double act. Now, twenty years later and in his seventies, Tobias's appearance had mellowed, and the Radical brothers still guaranteed a crowd for area merchants.

Alisha was particularly excited this Saturday morning. They were finally on the bus. Alisha watched intently out of the bus window for the piano store, gripping Nancy's hand tighter as they got closer to town. Without taking her eyes from the window, Alisha let go of Nancy's hand and pulled out her thumb. "Nancy," she said, "stop shucking thumb."

Nancy clipped the words, "Tum, tum, tum, tum, tum," before reinserting her thumb.

"That's okay," Alisha said and put her arm around Nancy's shoulders but still looked out the window.

"Beatrice, she's looking for something," Elfie said.

Beatrice glanced at Alisha in the rear-view mirror. "She's always looking for something; just keep watching her."

Alisha turned and whispered to Nancy "I hear what Miss Effie say."

Nancy leaned against Alisha, removed her thumb, looked at Elfie, said, "Sa," and reinserted her thumb.

"Nancy, take thumb out!"

"Ou, ou," Nancy said and quickly reinserted her thumb.

"Nancy, stop shucking thumb! We're almost there."

"Ter, ter."

"Keep trying," Alisha said, holding onto Nancy's favorite thumb.

"Tie, tie."

I'm scared, Alisha thought and squeezed Nancy's hand much too tightly. Nancy twisted out of Alisha's grasp and reinserted her thumb.

Beatrice turned the corner and parked in their usual space on a side street near the center of town. Just as she stopped the bus, Alisha spotted the store window and the piano.

"There," Alisha whispered, pushing Nancy into the aisle. "Hurwe."

Nancy jumped down and slipped her thumb out long enough to say, "We, we."

Beatrice pushed herself out of the driver's seat, pocketed the ignition key, and said, "Okay girls, let's go for a walk," as she stepped off the bus.

Elfie slung a small supply bag over her shoulder and said to each girl walking by her, "Stay in line behind Miss Beatrice."

Tobias Hurley made the people on Main Street feel like they were at the circus when he played the calliope. Beatrice and Elfie chatted with merchants who stepped out into the warm May morning to greet shoppers strolling on the sidewalk. Beatrice turned to account for all her girls and smiled at the ones pressing their faces against the toy store window. Others were brave enough to wander inside, and still others skipped along the sidewalk enjoying the unique sensation of being in town.

Nancy followed at arm's length as Alisha pulled her along and they drifted further behind the group. As soon as Elfie turned her back to talk to someone else, Alisha slipped around the corner, down the block, and into the Van Horne Music Store with Nancy in tow. She tiptoed to the corner window where the piano sat. Holding onto Nancy with one hand, she counted keys with the other and whispered a mixture of numbers as she touched each key.

Beatrice detected the missing girls almost immediately. She darted into several stores, calling their names. Elfie and a police officer joined the search. Beatrice almost missed the Van Horne Music Store, but as she rounded the corner, she saw Alisha and Nancy standing by the huge black piano Ed Van Horne loved the most. She rushed through the door and scolded loudly, "Alisha, Nancy, what are you doing here? You're supposed to stay with the other girls."

Alisha was too excited about the piano to care about being scolded. "Miss Beatrice, look at this piano. Isn't it pretty? It has a thousand keys. Can we take it home with us?"

Ed Van Horne rushed to the front of the store. "Miss Newberry, I didn't see them come in; they didn't make a sound."

"I figured as much, Ed. Go down the street near the

calliope and tell Elfie and the officer that Alisha and Nancy are all right." Then relief and compassion made Beatrice add, "I might as well let her hear how it sounds."

Alisha knew she had been bad, but she also knew Beatrice could be a softie.

"Alisha, I'm going to let you count the keys once more. This time though, press the key hard and listen carefully to how each note sounds."

"Okay," Alisha said, wide-eyed. She started on the treble end, hit each note as hard as she could as Miss Beatrice counted each key. "Is that how you play the piano, Miss Beatrice?" Alisha asked, more than a little disappointed that she didn't produce a melody.

"Well, it's a start, but we can't take the piano home with us. You'll just have to keep playing your pretend piano until you have a real one. Then you'll learn rather quickly, I would imagine."

"That's okay. My piano sounds better," Alisha said, sliding off the bench. "How many keys does it have?" she asked, looking back toward the store window until Beatrice had tugged the two girls around the corner.

"Eighty-eight!"

After Alisha had seen the real piano, she began putting the image of the keys with the sound of her songs. Her imaginary piano sounded much better than Mr. Van Horne's piano. She was sure of that.

Determined to find her a family before Alisha turned five, Beatrice began an active campaign. When the girls turned five, the County Adoption Board transferred them to an orphanage closer to a school, and Beatrice worried about Alisha being ridiculed as an orphan, as well as for her continuing compulsion to hide. Children with an unexplained behavior, who were otherwise normal or even exceptional, were sent to the State Mental Hospital because no one knew an appropriate treatment. Confined in an institution, the unusual behavior often became the child's predominant behavior. If Beatrice did not act soon, Alisha might spend the rest of her life in such a place. Beatrice vowed to protect her in the best way she knew how—find a family, and soon.

Beatrice continued to suggest activities to replace Alisha's penchant for hiding, but the child was stubborn. Except for Nancy, Alisha allowed no one to interfere with her music "practice," telling the world it seemed, that her music belonged to her and no one could take it away. Beatrice interviewed family after family, but would not allow Alisha to go to anyone's home on a trial basis, nor would she force her to go with any family. Beatrice was determined that Alisha must voluntarily accept a family—no coercion allowed.

After a few families came and went, Alisha had the routine down like a well-rehearsed play. She grasped Beatrice's hand with both her hands, turned her head toward Beatrice, closed her eyes, and marched into the living room beside her protector, feeling her heart beating faster with each step. She sat as close to Beatrice as possible and kept her eyes tightly shut. When the discussion turned toward gathering up her toys and leaving, Alisha opened her eyes, jumped up from the sofa, and ran to the storage room.

The most recent prospective mother said, "Well! She's not going with us."

"That's right," Beatrice said.

Nancy waited in the hallway with her thumb securely in her mouth and slipped into the storage room as Alisha closed the door. Alisha gulped, scrunched herself into her familiar corner, and squeezed her eyes shut. She felt a tug on her arm and opened her eyes to see Nancy holding her thumb in the air, grinning at her accomplishment.

Alisha was in the only home she had ever known and did not intend to leave with those people—any of them. When she heard other girls talk about mothers, she concluded that Beatrice was hers and felt defeated to hear her *mother* talk about someone else taking her away.

A door slammed. The people were gone. Alisha knew the routine. She waited to hear the banging noises of pots and pans on the shelves and Beatrice calling, "Alisha. Where is that Alisha?" But she heard the other girls calling, demanding Beatrice's attention. "We're not leaving without Miss Beatrice," Alisha whispered to Nancy, who had fallen over in the opposite direction, asleep and sucking her thumb.

Chapter 12

Almost five years had passed since Asyah and Angeni died, but sadness clung to Sarah Copper Devinwood, like a second skin. Her childhood home beckoned, so she and John left their young daughter, Belinda, with Maggie, their oldest daughter, and traveled to the Copper farm, this time for a vacation. The beauty of Koasati Springs renewed her spirit like no other place, but the distance made frequent visits difficult. Still, Sarah and John had managed to make the trip in the spring or fall for the ten years that Asyah and Angeni were married. They had carried jars of fruits and vegetables that she knew Asyah enjoyed and clothing her sons had outgrown that now fit Robert and the twins perfectly. Sarah so wished she had visited that year before Asyah and Angeni died, but she had postponed the visit until Belinda turned two, and now she would always regret that decision.

Sarah uncovered furniture she had transformed into ghosts with sheets. She opened windows to freshen the air and cleaned house while John trimmed trees and shrubbery. One day, they pulled weeds and raked the small cemetery and garden where the spirits of three generations of the Copper family rested. Roses were again blooming profusely along the fence line near the graves of Asyah and Angeni.

Driving home from Koasati Springs, John slowly worked himself into a rage. He was still furious at Hank and held him personally accountable for getting rid of the children, but could not entirely hold himself blameless either.

"Sarah, we have to stop talking about bringing Alisha home and do something. She's been in that place for nearly five years, and I don't want her going to school from there. I want her with us so she can go to school with Lindy. I just hope those boys are with a family and in school, wherever they are."

"While you're working up your anger, John, remember that in her last letter to Kate, Angeni also listed us among the relatives she believed would take care of her children," Sarah said.

"We could have, if she had not insisted that all the children stay together," John said as his anger settled into mild annoyance.

"I know," Sarah said, "and with eight of our own, we didn't have space for four more."

"Hank took the children away to orphanages so fast that nobody had a chance to consider alternate solutions."

As they talked about the situation, John became irate again. "If I had known Hank would get rid of the children overnight, we could have found a way to take the baby at least. She could've stayed in our room until she was old enough to share a room with Belinda. We could've also kept the boys until we found a suitable place for them somewhere near us. I'm angry with Hank, but I'm almost as mad at myself for not realizing what was happening."

Sarah wanted to comfort her husband but felt little comfort herself. "Well, I've been writing to Mrs. Newberry off and on for two years, so I'll write again tomorrow and ask if we can visit. Maybe she'll let us bring Alisha to our house since it's time for her to start school. You have to remember, she's still under the guardianship of the county orphanage. We can't just go by and whisk her away."

"That's exactly what I'd do if I thought I could get away with it."

"Well, you can't, John, so let's do it my way."

Sarah wrote a letter to Beatrice that she now had a room ready and waiting for a second little girl. The previous year, Sarah and John's youngest son, Erskin, had joined the Navy.

🎼

Beatrice read Sarah's letter with tearful gratitude. Her prayers were answered—she knew she'd never find a better-suited family. Two weeks before Alisha's fifth birthday, Beatrice talked to Alisha about her aunt and uncle. After listening to Beatrice, Alisha wanted to like Sarah and John. Maybe she would and maybe she wouldn't, but she didn't understand why she couldn't just stay with Beatrice.

When the Devinwoods arrived, Alisha gave Beatrice no indication that she would react any differently toward them than she had other families, but she promised to try. Two details about the Devinwoods appealed to her:

she would have a room of her own and she would have a sister.

Beatrice tugged Alisha forward into the living room to greet the Devinwoods. Alisha squeezed one of Beatrice's fingers in each hand as they headed for the same familiar sofa. When the conversation began, Alisha looked up quickly, then hid her face behind Beatrice's apron and listened to the voices of the Devinwood family.

Sarah and John had brought two of their children, Erskin, a Navy ensign, and Belinda, their youngest daughter. Erskin was excited about a new car he bought the first day home on leave, and he described every detail. He talked about his life aboard the U.S.S. Roosevelt, which had anchored in a South Carolina port.

Alisha still kept her face hidden behind Beatrice's apron. Beatrice asked about Tawasa Springs, a community not far from the rural area where the Devinwoods lived.

When Sarah introduced Belinda, she added, "Everyone calls her Lindy."

"Hello, Lindy. Do you go to school yet?"

"I'm in the first... well, I'm almost in the first grade and I can read and spell and Mom takes me to the library sometimes." Belinda spoke rapidly, running all her sentences together.

Lindy got Alisha's attention. Alisha turned her head sideways, released one of Beatrice's fingers, and peeked through the keyhole she made with a thumb and finger. She focused on Belinda's French braids. *Her hair is like the girl in my storybook. We're the same old... I'm taller. She stays close to her mother. Maybe she's shy.* Alisha watched Belinda look at Sarah before answering Beatrice's questions and then she swung her keyhole around the room and saw everyone was looking at her. *Why are they looking at me? Lindy's talking, and she's not slowing down one bit.*

As everyone spoke, Sarah watched her daughter but also kept an eye on Alisha and wondered what the child was thinking. Sarah had also wondered how she would keep up with two girls. John earned enough money from his apple orchards to support them adequately—one less worry, but she knew taking on an additional responsibility would be taxing. Seeing the two girls warming up to each other gave her confidence that adopting Alisha would be a good decision.

Alisha shifted her keyhole back and forth from mother to daughter and wondered if she looked like Miss Beatrice. She looked from mother to daughter—both had chubby faces, blue eyes, and dark hair. Alisha dashed out of the room to find a mirror and then hurried back to her seat. She twisted the mirror until she could compare her face to Beatrice's face.

"Miss Beatrice? Do I look like you? Like Lindy looks like her mother," Alisha said.

John and Erskin laughed. "Alisha, nobody looks that much alike except twins," Erskin said, "but you do look like your mother. I remember seeing her once before you were born—"

John swung his foot around and tapped Erskin's leg.

Alisha looked at them, surprised. *I have a mother somewhere and … she gave me to Miss Beatrice. Miss Beatrice is giving me to Aunt Sarah.*

Alisha's exposure to males had been very limited and she suddenly realized Erskin and John would also be at her new home, but then decided that if Lindy lived there, it must be all right. *Erskin was talking about my mother—I want to go.*

After Erskin's revelation, Alisha looked suspiciously at him, but he was avoiding her eyes and focusing on Belinda. Erskin felt Alisha's stare, caught her eye, and glanced at his watch. He smiled and winked giving her an, I'll-tell-you-later look.

Beatrice, concerned that Alisha was about to disappear again, prodded Belinda to keep talking. "Lindy, you must be about the same age as Alisha. I'll guess you're about six?"

"Yes, ma'am, I'll be six in June. I have to be six to go to school." Shifting in her chair and suddenly turning shy, Belinda pointed toward Alisha. "How old is she?"

Alisha held up all of her fingers and said, "I'll be five tomorrow, but I'll be six next."

"Not tomorrow," Beatrice said, "but in about two weeks you'll be five." Then sensing Alisha's apprehension, she said, "Lindy, what do you like to play?"

Belinda immediately lost her shyness and with exaggerated animation began describing her dolls. "My favorite doll is Molly. She did have lots of hair, but I combed most of it out. I put a different dress on her every day, and she sleeps with me, and she goes with me everywhere." Glancing at her mother, Belinda confided, "But I dropped her in the mud today and Mom made me leave her in the car."

Alisha relaxed her hold on Beatrice and moved

over slightly as Belinda regaled her with stories of her dolls. Beatrice held her breath. Sitting forward on the sofa, Alisha smiled at Belinda, and both girls suddenly exploded in giggles.

Alisha wanted to go with Belinda but realized that also meant leaving Miss Beatrice. Alisha cupped her hands close to Beatrice's ear and whispered, "Can I go with them?"

Beatrice kissed her cheek and whispered to Alisha, "Yes, my love, that's what we've been planning for, now isn't it? I want you to go, but only if that's what you want to do. We'll still always love each other."

"Can Nancy go?"

"No, Alisha, Nancy needs to stay here with me."

Alisha edged herself around the back of the sofa and squeezed in between Sarah and Belinda, who stopped talking long enough to take Alisha's hand before their giggling re-ignited. *She's really* going, Beatrice thought, watched the girls for another moment, then said, "Okay, let's go pack."

With a nod from Sarah, Erskin and John went to the car. Sarah stood, and after Beatrice informed her the adoption papers would be mailed soon, she took Belinda's hand and joined John and Erskin.

"Miss Beatrice, does Erskin know my mother?" Alisha asked.

"Maybe, but I don't know a lot about your family, Alisha. Your Aunt Kate brought you to live here when you were six months old. When you get settled in your new home, Aunt Sarah and Uncle John will tell you all about your family."

"I pretended you were my mother."

"I know. I was for almost five years, but you did have a real mother. Come on now; let's get your clothes and toys."

Erskin backed up the car to the front porch and placed Alisha's boxes in the trunk of the car. Alisha and Belinda stood on their knees in the back seat looking out the small rear window of Erskin's new car. Alisha waved goodbye to Beatrice and the other girls who were waving from the front porch. Nancy stood away from the others, watching the car drive away and sucking her thumb.

"Nancy, stop shucking your thumb," Alisha whispered.

Chapter 13

For the past few miles, Sarah watched the setting sun slowly illuminate patches of translucent clouds with red and orange streaks. Just as Erskin drove into their gravel driveway, the sun suddenly disappeared over the mountain range behind their house. Sarah thought the scene was fitting for the end of Alisha's life at the orphanage. Erskin stepped out of the car and moved aside quickly to make room for Alisha and Belinda darting around him to get out. Belinda grabbed Alisha's hand. "Come on, let's go to my room," she said, and they took off running.

Alisha had little time to see the features of her new home. She could only glance at the flowers and plants in cans and buckets on the edge of the front porch, the rockers and straight chairs, and hanging from the ceiling, a swing. But when they entered the house, Alisha pulled back on Belinda's hand for a better look. She stepped into a long hallway and looked to her left through an open door into the living room. She stopped at the door, and before Belinda tugged her forward, she caught a glimpse of a dark mahogany upright piano, and felt the first tug of her new life.

While Erskin unloaded Alisha's belongings from the car, John went around the house to his tool shed. Sarah went to the kitchen to prepare dinner and heard the girls' first argument.

"Which one can be mine?" Alisha asked and picked up Belinda's favorite doll.

"Not that one. I told you she's my favorite. Pick out another one," Belinda said.

"No. I like that one." Alisha said, placing the doll back on the chair, and then she rushed to meet Erskin coming through the front door with her belongings.

Belinda called after her, "You can't have it. Get your own. You did bring your dolls, didn't you?"

"I only have one," Alisha called back.

Alisha went back to Belinda's room while Erskin removed Alisha's things from the box and stacked them on the bed. When the last of Alisha's clothes were in her dresser, Erskin hung her small coat in the wardrobe and picked up a package from the top shelf. He removed a soft blanket and a new doll. Erskin smiled, remembering discovering all the packages his mother hid from him while he was growing up. He laid the new doll on the bed and took Alisha's well-worn doll to Belinda's room.

The girls sat on the floor looking through Belinda's books, their argument forgotten. For a while, Erskin watched from the doorway and then said, "Alisha, look what I have for you."

Alisha jumped up, took her doll, and sat back on the floor beside Belinda. She hugged her doll, looked up at Erskin, and said, "Thanks," and without hesitating, she asked, "Do you know my mother?"

He knelt down and met her eyes. "I do ... I did ... yes," he replied.

"Where is she?"

"She's in heaven now."

Alisha jumped up. "Let's go see her! Help me find a mirror. I want to see if I look like her."

"You can't do that, silly," Belinda said. "You have to die first. Heaven's where you go when you die. Didn't you ever go to church?"

"Sometimes, but they didn't teach us dying. Did my mother die?"

"Erskin, come here a minute," Sarah called.

"Yes, she ... uh-oh, Mama's calling." Grateful for the summons, he took Alisha's hand and said, "Let's go see your room."

Alisha looked around her room and exclaimed, "Where did *that* doll come from?" She hopped on the bed and reached for the doll, but jerked her hand back. "Whose is it?"

"It's yours; do you like it?" Sarah asked.

"Oh, yes! We can sleep together." She called to Belinda, "I have two dolls now, Lindy. I'll bring them to your room, and we'll sleep with all our dolls."

"You have your own room now, Alisha," Sarah said. "This is your room. You can sleep in your bed."

"Oh, I forgot." Alisha looked at Erskin, then toward Belinda's room. "Can I sleep with Lindy sometimes?"

"I'm sleeping with Alisha sometimes too," they heard Belinda say from the other room.

Erskin hugged his mother's shoulders. "Momma, this is your battle and you're going to lose. I'm going outside to chop firewood; it's easier." Erskin laughed, drawing a big smile from his mother.

Sarah checked on the girls for the next several mornings and found Alisha sleeping with Belinda or Belinda sleeping with Alisha.

"What'll I do, John?"

"Nothing. Leave them alone; they'll work it out."

Soon after Lindy began first grade, Alisha finally approached the piano in the living room. None of the family led her there—not by design. Because Sarah and John's philosophy was to encourage their children to make their own choices, they left Alisha alone to integrate into the family at her own pace.

The dark mahogany upright piano was centered against a living room wall, leaving a perfect corner for Alisha when she wanted to be alone. Seduced by the smell emanating from a combination of aged piano wood, ivory keys, felt-covered notes on metal rods in the hollow well of the upright, and the silence of the room, she found a safe corner to hide in the living room—and at last Alisha became acquainted with a real piano.

When she first arrived, Alisha was afraid to lift the cover of the keyboard. The piano had been polished until it gleamed like new, almost untouchable, like the piano in the music store, except much larger. Alisha hoped her aunt Sarah wouldn't mind if she touched it some day. Memories of counting the keys in the Van Horn Music Store that Saturday morning made her want to get to know the keyboard better, especially the elite black notes.

One day, she sat in the corner beside the piano, singing and playing her imaginary piano on the wall. Out of nowhere, she heard, *Watch your fingers. Listen closely now; can you hear the music you're making on your piano?*

"There you are; stay with me please," Alisha pleaded and kept tapping her fingers in rhythm to her song. She abruptly stopped tapping. "Can you hear my music?"

Yes, I can. Your song is beautiful. Don't you know that? Do you remember how excited you were to count the keys on the piano the day you were lost from Miss Beatrice?

"I wasn't lost! I was looking at the piano I found … it was pretty. But I thought all those keys would sound better."

You'll like this piano. Maybe these keys are waiting for you to make beautiful sounds some day. If you play and play, and don't ever stop, you'll find your song, and you'll be a star someday.

"I've already been looking at it, but it's not my piano … I watched Uncle Francis play when he visits. Miss Beatrice was really mad at me that day in the shop."

She wasn't mad. She was afraid you and Nancy were lost. You can play this piano just like Uncle Francis does. It doesn't belong to him either.

Alisha argued, "No, I can't. My hands are too little. Uncle Francis has big hands and he can reach all over the piano keys."

Betcha can.

"Okaayy … I'll show you."

Alisha slipped out of the corner, quietly tiptoed to the piano, and climbed on the bench. The cover was open. *Aunt Sarah always closes this cover. Who left it open?*

Alisha leaned her head close to the piano keys. She had watched Francis as he stretched his long fingers to play—it looked as if he could cover the entire keyboard and play all the notes. *I can't play like him until my hands get bigger.*

Alisha swung her legs around to face the piano, stretched her fingers as far as she could, turned her hands over to examine their reach, and then relaxed and looked around, demanding, "Where are you? Come back. You wanted me to play; come back and show me how!"

Alisha waited...and listened. She could hear the melody of the song she had been singing in the corner. *Okay, I'm gonna try it.* She placed her hands wide above the keyboard, stretched her fingers as far as she could stretch, and hit all the notes within her reach at once. Discouraged by the frightening sounds, she began to climb down from the bench. "I knew it; I'm going back to my piano," she whispered.

Wait. Stay and try once more. When Uncle Francis was your age, he taught one finger to play... and then two... and then three. He learned to play with both hands after he had taught all his fingers to play.

"Oh, all right," Alisha whined. She positioned herself again, pointed her forefinger, and began to sing and search for a key until she found the same sound to match the note she was singing. When she missed a note, she stopped, held her hand directly in front of her eyes, and chastised her errant forefinger. "Bad, bad," she scolded, and started over again. Her voice wasn't missing the note—it was her finger.

"I hope Aunt Saran can't hear me talking to my finger— she might take me back to Miss Beatrice," she whispered.

They're not going to send you away. Sarah and John really want to be mother and daddy to you ... pay attention now to what you're doing. If you'll say nice things to that finger when it does a good job, it will play better and better.

"Will you stay here with me, will you please? Why can't I see you anyway?" Alisha continued to search for the exact note to match her voice until her forefinger could play the entire song without missing a note. When she stopped, the sun was setting and casting sparkling rays through the room and onto the piano.

Sarah stopped at the living room door, amazed. Alisha had been at the piano for over two hours and was quickly finding the melody that sounded exactly like the song she had been singing around the house for a week. Sarah listened as she swept the long, wide hallway that went through the house from front door to back. She recalled Beatrice's earlier letters describing how Alisha turned stories into songs and how she practiced on her imaginary piano. After hearing Alisha, she could also hear the excitement in her son-in-law, Francis's, voice and understand his enthusiasm about playing the piano for Alisha.

"Sarah," Francis had said, "I had my hand on the doorknob to go into the living room when I heard her singing to herself. I cracked the door just enough to see that she was sitting in the corner beside the piano. I closed the door, waited for her to come out, and I then tried an experiment. When she went to her room, I went to the piano. I played loud and jazzy songs, watching the doorway. Just as I thought, she came back—like following the Pied Piper. She slipped into the room and stood at the side of the piano. She must have thought she was out of sight, but when she peeked around the corner, I picked up the beat. She finally eased around the piano and sat on the edge of the bench. I had to convince her it was all right for her to be there, but then her attention was drawn fully to the music—I think she forgot I was there. She watched my hands and tried to see underneath my finger, trying to figure out how I was playing, I guess. I hope you find her a music teacher soon."

Sarah's intuition had been correct—the open keyboard—she would continue leaving the cover open for a long, long time. Sarah stopped sweeping the hallway and stood outside the living room door until the music stopped. When Alisha walked into the hallway, Sarah asked, "Where did that beautiful music come from?"

"You could hear my music too?" Alisha asked, her voice barely audible, tapping all her fingers together in rhythm with each word.

"Your music sounded *so* pretty."

Alisha stopped tapping. "Are you taking me back to Miss Beatrice's house?"

"Oh *no*, as long as you want to stay, we *want* you to stay, Alisha. Will you play for me again sometime?"

Alisha skipped away. "Okay, I'll play again. Where's Lindy?"

Sarah breathed a sigh of relief for the first connection to Alisha. Sarah believed Alisha would find her way in music, just like Asyah.

Chapter 14

Robert slumped his gangly body on the chair, elbows on the kitchen table supporting his head. "Where's Lester? I thought we were going fishing," he said, gradually waking up. Over the past couple of years, he had become an avid fisherman, much to Lester's satisfaction.

"George came by earlier and they left," Bess said. "You were sleeping, and Lester didn't want to wake you. He knows how you boys like to sleep."

"He should've blown the horn like he usually does. School's out, we *wanted* to get up."

Joe came in the door behind Martin and James, saying "Oh, so that's how that works. I should've figured that one out by now."

If anything, James and Martin looked more alike as they grew into adolescence, and they took full advantage, wearing one another's clothes, pretending to be each other, and generally keeping everyone, particularly Bess, confused. The two they could never fool, although they tried constantly, were Robert and Lester.

James passed by Robert and thumped his head. Robert was quick. Without turning, he reached over his head and grabbed James by the hair. James yelped,

Martin jumped into the melee, and all three fell to the floor, wrestling.

Joe ignored their rowdiness until Bess set a platter of ham and eggs on the table, then he shouted, "Umm, umm, good. Smell that food! Bess, you should've cooked enough for the boys." He heard voices from the pile saying, "Get up. Ouch, turn me loose! Move, get off me!" The boys instantly scrambled for their chairs.

"Not so fast," Bess said. "Go wash your hands and hurry back before your food gets cold."

Robert ran out of the kitchen with James and Martin right behind him. They were back in thirty seconds and digging into their food.

Bess refilled glasses with juice and announced to the boys, "Helen Snow, our neighbor over on Highland Road, has a new baby girl. Joe and I want to take you to see her. We have presents for all three of you to give to the baby and one for Helen."

Robert shoved his chair back, crossed his arms, and frowned. "I'd rather go fishing," he said.

James and Martin looked at their brother. "Me too," they said, mimicking his expression.

"Joe, don't you back out on me," Bess pleaded.

"Tell you what, guys," Joe said with his usual smile, "go with us this afternoon, and when we get back, we'll ride horses down to the river and see if George and Lester are catching anything."

"Can't we just ride horses? That's more fun than fishing," James said.

Robert took his last bite of food, quickly signaled for

their yum-yum-good routine, and said, "Martin, you and James ride; I'll wait for Lester," and the boys scurried out of the kitchen.

Joe, apprehensive about his wife's plan, said, "Bess, don't be so sure this is a good idea."

"If it disturbs them into thinking about their sister, it'll be worth it."

"What makes you think they don't remember her?"

"Because they never talk about her or their parents."

"To us, they don't."

The brothers had not forgotten their sister. Memories of her hung over them like a heavy cloud, and led by Robert's influence, James and Martin wanted nothing to do with the baby they were about to visit. The brothers inherited their father's playfulness and optimism that usually carried him through the worst of times. For a few weeks after their father died, they clung to one another, slept in the same bed, and walked around the farm as if Asyah would magically reappear. They were able to return to their playful behavior when they gathered around their baby sister. They wiggled her tiny fingers and tickled her nose and ears until she woke up to their silly faces and funny made-up songs. Alisha delighted in their antics and watched every move they made, as if they were performing just for her. They made her laugh and tried to get her to mimic what they did.

The boys helped Bess wrap presents for the new baby, while Joe kidded around trying to convince them they would have fun. But in the car, Joe watched Robert in the rearview mirror become more sullen the closer they came to the Snow's house, and he knew James and Martin would take on the same mood.

When they arrived, Joe opened the door and said firmly, "Okay, everybody out," and stood by until James and Martin slowly followed Robert out of the car.

"We'll wait out here," Robert said on the Snow's front porch.

"What about you, Martin? What about the present you have for the baby?" Bess asked.

"I'm James."

"Sorry...*James.*"

"Maybe we could come in later," Robert said. "Give her your presents first, okay?"

"Sure," Joe said, and knocked on the door. "Come on Bess, let's go inside; they can come in when they're ready."

Joe greeted Helen, looked around, and said, "Where's Frank? I thought the proud papa would be here today."

"Come in, Joe. He had to go over to the mill to help install the new grinding wheel. They're trying to get into full production."

Bess's spirits lifted when she saw the infant. "What a beautiful baby, what's her name?"

"We named her Julia, after Frank's mother, but we call her Julie."

"Do you mind if I hold her?"

"Of course not," Helen said and placed the baby in Bess's arms.

Joe presented a gift for the baby and went to the window to watch the boys sitting on the edge of the porch, swinging their legs, tossing their gifts in the air, and taking turns catching them.

"How are the boys...twins, aren't they?" Helen asked.

"Yes, twins, and Robert's their older brother."

Bess added, "The twins look so much alike, I'm having trouble remembering which one has the freckle on which side of his face. I'm forever mixing up the two."

"They've developed quite a repertoire of tricks to keep us confused," Joe said.

"Joe, see if you can get them in here," Bess prodded. "They have presents for the baby."

Joe tapped on the window. "Come in, guys, and see the baby; she's a cute little thing."

The brothers looked at one another, but made no move to come inside the house.

"Joe, if you can convince Robert, the twins will follow," Bess said and carefully placed Julie back in the cradle.

Joe stepped out on the porch and said firmly, "Boys, come in now, and bring your gifts."

Joe watched them walk grudgingly toward the cradle with Robert leading the way. "Boys, this is Helen, and the baby's name is Julie," Joe said matter-of-factly.

"Hi, Miss Helen," Robert said and handed her his gift. James and Martin followed their brother's lead and handed over their gifts. They looked at the baby, unable to restrain a grin. Robert reached down and touched the baby's hand with his finger. Startled when Julie wiggled and moved her hand, Robert turned to his brothers and said, "Let's go." James and Martin glanced once more at the baby and bolted out the door in front of their brother.

"I had no idea this would upset them. Did they leave a baby at their home?" Helen asked.

Joe looked at Bess and mumbled through his pipe, "They don't remember, huh?" He followed the boys and left Bess explaining to Helen.

"Yes, we believe they had other siblings, but we could not get the information from the Boys Home. We thought enough time had passed and that this would be a good idea, but apparently not. We'll visit again, Helen, just Joe and me with you and Frank."

"We'll be happy to see you—and the boys—anytime," Helen said as she walked Bess to the door.

Joe found the boys standing against the side of the house, rubbing their eyes. Robert was the most upset, but Joe could not tell for sure if the twins were crying because of the baby or if they were crying because Robert was crying.

Joe put his arm around all three boys. "All right, let's go home," he said and led them to the car.

When Bess got in the car and saw that the boys had been crying, she cried. Joe returned his downhearted family home and left immediately for his office to escape the distress and finish a work project before leaving on a trip.

The boys silently crept out of the car and went straight to their rooms. Bess started toward her room but then heard someone coming in the back door and knew it was Lester by the smell of fresh fish. He held up a string of large trout.

"Smelling up the house again, are you?" Bess chided.

"Guess I am, but somebody's gotta bring fish home. James can't catch 'em. Robert can't catch 'em. Martin can't—guess I'll have to teach you to fish, Bess."

The boys heard Lester's voice and ran into the kitchen. "You're going teach Miss Bess to fish?" James asked.

"Got to," Lester said while laying the string of fish in the sink and covering his catch with water. "Hey, who punched you guys in the eyes? Looks like somebody punched all three of you. Who did that?"

James and Martin hung their heads and looked toward Robert, who glanced up at Lester but didn't answer either.

"Okay, let's go to the barn and clean these fish before Bess kicks all of us out of here. Boys take these fish and start cleaning—I'll be there in a minute."

Robert took the string of fish and, with his brothers in tow, headed toward the barn. Lester listened as Bess told him how the boys were reluctant to go inside Helen's house and how upset they were after seeing the baby.

"I knew it. We should have talked to them about their family long before now." Lester sighed and went out to the barn. The fish lay on the cleaning table untouched and the boys were in the hayloft. *They're sure talking now,* he thought and listened awhile to their conversation before slowly climbing the ladder. He eased down on the bale of hay next to James.

"Lester, you have to believe us. We do have a sister," Robert said as he walked away and grasped an overhead rafter. "Her name is Alisha."

James moved closer to Lester. "You can find her, Lester, I know you can. You can do anything…please."

"You *do* remember your sister, don't you?" Lester began.

"Yeah, I mean, yes sir, we remember. Her name was Alisha, but we called her 'Sis' and made up songs for her."

"And James made silly faces," Martin said.

"You did too," James said.

"Remember how she would smile at us when we touched her fingers and ears," Robert said, without turning around and revealing a slight grin.

"Why haven't you talked to us about your family before, Robert?" Lester asked.

"We thought you didn't want to talk about them."

Lester shook his head, bothered by his own oversight. "I guess we assumed you didn't want to talk about them either. Where are your parents?" he asked gently.

The two younger boys looked to Robert. "They're dead," he said, looking at Lester with eyes that spoke of a broken heart but also of an unbreakable spirit.

"I'm sorry about your parents, Robert."

Robert said. "Father O'Kelly wouldn't tell us where our sister is. He said he didn't know, and I guess he didn't. Uncle Hank left without telling him anything. James, remember how fast he drove off?"

"Yeah, but girls couldn't live there anyway," James said.

Lester leaned back on the hay bale. "I want all of you to know that even if your uncle had stayed around long enough to tell Father O'Kelly about your family, the orphanage was bound, by law, to keep it confidential. Would you be okay telling me about your family now, and maybe where you lived?"

Lester listened patiently as the brothers opened up. They alternately told how their father fell down the steps and didn't respond to their pleas to wake up. Unlike Robert, James and Martin remembered only a few details of their father's funeral.

"I remember how good the flowers smelled in the church," James said, "and the sad songs. I didn't even know there was a cemetery behind our house until we buried Dad. He wouldn't let us go back there, we always went the other way—toward the river."

"He fell down the steps and didn't saying anything but, *oh no,*" Robert said. "I called Mama and when she saw him, she screamed so loud I thought she was going to die too … well, she did die but not then; that was later. Dad looked like a wax person in the casket. I didn't believe it was him at first," he said and paused.

James took over with his remembrances. "He used to play his banjo a lot and help us make up songs. He helped me catch my first fish, and we worked on the barn and fences with him too."

"We kept looking for him to walk in the door or wake us up in the morning," Robert said. "When they closed the lid on the casket, I still believed I would see him again—it still doesn't seem real."

"He helped us gather eggs," Martin said, moving off his hay bale to stand near Robert.

"You broke 'em," James reminded him.

"You did too," Martin quickly reminded his brother.

Lester sat up and asked, "Did your Daddy teach you to rub your bellies and do that 'uum, uum good' thing you do after you eat?"

"Yeah," they said. The question produced a smile from all three boys before they corrected "yeah" to "yes sir."

Lester leaned forward, propped his arms on his knees,

and asked with caution, "What do you remember about your mother?"

Robert spoke up angrily. "She took good care of us; I don't care what anybody says."

Lester stood and reached to touch Robert's shoulder. When Robert flinched, Lester said, "I'm sure she did, son. Your parents must have loved you all very much."

James rolled over on the hay bale, hiding his face in the fetal position. Lester almost missed his whispered, "Mom died in the river." Lester sat back down on the hay bale, drew James close, and hugged him.

Desperate to change the subject, Martin said, "Robert, tell Lester the Indian story Dad used to tell us."

Robert shook off his renewed grief and continued with his father's habit of telling the Indian story. "Okay. At first, the People lived in a great big underground cavern. One day, they came to the top and found a huge tree at the cave's entrance. Daddy called it the dividing tree because when the People walked out of the cave, they divided. Those going to one side of the tree became the Alabamas Indians and those to the other side, the Coushatta. In the late 1700s, the Coushatta, later called 'Koasati,' and the Alabamas Indians began moving toward east Texas near the Angeni, Neches, and Sabine Rivers. But for a long time everybody settling in the area where we lived still looked like the Coushatta."

James freed himself from Lester and reported softly, "Dad said that's why we look like Indians … well, Mom was the one who really looked like an Indian, especially when she braided her hair."

"She was pretty," Robert said.

Martin looked pensive before he spoke. "Dad took us all over the mountains looking for a tree standing in the middle of the entrance to a cave."

"Did you ever find the cave, Martin?"

"We found plenty of caves, and some of them had a tree in front, but he would never tell us which one was the cave in the story."

"Probably because he wanted to keep on looking," Robert said. "He liked the woods—we did too, but the caves were so dark we crept in a few feet and ran back out. It was too scary."

"Not for me, I wasn't scared," James declared.

"Yes, you were," Robert said, and they all laughed.

Lester stood up. "All of you listen to me. Someday we'll look for that cave again, and some day you'll see your sister. Right now, let's go clean those stinking fish and cook them at my house so Bess won't be mad at us for smelling up her kitchen."

Chapter 15

The birthday party was in full swing on the Devinwood's front lawn. Alisha was six in May, and Belinda would be seven in June. Each girl pleaded for her own party, but Sarah chose the midpoint for a shared birthday party. She watched Alisha and Belinda run across the lawn in white pinafores she had embroidered and shook her head at their unconcern for her carefully tied hair bows, now reduced to pink streamers flying as they ran.

John brought out his ice cream maker, filled the canister with Sarah's mixture of cream, sugar, and vanilla flavoring, and then packed ice and rock salt around the canister in the wooden bucket. He kept the children occupied with turning the handle until it became too frozen and difficult, and then he took over until the ice cream was firmly frozen.

Kate and Hank were there, and Sarah was relieved to see Kate looking healthy and even Hank behaving with more kindness than she'd ever seen him display. Kate helped her decorate the table with a white cloth and pink and white crepe paper, which showed off the three-layer birthday cake and thirteen pink candles. Hank set up a camera on a tripod, covered his head with a blackout hood, and began adjusting the lenses. Nine children stood behind the table, waiting impatiently for John to light the candles so Alisha and Belinda could make wishes and Sarah could slice the cake. But first, Hank *had* to take his pictures.

"Hurry up, Hank, take the picture. The children can't stand still much longer," Kate said.

"Be patient. They can wait," Hank mumbled, absorbed in his hobby. "I'm trying to photograph the table and kids, not the shadows behind them."

"Stand still, girls, so Hank can take your picture," Kate said.

As soon as Hank came out from under his blackout hood, Sarah cut the cake, Kate filled paper cups from a pitcher of Kool Aid, and John added a scoop of ice cream and served the eager children.

John returned to the porch and watched the children playing. Hank gathered up his equipment and headed to the car, where he read a newspaper to avoid hearing— again—John's opinion about taking the children to orphanages.

Kate and Hank had visited the Devinwoods almost weekly the first summer Alisha arrived, and after a particularly long visit, John warned Sarah, "Kate's trying to edge in on your territory. You'd better watch her; she'll try to take that girl away from you."

"*Us,* John…take her away from us. She's your daughter too."

"If you think I don't know that, just watch me if they try to take her from *us.* In their case, it won't be *they;* it'll be just *Kate.* I believe Hank would be happy to never see

Alisha or another child again, else he'd go get those boys from wherever he took them."

Alisha and Belinda began first and second grade in a one-room schoolhouse called "Choccolocco," a name derived from the Cherokee Indians whom the local people had thought were "loco" when first encountering the Indians. The teacher, Miss Gussie Borden, drove a black Ford, which she kept spotless. At recess, students took turns polishing the car with scraps of cloth she kept in a bag near the door. Each morning she stopped at the Devinwood driveway to pick up Belinda and Alisha in her shiny Ford, as she did a few other students along her route, and then returned them home after school.

Gussie had started teaching first grade in the one-room schoolhouse thirty years earlier. She added a second grade and then a third grade as the original six students progressed through their lessons and assignments. Students rarely missed a day of school, even in the harsh winters. They warmed themselves and their lunches by a black coal heater situated in the center of the room. Local men kept up the building and not much changed through the years, except the trees and shrubbery that Gussie planted that first year had grown to maturity and the number of students had increased. The past summer, the men gave the schoolhouse its first coat of white paint, making it strikingly visible for quite a distance.

Gussie arranged her growing student population, now

up to eighteen, by row and grade, keeping the grades as separate as possible given the space limitations. Belinda considered herself an experienced student this year and sat proudly in the second row, reminding Alisha that she was *only* a first-grader and must sit in the first row.

The children arrived at school squeaky clean because they knew their teacher often walked up and down the aisle inspecting ears and fingernails. In the spring, she added a necessary inspection for head lice, which she knew were easily transmitted by swapping wool hats and while playing together on the playground.

Gussie greeted her class each day with the same words, "It's time to begin." She smiled and rapped the edge of a ruler on the top of her desk. She began by calling the roll from a black book, and with each "here," she checked off the name in a narrow column to the left of six other columns labeled, *Name, Reading, Writing, Arithmetic, English,* and *Deportment.* By the end of the day, the students had an *A, B, C,* or *D* entered by their name for each subject. Gussie considered it impossible for anyone to fail and did not give an *F.* When a student's grade fell to a *C* in any subject, she paid special attention to that student on Fridays while the others played outside. If the student's grade did not improve, she made a surprise visit to their house on Saturday morning for a drill in English or arithmetic, just to make sure she had the attention and the cooperation of the parents.

After her daily roll call, Gussie began the day with reading, sometimes combined with a short lesson in English.

"Remember, each of you must read a paragraph. Gene-Claude, tell the first graders just what a paragraph means."

Gene-Claude, a third grader, loved to perform, especially for first-grade underlings. He popped out of his desk and stood pencil-straight. As fast as he could, he said, "It's a bunch of stuff on one subject written about one … uh … thing, with what you're really talking about in the first sentence and the rest of what you're going to talk about in the next bunch of sentences and in the last sentence … well, that takes you to the next paragraph."

"Gene-Claude, you're absolutely right. Now, when you go home tonight, write down what you said. I'm going to ask you to do that again tomorrow morning, but I want you to repeat what a paragraph means—in the four *proper* sentences that you've written."

"Yes ma'am." Gene-Claude slipped quickly back into his desk and immediately stood again asking cautiously, "Miss Borden, are you coming to my house on Saturday?"

"Not if your sentences are *proper*," she replied.

Gussie also insisted on order. She sent students out to play one row at a time while the remaining two rows worked on their lessons and took tests. Each afternoon, she practiced a hymn with the students, which they sang together in church the following Sunday.

Mary, another first-grader, sat behind Alisha. To get Alisha's attention, she poked her with a pencil eraser. Alisha leaned back against the desk to hear Mary whisper secrets. The girls had become friends on the first day of school and found it difficult to confine their chatter to the playground. Mary's gregarious nature matched Alisha's, but their behavior often landed them at their desks during recess.

In the third month of school, Alisha still persisted in reading her lines while sitting in the coat closet. Gussie was perplexed and noted Alisha's behavior in her daily log but gave no indication that sitting in a closet to read was abnormal or unacceptable.

"Alisha, stop listening to Mary and read the first paragraph. Mary, you'd better stop talking and listen, or you'll both spend recess inside today."

While Gussie chastised Mary, Alisha slipped into the closet to read her paragraph. On the second line, Mary began reading along with Alisha. Gussie glared at Mary, as all eyes turned to the open closet door. Alisha peered around the corner of the door. Matching each other's volume, Mary and Alisha finished reading the paragraph. Alisha returned to her desk, turned, and smiled a "thank you" at Mary.

Gussie gave both girls an *A* for reading, thought for an instant, and added another *A* by Mary's name for deportment. A few weeks later, she noted that Alisha was no longer sitting in the closet to read.

At home, Alisha still had the need to hide. Sarah did not allow anyone to disturb her, often insisting that the family wait on dinner until she came to the table, realizing the smell of food most often got Alisha's attention.

𝄞

Maintaining the Devinwood property around the apple orchards required controlled burning, one of John's favorite jobs. Typically, he would light a small fire to burn underbrush from one area of the woods and spend the day confining the fire to that area before moving on to the next. Most of the time, his burning projects worked out that way, but not on one particular autumn day.

Alisha sniffed the air and asked, "Lindy, do you smell smoke?"

"Yes, the smell's getting worse. Look at all that smoke on the hill."

"I guess your dad is building a bigger fire," Alisha casually replied and continued placing furniture made of stones in their imaginary playhouse. "Can I put the piano in my room so I can play more?" she asked.

"It won't fit. You should make a separate room for your piano," Belinda suggested.

"If I do, will you stay in the room with me while I play?"

"Okay," Belinda said, distracted by the smoke. "Dad's sure working hard; his fire's getting bigger."

Alisha and Belinda were much too busy to be bothered with the distraction and did not understand the enormity of the situation. They continued arranging stone furniture and chatting about their cooking, dolls, and make-believe friends.

Sarah looked out the kitchen window, eyes wide

with alarm. She had not checked on the girls since John started the fire, which now looked out of control. She immediately headed in the general direction of where they played. Neighbors, seeing the smoke, hurried over to help battle the blaze without hesitation, knowing they could always count on John to be there when they needed help. When the neighbors learned the girls were out beyond the fire line, they grabbed green pine tree branches and beat the fire with more urgency than usual.

Unaware of the attention they were generating, it was not until Alisha and Belinda felt the smoke burning their nostrils did they abandon their playhouse. They moved to another area, in a direction away from the smoke, taking them farther from home and away from familiar surroundings. When the smoke obscured their sense of direction, they became frightened and ran until they exited the woods onto a nearby farm.

Belinda stopped running. "I know where we are now," she said, breathing hard.

"Me too," Alisha said. "This is where Miss Dorothy lives. She bakes good cookies. Let's go knock on her door and see if she has some."

"Miss Dorothy," Belinda called as she knocked. "Are you home?"

Dorothy Brown came to the door. "Hello, girls, what are you doing this far away from home?" Looking with concern at the smoke rising behind the girls, she said, "Oh, I see Mr. Devinwood is burning off the underbrush again."

"Yes, ma'am," the girls replied simultaneously.

"He's working hard today," Belinda added.

Alisha raised her nose, sniffed a long exaggerated sniff. "Hmm, your cookies sure smell good, Miss Dorothy." Belinda seconded the appreciative sniff.

"I think I'd better give you some cookies to eat on the way home. Your mother is going to be worried about you—very soon." Dorothy put four cookies for each girl into two small bags. "Now, be on your way before you scare Sarah half to death."

Alisha and Belinda walked slowly toward home, finishing the cookies before turning into the dirt road leading to their house. They kicked stones, trying to out-kick each other, and picked flowers along the side of the road, feeling no sense of urgency.

Maggie, their older sister, saw Alisha and Belinda strolling toward the house. She called out, "You two had better hurry and get home. You're in big trouble. Mama's looking for you, and she's mad!"

When they reached the house, Alisha and Belinda jumped onto the front-porch swing to wait for their mother. They held flowers they had gathered on the way home as they swung. When they saw Sarah swinging her arms and walking as fast as she could toward the house, they realized Maggie was right; she looked really mad. They released the chains and slowed the swing.

Sarah pointed at her girls with a small green switch that she had snapped off a bush. She went straight to the swing, stopped it completely, and switched Alisha and Belinda's outstretched legs, ignoring the flowers in their hands. Belinda started crying immediately but stayed in the swing. Without a tear, Alisha jumped out of the swing and ran straight to her corner by the piano.

"Oh no," Sarah exclaimed, exasperated. She was angrier with John than at Belinda and Alisha. *I've set back whatever progress I've made in getting her out of that corner. Why can't she just cry like other children?*

Alisha sat alone by the piano examining the red stripes on her legs. No one had ever hit her. She touched her finger to her tongue and gently patted the stinging stripes with her fingertips, but she felt a new kind of hurt that had nothing to do with the red stripes. She decided she would stay in the corner forever. She relaxed and fell into a slumber, felt the familiar warmth cover her like a soft blanket and heard a whisper. *She loves you, Alisha. She was afraid, like you are now.*

The room was almost dark when Alisha woke up to the smell of food. *How long have I been here,* she wondered. She did not want to face her Aunt Sarah and the possibility of the switch again, but hunger forced her to change her mind about staying in the corner forever.

Sarah stood just outside the door, listening. When she finally heard movement, she knew Alisha would be out soon. She watched the light come on beneath the door, heard the piano bench scrub the floor as Alisha pulled it closer, and then heard Alisha begin to sing and search for notes. Sarah breathed a sigh of relief. She was convinced that if Alisha's interest in music continued—and she had a feeling it would—playing the piano would replace that annoying habit of hiding.

Sarah walked by the dining room and saw John in

his chair at the opposite end of the table where he had positioned himself soon after the fire was out. As was her habit on nights like this, Sarah prepared a simple meal she knew everyone would enjoy. As long as she could remember, she had insisted on ending the day in harmony, and that seemed to be easier to accomplish at the dinner table. Battling the woods fire had taken a long time and a great deal of help from the neighbors, but caused no damage other than burning off more of the woods than John had planned.

Alisha and Belinda sat on their chairs, watching their mother's every move while stealing glances underneath the tablecloth to compare their red stripes, which by now had almost disappeared.

As Sarah cleared the table, Alisha whispered, "Lindy, does she still have that stick?"

"No," Belinda whispered.

"Why did she hit us?"

"She wanted us to come back home."

"We *were* home."

"I know … I don't know why."

"Do you think she loves you?"

"Yes, she's got to love us; we're her kids … well, I think so," Belinda whispered, unsure now that Alisha had brought it up.

"Does she ever hug you?"

"Sometimes."

"Then she loves you," Alisha whispered. "Why doesn't she hug me?"

"I don't know that either."

"My mother hugs me," Alisha whispered, remembering the comfort of the unseen whispers.

In the summer of 1943, Sarah convinced John to sell their home and the apple orchards and buy another home in the mountainside village of Tawasa Springs, Tennessee. Belinda had completed the third grade, and Sarah met with Gussie Borden for the last time. It was time to move. Sarah hoped the girls would adapt to their new home in the larger town of Tawasa Springs and the new school.

Alisha was initially excited about moving, but when she realized it meant leaving her teacher and friend, Mary, her episodes of withdrawal returned, but so did a rising passion for the piano. She practiced on the piano with one finger until she mastered all the melodies she knew then tried playing with two fingers, then four. She began making up songs that were, more often than not, tales about their former teacher and classmates. Belinda sat nearby and occasionally looked up from her book to suggest a word or phrase when her sister struggled. Their routine went on day-after-day until movers took the piano away.

The first morning in their new home, Alisha awoke to the unfamiliarity of her new surroundings. She jumped out of her bed and looked through the house for the piano. Ignoring Sarah and John's conversation, the clatter of dishes, and smells of breakfast, she ran to the front door and breathed a sigh of relief. There was the truck with its lumps and odd shapes covered by a canvas. Then she remembered the movers agreed to load the piano last so she could finish playing her new song.

The two-story white house was poised near the top of a grassy plateau with the Chattanooga Mountains as a backdrop. Ancient oak trees framed the property on each side with smaller maples and fruit trees scattered over hills behind the house. A quarter-moon-shaped driveway provided access from the main street.

Alisha and Belinda transferred from their one-room school with less than twenty students to Tawasa Springs School with three hundred students and twelve grades.

The springs, giving Tawasa its name, flowed from under a ledge of a centuries-old rock, forming a natural bridge over the streamhead and a brook that ebbed and flowed around the hilly community, eventually running through the center of town. Over time, a natural park evolved into a rich tapestry of purple, gold, and claret wild flowers. In the center of the park, a new bridge rose across the deepest part of the creek, serving as a school crossing.

Kate and Hank arrived after Alicia and Belinda's eighth and ninth birthday. Sarah had ironed clothes and supervised the girls' packing suitcases for the summer vacation to Kate and Hank's house. On the day they were to leave, Belinda awoke with a fever. "I'm sorry, Alisha," Sarah said, "but Lindy will have to stay home, but I want you to wear your new dress and sandals, the ones from Kate."

Alisha went to the front porch where Sarah and Kate

waited. She handed Sarah her hairbrush and announced, "Lindy's going to be a nurse."

"I hear she needs a nurse herself today," Kate said. "What brought that on?"

"She's reading about Clara Barton taking care of her brother." Alisha took a hair clip from Sarah's apron pocket and held it up. "Mom, why does Lindy have red spots on her face and arms?"

Sarah and Kate looked at one another and cried, "Measles!"

Sarah quickly fastened the clip, adjusted Alisha's hair for the final touch, and rushed inside to see about Belinda.

Alisha followed behind the flustered woman. "You look awful, Lindy."

"Tattletale! I told you not to tell," Belinda said, glancing at her mother.

"*So...*"

Belinda kept reading. "Listen to this, Mom. Clara Barton took care of her brother when he was sick, and she was just eleven years old—that's not too much older than me. I'll bet I could do that too."

"I'm sure you could, Lindy." Sarah said goodbye to Kate and Alisha, rearranged the covers, and sat beside Belinda to listen to the nursing adventures of Clara Barton.

"Aunt Kate, why did Uncle Hank buy such a big car?" Alisha asked, looking over the inside of Hank's new Packard.

"For long trips, I imagine." Kate said as she watched

Hank dash to the front porch and return with Alisha's suitcase just as John came out of the tool-shed.

As they drove away, Alisha slid down on the floorboard behind Kate and began singing and tapping in rhythm on the seatback.

"When will we be at your house?" Alisha asked.

"In about an hour," Hank said. "Are you going to sing *all* the way home?"

"If you want me to," Alisha replied innocently. "Do you have a piano?"

"No, thank goodness," Hank replied.

"Where do you live?" Alisha asked.

Kate answered quickly, "Bremington, on Lake Vista."

"Vista's a pretty name," Alisha said and resumed singing.

The next time Alisha paused, Kate said, "Alisha, I think you're old enough for a sleep-over party? We could invite the two girls who live down the street."

Hank groaned and clutched the steering wheel. "Oh no, those kids drive me crazy."

Alisha propped her elbows on the back of the seat. "Uncle Hank, you could play kickball with us."

"Oh no, he can't. You might get hurt," Kate said, alarmed.

"Are all adults afraid, Aunt Kate? Uncle Hank's afraid of Uncle John. Mom's afraid to let Lindy come with us because she had the measles. You're afraid I might get hurt. Miss Beatrice was *always* afraid we'd get lost on our trips to town. I'm not afraid!"

"Well, maybe you should be afraid sometimes," Hank replied.

"If the girls upset you that much, just what do you suggest, Hank?" Kate said, fed up with his sarcasm.

Alisha stretched out on the back seat, soothed by blurring trees whizzing by the window, and soon fell asleep. Hank drove in silence, staring straight ahead while Kate quietly pointed out the magnificent oak trees surrounding farmhouses and red barns and beautiful still lakes with cows and horses grazing in lush green pastures nearby.

"Alisha's asleep," Kate said, giving up on sharing her appreciation for the countryside. "Hank, maybe leaving the orphanage has affected Alisha more than we realize. I think we should take her back for a visit; I'll bet she misses Beatrice, don't you think?"

"Of course she does; she *was* her mother for five years," Hank said loudly. "But why would you want to go back there now, Kate? You didn't exactly endear yourself to the woman."

Kate matched Hank's volume. "What about yourself? You didn't endear yourself to anyone by forcing me to do what I did! You didn't care what taking her to the orphanage would do, did you Hank? Anyway, what do we have to lose now?"

Alisha rolled off the seat. *How can they argue so much?* The thought of visiting Miss Beatrice was a surprise, but Alisha realized she did miss her. When she remembered Miss Beatrice saying *you'll just have to keep playing your pretend piano until you have a real one; then you'll learn rather quickly, I would think,* she wanted to see her.

"Hank, turn this car around," Kate demanded. "It's early. We're going to see Beatrice." She turned toward Alisha. "Alisha, how would like to go visit Miss Beatrice?"

Alisha was suddenly frightened. "Okay, I guess … are you going to leave me there?"

"No, of course not; what makes you think that?"

"The day I left and we were packing my stuff, I asked Miss Beatrice why I lived with her instead of my own mother. She told me *you* brought me there."

"Humph," Hank mumbled, and Kate looked at him with renewed anger. "Well, this time we're going in to visit for a while and then you're going to our house. I promise."

"Uncle Hank, are you going in?"

"No, I'll wait in the car. Don't stay very long or I'll leave you both," Hank said, but he was not smiling.

"No, you won't. You're teasing, aren't you? You wouldn't leave Aunt Kate." Alisha tried to remember more about Miss Beatrice and hoped Uncle Hank really was just teasing.

More than three years had passed since Alisha had seen Beatrice, and memories of her life at the orphanage were fading. At times, she had to try hard to remember what Miss Beatrice looked like. Now, going back to visit, Alisha felt her loyalty divided between Sarah and the woman she thought—or pretended—was her mother. As soon as she saw the house, though, she forgot about loyalty as memories rushed in. She felt Beatrice's affection, saw the summer backyard baths, tingled at the thought of the Saturday morning bus rides to town … and oh, the stories … learning from Miss Beatrice to tell stories would always delight Alisha.

Just as Beatrice reached for the string to start the attic fan, bringing in a cool gentle breeze, she glanced out the open window to see a car arrive. Kate and Alisha were getting out of the car, which almost made Beatrice faint. Her memory flashed back to the day Kate arrived to hand over a tiny baby, and illogical thoughts ran through her mind. *Oh my Lord, what if she thinks she can bring that child back … nonsense … Alisha's eight years old now.*

Alisha bounded up the front porch steps. Beatrice rushed out the front door, struggling to hold back her tears. By the time she collected her wits, Alisha was already on the porch. She gathered Alisha into her arms, as she always had. "Just look at you, Alisha. I had no idea you would've grown this much. I can't pick you up any more." She squeezed Alisha tighter, then held her slightly away to get a better look. "I'm so happy you're here, I've missed you a lot."

Alisha did not feel the same comfort of Beatrice's arms. She looked back toward the car. *Uncle Hank is still there. Why is Miss Beatrice crying?*

"How do you like your new home?" Beatrice asked.

"Okay, I guess … Lindy and I go to school Miss Beatrice—and *I* have a *real* piano."

"I'm so happy for you, Alisha. Did you count the keys like you did at Mr. Ed's?"

"I counted them a few times to make sure there were

eighty-eight like you said, but now I can play songs," Alisha said proudly. She looked around. "Where's Nancy?"

"Nancy had to go to a hospital. We couldn't keep her here any longer."

"Was she still sucking her thumb?"

"Yes."

"I'll bet I could have made her stop if I hadn't left."

"No, Alisha. No one will ever be able to do that."

"I could have," Alisha said. "Can I go inside?"

"Of course you can," Beatrice replied and watched as Alisha skipped into the house and disappeared into the hallway and rooms. Beatrice turned to Kate. "Come on in. You seem different from when I first saw you coming up that front walk eight years ago."

"I *am* different, Beatrice. I hardly know where to begin apologizing."

"I never understood your actions, Kate, but time moves on, things change. Maybe it would be best if you and I start over from where we are right now. Let's go in the kitchen, I'll make coffee, and we'll talk."

Alisha walked into the room with the brick floor, smiling when she went over to the fireplace and remembered nighttime baths in the big tub of soapy water. She was surprised to see the tub beside the fireplace now filled with flowers. *Where do they take a bath?* Across the hall, Alisha opened a freshly painted door, peeked into the long, narrow room that she remembered as Miss Beatrice's office, and flipped on the light switch. Four fancy scroll light fixtures lit the room, and she drew in her breath at what she saw. The room was painted pale pink. The walls were papered with tiny wildflowers and an occasional pink lily rose from the center molding to the ceiling. Two large claw-foot bathtubs sat end to end along the long wall, and child-sized lavatories sat on each end wall, graced by gold-framed oval mirrors. A small rack above each lavatory held five toothbrushes, all different colors. *This is very pretty, but I'll bet they miss the bubbles in the old tub—well, maybe not Miss Beatrice.*

Alisha found her way up the steps to the second floor and stepped into the part of Beatrice's room that she called the children's music room. Besides the kitchen where she and Miss Beatrice played the talking game, Alisha liked the music room best. She could hear Brahms Lullaby, *Go to sleep ... go to sleep, go to sleep and rest good night ...* coming from the shiny Victrola horn while she and the other girls napped on the pretty rug. Alisha stood by the window, looking out over the front yard and thinking, *Everything in the room looks just the same, except Miss Beatrice; she looks ... different ... smaller than before. Maybe she's lonely. She was crying. Wait a minute, why didn't I cry—why don't I cry. I don't remember ever crying, but I must have when I was a baby.*

Alisha sat on the steps at the third floor landing for a while and then went into her former hiding places. She found the closet where she fell asleep, causing Miss Beatrice to block off the third floor; then she went back to the first floor storage room and sat on the old familiar wooden box.

Parts of the house felt soft and easy—homey—but the storage room where she spent so much time no longer felt like the hiding place she had claimed for her own. Alisha hurried to leave, but when she peeked out and saw curious faces waiting in the hallway, she quickly closed the door and went back to her box. Those faces represented a life from which she suddenly recoiled. *If I joined them,* she thought, *I'd be like them again.*

Alisha returned to the box in the corner of the storage room remembering Miss Beatrice making her sit in the highchair day after day until she finally talked and then rocking her fears away in the front porch rocker. Alisha was sad, but when she closed her eyes, no tears came. She heard, *Crying is just one way to behave when you're sad. Your ways are right for you—playing too hard, playing the piano, singing… and, yes, hiding in corners. You'll learn other ways as you grow up.*

Alisha realized she now belonged with the Devinwoods—there, not here, alone. A new energy flooded her heart, and she did not want to remember anything more about her life in the orphanage.

Beatrice remembered Kate from that wintry day in 1935 when she wobbled up the walkway and deposited six-month-old Alisha in her arms. Kate had been very upset that day, rushing back and forth to the waiting car. Beatrice believed then that Kate would always suffer for what she was doing, but exposing old wounds would help no one now.

Beatrice made a fresh pot of coffee to extend the visit. She wanted to relieve Kate's concern about Alisha secluding herself during the years she spent in an orphanage. "That's how she worked things out, Kate. It's not everybody's way, but it worked for her. Let's hope she'll find better ways of solving problems as she grows older."

"Maybe she's already found one way," Kate said. "Learning to play the piano has certainly helped. So far, she's playing the piano with four fingers, and she's adamant about practicing."

"Then my hunch was right. The Devinwoods are good for her, aren't they?"

"They were absolutely the right choice. Alisha and Lindy play well together, and Sarah, being the voracious reader she is, keeps them supplied with books from the local library. As a result, they both love reading, especially Lindy."

"Where is Lindy? I would like to see her, too."

"She has the measles or she would've come with us today."

"You'd better watch Alisha for red spots; she'll probably get them, too—my girls have all had them. Most of the time bed rest is all that's necessary." Beatrice paused for a moment, thoughtful.

"Kate, I'd like to ask you a question. If you don't want to answer, don't; but why didn't you keep Alisha or visit her or ask for her to come live with you when we were looking so hard to find a family?"

Kate turned away, unable to meet Beatrice's eyes. As if she were struggling to stay away from the past, Kate sat frozen, quietly explaining, "Angeni, Alisha's mother and my sister, committed suicide. After she died, I wanted to keep Alisha; I really did ... and her brothers, too. I would have loved those children like my own. I was so sure I would finally have a family, but Hank wouldn't hear of it.

It sounds strange and it has to do with his childhood, but although he's a pediatric surgeon, he doesn't like children and will not have them around. Giving Hank some credit, though, he knew Angeni and I inherited a... *condition.* Unfortunately, Angeni didn't encounter it until after her husband died. No one knew how ill she was, and she was never the type to ask for help anyway. I was more fortunate in a way because Hank detected a problem soon after we were married. I don't expect exoneration, but I believe Alisha is much better off living with Sarah and her family than with Hank and me."

Beatrice nodded. "Thank you for telling me that, Kate, and for bringing Alisha to visit. She looks healthy, and I'm so happy to see she's doing well. But I certainly do miss her; she kept us hopping, but the place was alive—do you know what I mean?"

"Oh yes, she's active all right," Kate said, smiling at last.

"I do hope you find Alisha a music teacher, Kate. She really needs one. I remember her singing nursery rhymes instead of just speaking them... and the Saturday morning she got lost downtown, how fascinated she was with the piano in Ed's shop," Beatrice said, laughing

"She still sings—a lot. I think you're right. Music lessons may be the only way to get her out of those corners once and for all."

Just as Alisha started to leave again, Beatrice swung open the door. The girls gathered behind Beatrice and Kate, trying to see the girl they thought was there to join them. Beatrice entered the room, moving a few pans around on the shelf. "There's my girl. Remember me rattling these pots and pans, Alisha?"

Alisha laughed and said, "Yes ma'am, I remember."

Beatrice explained to Kate, "That's how I got her to come out of the storage room."

Even though Kate thought this ritual had reinforced Alisha's behavior, she conceded, "I couldn't have thought of a better way myself."

Chapter 16

Kate leaned against the wall in Hank's hospital room, watching dust particles dance through the open window in the April sunlight. The sunrays streamed toward her husband's chest as if the task of each particle was to seize a tiny piece of Hank's life and carry it away. She knew that with every rise and fall of his chest, Hank was giving up possession of his life.

Hank's irregular arm twitches and an occasional puff when he exhaled were mesmerizing. Now, years after deferring to this sometimes-cruel man and losing her chance to have children, Kate was losing her husband as well. She had kept a deathwatch for the past three months, when the doctor told her Hank's stroke was incurable and his coma irreversible.

There were good times, of course, and Kate forced herself to focus on those times, but even that seemed like such a waste of time, now. Hank could not know how tired she was of waiting, could he? Kate said aloud to her unconscious husband, "I'm tired of it all, Hank...aren't you, too?" She returned to the thoughts that had induced overwhelming guilt since her sister's death and settled into her familiar state of blame and pity. *Angeni's gone. Now that Hank will soon be gone, I'll bear the guilt alone. I will never forgive my sister for her part in this, but on the other hand, I'll never get over the callous way Hank—and I—failed those children. We abandoned those four children to strangers.*

Unlike most girls her age, Kate had not married young. After her parents died, she contented herself with taking care of Angeni, her baby sister. Then when Asyah married sixteen-year-old Angeni, Kate suffered as if someone had stolen *her* child. In anger and hurt, she moved to Bremington, which was far enough away that she wouldn't be tempted to return home. Kate was in her mid-forties when she married Hank Parker, a fifty-year-old widower.

After she married, Kate continued her job in the Bremington Style Shop. She became fascinated with stylish hats featured in the shop and knew how to complement any dress with the perfect hat. Kate wore her creations in the shop, and soon window shoppers drifted in and out of the store to seek her advice about their clothing. The more demanding customers shopped with her exclusively. Soon after their marriage though, Hank bought the shop and monitored Kate's health, allowing her to open the shop only a few days each week.

Kate visited her married sister twice, and on her last visit, Angeni exaggerated the family resources, leading Kate to believe they were financially well off. Kate was shocked by her sister's suicide and angry over the responsibility it imposed on her. The anger fueled her frustration and inability to do what she knew to be the right thing—provide a home for her nephews and niece. She allowed Hank's authoritarian personality to dominate, conceding to his demand to keep their home free of live-in relatives, especially children.

Kate was somewhat comforted by the past few years—ever since Alisha moved in with Sarah and John—because she appeared secure and happy. But Kate could not get over her shame that Alisha and her brothers were isolated from one another because of her.

By Kate's measure, though, another tiny light shone brighter: she and Sarah had grown closer because of their visits and long conversations. She also instinctively knew what clothes Alisha and Belinda liked and assumed the responsibility of supplying their school wardrobe, augmenting Sarah's handiwork. On holidays—Easter, Valentine's Day, and especially at Christmas—she brought gifts of the season for the girls and included enough extras to share with their friends and other family members.

Best of all, Kate could now have Alisha and Belinda at her house for a two-week summer vacation, which she enjoyed even if it was only a short time. Kate remembered when the visits began, how she waited patiently for Alisha to emerge from her hiding place. She had used that time to visit with Sarah. Hank, as usual, sat in the car reading his paper, watching for John, who seldom missed a chance to chastise Hank.

Hank barely tolerated Alisha and Belinda's summer visit, but Kate could count on Hank to go with her and the girls to the park built on the bank of the tranquil Lake Vista. The girls were eager to take their first ride of the summer on the Ferris wheel and paid no attention to Hank's grumpiness. Hank seemed proud of the Ferris wheel rising high in the middle of the park and repeated its history as they walked to the park. "Remember, girls, George Washington Gale Ferris invented that wheel for the Chicago World's Fair of 1893 from a drawing on a dinner napkin," he would say. "During the nineteen weeks it operated at the World's Fair, the Wheel carried over a million-and-a-half riders."

"Where is he now?" Alisha wanted to know.

"Who, George?"

"Yes."

"Well, old George died a long time ago, three years after the Chicago World's Fair. He was only thirty-seven years old," Hank would say sadly, ending his story and his conversation with the girls. Kate remembered those trips to the park as some of her most pleasant times with Hank and the girls.

A movement brought Kate's attention back to her dying husband. She had stayed by Hank's bedside since the stroke, leaving only a few hours each day to go home, refresh herself, and sleep for a while. She watched her husband stir from his unconscious state and motion for her to come closer. Kate stilled Hank's hand and held her ear close to his moving lips. His voice, barely audible, whispered one word with each gasping breath. "Take...medicine...ev...day...Kate" and, in fading words, "boys...Holy...Cr..."

All the anger Kate harbored since they abandoned the children welled up inside, and she would not let him finish. She placed her hand over his mouth, quieting his words, rejecting his final gift. That evening, Dr. Hank Parker died at age sixty-five, leaving Kate alone.

When she realized that Hank was gone, Kate rested her head on his chest and waited for the nurse to arrive for her rounds. It seemed the world had opened up and swallowed Hank's goodness years ago and the earth had finally taken his body. In the end, she desperately wanted him to know that she rejected his final attempt at a gift, too late offered. *We both lose, Hank.* Kate repeated Hank's last words to one person—Sarah.

By Christmas, Kate learned to drive and began enjoying her visits with Sarah again, as much as she could enjoy anything anymore. Guilt had replaced loneliness after Hank's death, and the humiliation that began festering when she and Hank abandoned her sister's children grew until Kate had created a dead zone within, where she dared not go.

Sarah sat with Kate at the kitchen table, where they often sipped coffee and had long talks. Even though Sarah could see Kate was embarrassed about not knowing the boys' location, she persisted in discussing Alisha's brothers anyway. "I won't give up on reuniting these children, Kate. We must find out where they are."

"Sarah, I only know what Hank mumbled before he died. Anyway, those boys experienced a very traumatic event at such an early age, and since it's been this long, let's please not disrupt their lives until they finish growing up."

"I don't understand your insistence on delaying, Kate," Sarah retorted, "Hank's the one who didn't want those boys in your home, and it was *his* attitude and *his* actions that landed them in an orphanage. Why can't you at least face that much and relieve yourself of some of that burden you're carrying around?"

Kate was trembling but steady. "You're right, Sarah, Hank was convinced that it would be a terrible mistake for the children to live with us, and I couldn't change his mind. Now that he's gone, the best I can feel is regret."

Sarah, anger spent, said, "I realize what's done is done, but those boys are growing up fast. They're already teenagers. If we could somehow locate this Holy Cross orphanage or home, or whatever it is, we could find out if the boys have been adopted and get to know them before they go out into the world and we lose all chance of finding them."

"We don't have much of a chance now, Sarah. Let's talk about this again, another time," Kate said and picked up her purse to leave.

Although common sense reminded Sarah that even though it was Kate and Hank who physically cast off the children, all the families on Angeni's list of desired homes must share the blame, including her. Those who should have welcomed the children dismissed their responsibility. Rather than ask Kate for help in the future, Sarah decided that she would reunite the children on her own.

After Kate left, Sarah began preparing dinner. Being alone in the kitchen invited reflection on her childhood. Born in the late 1800s, her family depended on gardening and farming for their livelihood, and their only resources were human power and farm animals. Sarah painfully recalled her parents taking her out of school after she finished the third grade to help with housekeeping, while her brothers worked in the fields and orchards. In her regret that never died, it seemed to Sarah that families gave birth to children primarily to populate a workforce.

Except for their feisty and doting grandmother, an impassioned retired schoolteacher who never forgot her calling, Sarah and her siblings would have been denied any further education. Grandma Copper was crafty at luring her grandchildren into games requiring English and math, during which she also polished their penmanship and social skills. Most importantly, as she left, she gave each child a book from her personal library, instilling a love of reading in her grandchildren. *I should look through Asyah's house again someday for Grandma Copper's books,* she thought.

Sarah married John when she was fifteen, and they had their children in quick succession. Years later, when Sarah was sure that her childbearing years were over, much to her surprise she became pregnant again. Although she was apprehensive about bearing a child at her age, her new baby, Belinda, became the light of her life.

John Devinwood was a good man, capable of extracting maximum harvest from his apple orchards, and with an abundance of workers, he produced enough marketable fruit to earn an above-average income. Sarah never gave in to John's appeal to take the boys out of school to work in the orchards; nevertheless, her children paid dearly for their education, for John sent both the boys and girls directly to the orchards after school where they worked until dark.

Kate was determined that Alisha would soon have a piano teacher, and Sarah was determined to accelerate her efforts to locate Alisha's brothers.

Chapter 17

Mrs. Annie Flowers read the latest note from her daughter, Sally Baxter.

Kate Parker, one of your neighbors in Bremington, is looking for a piano teacher for her niece. I understand she has convinced the principal at Tawasa Springs School to hire a music teacher for the school. Do it, Mother!

Soon after World War II began, Mrs. Flowers became a widow. After the shock was over, she slipped into an abyss of denial, became reclusive, and was convinced her husband would soon be home. More dramatically, she gave up her passion for teaching music that had consumed her time during the years her husband served abroad.

When Sally went home for the summer, she saw her mother's world drastically altered. In a desperate attempt to reestablish normalcy, she began inviting her mother's widowed friends to dinner and learned that her reaction was common to wives of a husband or son deceased during wartime. When Sally recognized her mother's spirited personality returning, she arranged for this circle of widows to begin meeting weekly at a local restaurant. Sally also pushed her mother back to her first love: music.

After a while of teaching students at home, Annie Flowers secured the position of piano teacher at Tawasa

Springs School and began introducing her passion for music to new students. She was especially excited about one student.

It seemed to Alisha that Mrs. Flowers flowed, rather than walked, into the music room, saying, "Good afternoon, Alisha. How is my star pupil today?"

Alisha giggled and held her hands behind her back, moving around the corner of the piano just out of sight, but couldn't resist peeking enough to watch her teacher's fingers nimbly dancing over the keyboard. Mrs. Flowers was patient and knew plenty of fancy keyboard tricks to win over any student. She explained the music she was playing and invited Alisha to watch how she placed her fingers on the keys. When Alisha peeked around the corner again, Mrs. Flowers said, "Let's try it, Alisha."

"I'll try it when I get home," Alisha said and moved back out of sight. "I want to learn how first, and then we can play it."

"How will you know how if you don't watch my hands?"

"I just watched your hands," Alisha said and repeated Mrs. Flowers' movements on the side of the piano. "See, I can play it here."

"Did you play an imaginary piano before you had a real one?"

"Yes, ma'am; that's how I learned how," Alisha said and then reluctantly disclosed her secret for the first time. "My friend told me how when I lived with Miss Beatrice."

"Your friend? Tell me about your friend, Alisha."

"Well, she was with me at Miss Beatrice's and hid with me, especially when families tried to take me away. She started whispering to me a long time ago, and then I finally whispered back to her. Then she came to my house—you know, where I live now—and she talks, well, she still whispers to me—at least it sounds like whispers—when I'm alone. She's the one who talked me into playing the real piano."

"Do you ever see her?"

"No, but I can feel her right up here when she talks to me." Alisha moved around the corner of the piano to form a circle with her arms above her head. "See?"

"Yes, I do see," Mrs. Flowers replied and smiled.

For the first time, Alisha felt the whispers might be normal. "Do you have a friend?"

"Yes, I do, Alisha," Mrs. Flowers said gently. "We all do. They're guardian angels, but very few of us take the time to listen or talk to them. You're a lucky girl to be aware of yours so early in your life and to feel her close."

"Most of the time she's there when I'm alone and she talks to me, but sometimes I can't hear her and I think she's gone."

"Don't worry about that; just keep listening. She can hear *you* all the time, and she's there helping you even when you can't hear her or when you're too busy with other things to pay attention."

Mrs. Flowers was relieved. After a few lessons and clearing up the confusion about the friend, Alisha moved closer and then finally sat beside her for the lesson.

Once comfortable, Alisha wanted to show off and play what Mrs. Flowers had demonstrated. "Can we play this song together now, Mrs. Flowers?"

"I've been looking forward to it, Alisha. Let's play." Mrs. Flowers' greatest challenge was to instill the discipline in Alisha to read the music from the lesson book. She was a child-savvy teacher and knew that without that discipline, Alisha would stray from the written note and techniques and revert to playing by ear. Mrs. Flowers was acutely aware that Alisha's gift for music and time-proven teaching methods would evolve into an unstoppable blend of creativity.

Alisha's practice was a ritual of trial and error. The keyboard became as familiar to her as her fingers that swept over them, translating music from the written note into her own inimitable and distinctive style. When Alisha complained that practicing scales was boring, Mrs. Flowers suggested practicing a phrase from each piece of music, and Alisha quickly mastered the techniques.

As Beatrice had predicted, Alisha learned *rather quickly*. Her interest was so intense that Mrs. Flowers kept her as long as possible for the lesson. Alisha's schoolteacher, Mrs. Cobb, was not as enthusiastic about the piano lessons because throughout the school year she had to interrupt the music lesson to start her class. Mrs. Cobb would barge in and stand stiffly while Mrs. Flowers smiled, glanced at the clock in make-believe shock, and ended the lesson.

Alisha and Mrs. Flowers connected first with a smile, then with their talent, and finally with their hearts.

Mrs. Flowers and Kate's acquaintance was short-lived after Kate walked by the local restaurant on a spring evening, looked in, and gasped. Kate now realized why they never invited her into their widows' circle. There, in full view of the sidewalk strollers, Mrs. Flowers and her friends were having dinner, and a waiter was serving their wine.

After Kate's parents died and Asyah married Angeni, Kate moved away and exchanged her pain for a life of religious conservatism, which held that to drink alcohol or to keep company with those who did, was sure damnation. By the time Kate met Hank, her beliefs were well grounded. Hank never listened to Kate's religious rhetoric, but after he died, she wrapped herself in the same rigidity as a familiar means of survival until she could no longer summon another frame of reference on which to base her judgment of Mrs. Flowers.

Kate believed that, since she had exposed Alisha to this bad influence, she was responsible for getting her away from Mrs. Flowers. She would waste no time. The following day, she met with the principal, Edward Percival. Dressed in her best church dress, a pillbox hat, and matching purse and gloves, she stood straight and formal in front of Mr. Percival's desk. Without even a greeting, Kate shook her finger and said, "Edward, Alisha will no longer take piano lessons from that Mrs. Flowers. I will not have my niece drinking wine."

"Kate, your niece is eight years old. What makes you think she's drinking wine?"

"She's associating with Mrs. Flowers, and that's the same thing."

"You set up the association. Don't you think that's a rather ridiculous assumption?"

"I do not. I insist you fire her at once."

Percival had known Kate for years, but her flashes of anger always took him by surprise. He had an unkind opinion of her for taking her sister's children to orphanages but attributed the decision largely to Hank. He knew Kate loved her sister deeply, and he watched her frustration and guilt grow into bitterness through the years. He was now facing the full force of her unhappy life. Mr. Percival believed that if he did not fire Mrs. Flowers, Kate's revelation of Mrs. Flower's "shameful" behavior would not stop with his office. She would carry her complaint to the school board or to whoever was necessary to accomplish her goal.

Percival tried once more to change her mind. "Kate, couldn't you bring yourself to reconsider this decision?"

"No, I could not! I could never live with myself if I allowed Alisha to stay in the company of a woman who drinks whiskey."

Smiling to himself as he accepted defeat, Percival said, "Now it's whiskey. I thought you said she was drinking wine."

"It's the same thing as far as I'm concerned. I've already talked to two other parents, and they feel the same way as I do."

"Okay, Kate, you win; I'll talk to Mrs. Flowers today," Percival said, but his frustration resurfaced causing him to forget all decorum of his position. "This is in your interest alone, isn't it, Kate?" he added. "If you really had Alisha's interest in mind, you wouldn't be living alone in that big house, now would you?"

With her mouth open, Kate looked at Mr. Percival in disbelief. "Well I never … you can't talk to me that way," Kate said and stormed out of the school on her way to see Sarah and boast of what she had done to protect Alisha.

When she heard Kate's description of the now "drunken Mrs. Flowers," Sarah lost her temper. "Kate, why in the world would you do that? The lessons were going so well. I do not agree with you or any religion that would cause you to behave this way. You are placing your narrow interest far ahead of what Alisha needs. Now what are we going to do?" Sarah's anger was turning to tears. "Alisha loves Mrs. Flowers, and she needs her. She was learning *music,* Kate. You know very well you have exaggerated this experience into something very hurtful—why do you do these things?"

"Now you listen. I've been pa … "

"Don't you dare mention money to me," Sarah said, as she stood and paced the floor to ease her anger. "Those music lessons were far more important than any other *thing* you've bought. I appreciate you paying for the lessons and helping the girls with clothes, but you did that voluntarily and could have stopped at any time— besides, I think you did it as much for yourself as any of us. If you were going to take something from Alisha, you should have taken something that didn't matter as much as the music lessons."

John suddenly appeared in the doorway and said, "Kate, I think it's time for you to leave. Sarah needs to rest."

Principal Percival met with Mrs. Flowers, but he was uncomfortable with his task because he wanted her to resign rather than him to be forced to terminate her employment. Making it worse, he knew the students, particularly Alisha, adored their music teacher. He remembered walking by the music room and hearing the laughter as Mrs. Flowers and Alisha played a lesson together.

Mrs. Flowers saw Kate pass the restaurant and knew she would not ignore the wine, given her infamous religious fanaticism. She also knew what Mr. Percival was going to say before he began, but even so, the words left her shaken. She understood, but realized if she stayed, she would face a battle she could not win. And so, Mrs. Flowers resigned from the job she loved, sparing Mr. Percival and the school unwarranted criticism from those who might sympathize with Kate. They agreed she would stay another week for final lessons.

Alisha was Mrs. Flowers' last student of the day. As usual, student and teacher exceeded their scheduled time, but with no interruption from Mrs. Cobb. Mrs. Flowers gave Alisha two books and spent considerable time explaining the advantages of practice by reading the notes rather than playing by ear. She accompanied Alisha on a piano duet and ended the lesson, unable and unwilling to reveal that she would not be back. Mrs. Flowers taught

Alisha less than a year but knew Alisha would always be her star student.

At the end of the day, Mrs. Cobb surprised her students by announcing that Mrs. Flowers had taken a job at a new music school in Philadelphia to be near her daughter. Alisha knew well how to hide disappointment, but she did not know how to fill this void. After discovering she really could play the piano and now believing she could play well, her teacher and mentor was gone. After school, Alisha sat on the sofa beside Belinda, staring at the piano. Her world reeled.

"Lindy, what happened to Mrs. Flowers? Did I do something wrong?"

"No. I heard Mrs. Flowers saying good things about you to a teacher in the hallway, so it couldn't be you. Mom's upset about it, and she's in her room with the door closed, like when she's mad. She wouldn't tell me what happened, but I heard her tell Dad that Kate was wrong, but the principal fired Mrs. Flowers anyway."

Alisha leaned her head against Belinda's shoulder, neither knowing what else to say.

"I don't like Aunt Kate anymore," Alisha finally said.

Belinda twisted her curls while Alisha stared at the piano.

"Lindy, do you think I should call Aunt Sarah, *Mom?*"

Belinda jostled Alisha with her shoulder. "Try it. If she doesn't hit you with the switch, it'll be okay."

Alisha glanced at Belinda to make sure she was teasing.

"Yes, silly," Belinda said, "she's been wishing you'd

call her *Mom* for a hundred years. Get your sweater and let's go outside."

The school year was almost over and Sarah did not bring up the subject to Kate again but was far from through with the problem. She would solve this one in her own way.

The following Sunday, Kate arrived for a visit. Alisha stared angrily at her and emphasized calling Sarah "Mom." Sarah saw pain in Kate's eyes, but said nothing.

Without ceremony, Kate took a small package from her purse, opened the jewelry box inside, and handed a watch to Alisha. "Alisha, here's a gift for you. I know you're disappointed about the music lessons, but believe me, Mrs. Flowers' leaving is for your own good," Kate said just as John walked around the corner of the house.

"How so, Kate?" he asked.

Kate picked up her purse to leave. "I didn't expect you to understand, John."

"Then how in the world could you expect Alisha to understand?" he retorted.

"She'll understand some day," Kate said, rushing to her car as tears stung her eyes.

"Maybe, maybe not," John said, matching her pace.

Sarah saw the worried look on Alisha's face and nodded her okay. Alisha ran to the car. When Kate rolled the window down, Alisha said, "Don't cry, Aunt Kate. Thank you for the watch. It's pretty, and I'll wear it to school tomorrow, but I did like taking piano lessons the most."

Kate rolled up the window and drove away. Alisha

watched her aunt leave and thought, *and I'd rather have Mrs. Flowers back.*

The watch was gold and beautiful, and Alisha showed it to her friend, Caroline, the following day at school as they stood for morning assembly. "Aunt Kate gave it to me yesterday," she whispered.

"Why did she give you a watch?" Caroline whispered.

"I had to quit taking piano lessons because Aunt Kate didn't like Mrs. Flowers anymore and she left."

"Why did your aunt have to like her? I thought you liked her."

"I did … I mean, I do, but Aunt Kate made me quit. I don't think Mom liked it much either, because she had that I'm-mad-so-don't-talk-to-me look on her face. I guess nobody can stop Aunt Kate when she makes up her mind about something; nobody even tries."

Assembly was over and the conversation and laughter reached a solid buzz as the mass of students walked to class. Alisha felt encased in a fragile cocoon, accepting that Kate sent Mrs. Flowers away with no concern for what the music lessons meant to her. Believing she was helpless against such authority, Alisha willed herself power over what was hers: her music. "I don't care. I didn't need her anyway. I can still play if I want to," she said, partly to Caroline and partly to herself.

Throughout the day, each time she thought of Mrs. Flowers and looked at the watch, it grew uglier. At home, the watch choked her arm. She yanked it off and threw it on the dresser, vowing never to wear it again, thinking herself disloyal to Mrs. Flowers for wearing it at all.

When her sense of loss was not assuaged, Alisha picked up the watch with a forefinger and thumb, as if it were dirty, and dropped it beneath her clothes in the bottom drawer. Now that Mrs. Flowers had named the source of the whispers, Alisha longed for the presence of her guardian angel but feared she had lost her as well.

Alisha did not allow herself to think about Mrs. Flowers and did not keep her promise to read notes from the music books. Throughout the summer, she avoided the piano altogether but noticed new music books appeared regularly on the table near the piano. If she never saw Mrs. Flowers again, Alisha would not forget her first music teacher.

In the fourth grade, Alisha and Caroline became inseparable. In class, they sat at adjoining desks, played on the same softball and volleyball teams, and on weekends were often at one or the other's home. Memories of Mrs. Flowers receded in Alisha's mind like a filed away photograph, but as her anger toward Kate subsided, her world of music stopped.

The next school year, Tawasa Springs School had five hundred students and a junior and senior basketball team. The Huxley sisters, Caroline and Ellie, had wanted to be cheerleaders like their mother for as long as they could remember. Today, it was official. They were selected to be on the cheerleading squad of the Tawasa junior basketball team.

Alisha became bored watching Caroline practice cheerleading. She walked home and when she passed by the piano and impulsively tickled the keys she began playing around with a familiar melody. She was surprised at how much she wanted to continue. The urge to play took over, and she played as if she had never stopped, but she still could not go near the growing stack of music books.

Sarah had almost given up finding a music teacher until the next spring, she became acquainted with Natalie Maxwell, the church pianist. Natalie, had recently married Theodore Maxwell, the music director. Natalie and *Max,* as he was called, frequently invited guests to their home for dinner, and Natalie was frustrated because she could not cook well. Sarah proposed they combine their talents to help each other. Each week, Sarah would teach Natalie to prepare a complete meal, including a surprise dish for her husband, in return for a piano lesson for Alisha. The two women would tell no one their secret.

Chapter 18

When Robert turned sixteen, he had been driving for a couple of years, because Lester had given him the responsibility for purchasing supplies from the Huntington Ridge General Store and delivering them to the farm. Either Martin or James went along to help, giving Robert the opportunity to teach his brothers to drive. "Anyway," Robert rationalized to Lester when he discovered they were driving, "they'll have to know how to drive to get a drivers license."

"That's weak, Robert. You should have let me teach them."

"But Lester, you taught me, and I taught them the same way."

"From watching the way James drives, you didn't," Lester said.

Lester had good reason for concern, for while Martin was a careful driver and followed the rules, James was skillful, but wild and free, giving the impression that he was anything but in control. Lester knew George kept an eye on the boys when they were in town since the general store was across the street from the Bing Café. When George saw the boys loading supplies on the truck, he walked across the street, said hello, and watched them work.

James laughed and mouthed along with George as he said, "Try to keep the truck between the ditches, boys."

"Yes, sir, Mr. George," the boys replied in unison and saluted, eager to hurry off to see their friends before they were expected at home.

Lester came out of the barn just as the truck turned into the driveway, tires squealing. *Slow down, James,* he said to himself. Lester's life was absorbed in parenting the Copper brothers. In the fall, the twins would enter the eighth grade and Robert, the eleventh. Lester had watched them grow tall and strong and take on more and more responsibility for the farm work. Just last week, when Robert hooked up his chestnut brown mare to a wagon and the twins saddled their horses and they all took off to finish building the fence, Lester realized how mature the boys had become.

All three boys were good riders, but Martin excelled. He entered riding competitions, and although he did not always win, he was a fine competitor. When James and Martin began pursuing high school athletics with a "do or die" attitude, Lester tried to mellow their approach and taught them to play sports like the game of life— with toughness, fairness, and integrity.

Robert graduated from high school and turned his attention from the farm he loved to college life. Influenced by Joe, who taught him the importance of education, initially Robert was a good student. But even while he embraced the freedom of college and flourished among his peers, he missed his family, especially Martin and James.

Robert felt alone at school, and his memories were

sometimes chilling. He remembered holding his baby sister in the meadow, her bottle empty, waiting for his mother to come back and take them home. When they were young, Robert and his brothers talked about their sister as if she were still a baby. They made bold plans—secret plans— that made sense to children alone, but plans that kept their dream alive. In his darkest moments, Robert thought he could still be waiting for his mother to come take them home, but even knowing that time had erased a normal sibling intimacy with his sister, the reality of morning underpinned his determination to find Alisha.

Distracted by loneliness, the first semester Robert received poor grades. After the Christmas break at home with Lester and his brothers, Robert adjusted and applied what he learned from Lester about operating the farm. He concentrated on business classes until the middle of his sophomore year when he decided to pursue his passion—designing and constructing buildings. Only then, did Robert assimilate into college life, developing close alliances with his classmates and teachers alike. He recognized that, although he appreciated the Millers, it was Lester who helped him grow into a man.

Robert wrote Lester about his plans to study architecture, and Lester's response was to catalogue Robert's drawings from the first barn to a dream house, inspired by his high school sweetheart. Robert studied his forgotten drawings from the first crude depiction of the barn he drew in the second grade to the more skilled drawing of the dream house he had promised to build some day.

Normally, James was happy following Robert, but he was strong-willed and entertaining, often making him the center of attention and the subject of serious discussions between schoolteachers and Lester, or the Millers when they were home. In high school, James watched friends drop out of school to help on the farm or in their family business and decided it would be a good plan for him as well.

Lester became suspicious when James wanted to stay home from school under the ruse of helping on the farm. He drove James to school the following morning and discussed possible professions young men should consider these days, trying to dissuade him. The next day, James showed up at a friend's house and they drove around all day. Nothing seemed to establish his interest in school. The third time James skipped school, Lester, with a cooperating high school principal, wholeheartedly agreed.

"Let's just forget about school, James, but we'll have to make a plan."

"Great idea, Lester, I'm ready."

Lester laid out the plan. "James, you can work under the same arrangement I had when I began working for the Millers. You'll be an employee of the farm. You'll have a normal workweek. You'll earn wages."

Under Lester's supervision, James mended fences, cut underbrush, and performed a multitude of tasks, some necessary, some not. The work was hard; the hours were long. James began to miss his friends.

After two weeks of hard labor, Lester watched from the front porch as James drove the truck to a screeching halt in the barnyard and walked excitedly toward the house. He saw a remarkable change in the way James walked—a little taller and shoulders straighter. The boy had *hope* written on his face.

"Lester, I think I want to go back to school," James announced.

"You think you want to go back to school, son, or do you know?"

"I know."

Lester took James to school the following Monday. After what Lester had put him through, James began to appreciate school and concluded that schoolwork was not that boring after all. With a renewed interest in learning, he caught up all the missed lessons and won the favor of his teachers and coaches in the process. At graduation, Lester and the high school principal shook hands in honor of their victory.

Martin became preoccupied with Lester's Army memorabilia and secretly explored ideas about what to do with his life. Sorting through the treasures as well as raising and lowering the flag near the Miller's rose garden turned Martin's simple interest into an obsession. Then Lester took Martin to an air show. Martin was fascinated by the air show, and Lester was not surprised when he began talking about aviation being a calling he could not ignore. In 1948, soon after completing one year of college, Martin joined the United States Air Force, established the previous year as a separate service from the Army-Air Corps. When the recruiter came through Huntington Ridge, Martin knew with certainty what he wanted and left immediately for Aviation School.

Chapter 19

The first cooking class was over and Natalie Maxwell went from culinary student to piano teacher. While she waited in the living room for her young student to come home from school, she looked at Devinwood family photographs, carefully framed and arranged in groups on the walls and tables. One in particular caught Natalie's eye. It was a faded sepia print of Sarah and John leaving a small church, running in the rain toward a horse-drawn buggy. The photograph, centered above the fireplace, documented the happy couple's wedding day. The next picture showed Sarah and John with seven children standing underneath a tin roof overhang of an unpainted clapboard house. Another picture taken beside the same house, now painted white, showed the children much older and Belinda as a toddler, reaching up for her brother. Natalie smiled at the thought that Belinda certainly showed them that their family was indeed not complete without her. And of course, there were pictures of Alisha standing beside Belinda, assuming her status as a member of the Devinwood family.

Natalie sat on the piano bench and thumbed through a few of the music books—beginners, intermediate, and advanced—all classical. *Someone's trying to introduce Alisha to classical music ... very interesting.*

Then, the lessons began. After a few weeks, curiosity got the best of Natalie. She wanted to be told about the untouched music by Alisha, directly.

"Alisha, do you play from that stack of music books on that table?"

"Mom is saving them."

"For you, I hope."

Alisha shrugged.

"I'd like for us to try a few of the pieces of music from them when you're ready."

Alisha shrugged again. Natalie dropped the subject but noticed that as the lessons proceeded, the stack of books continued to grow.

The next spring, a year after the lessons began, Natalie raised her hand to knock on the Devinwood's front door when she heard Alisha playing her favorite Chopin sonata, *Piano Concerto in F minor.*

Sarah was watching out the window for Natalie. She opened the door, unable to hold back a satisfied grin. "I've been listening in the hallway; it's beautiful, isn't it?"

"Yes, it is," Natalie quietly said. "Chopin wrote that while he was still in his teens for a young singer he admired. Alisha makes it sound so easy—almost as if she wrote the music. How did that happen?"

"Alisha's friend Charlie Tumoro did it. Charlie lives

down the road. He's been attentive to Alisha since we moved here, but lately, his blond hair is always combed just so, and his blue eyes are shining. He's been extra attentive, if you know what I mean."

"Well, she's almost thirteen. Anyone would notice she's a cute girl and growing up fast."

"Yes, yes. I know indeed," Sarah said. "I'll soon have two teenagers living here. Anyway, a few weeks ago, Charlie came by and kept insisting that Alisha play something from one of the books Mrs. Flowers sent. Alisha refused, of course … until he left. As soon as he was out of hearing range, she started practicing the very song he tried to get her to play. You're hearing the result of that argument."

"I like Charlie," Natalie said.

"Me too," Sarah said with a smile as the two women walked into the kitchen.

The next spring, Sarah turned over meal preparation to Natalie and sat at the table, watching and dispensing tidbits of her kitchen wisdom. "Don't measure that salt, Natalie; just throw in a pinch. You don't have to measure everything—you'll be a happier cook that way."

They listened to Alisha practicing a concerto while Natalie cooked and Sarah reminisced about Alisha's first attempt at playing the piano. "You know, Natalie, I was so proud to hear Alisha discover the piano key that matched the note she sang. She was five years old at the time, and her little-girl voice was already pure and steady. In those years, I swept the hallway outside the living room door listening to her play and sing. I still sweep and listen."

"I know what you mean. I'm so proud of her. I believe

she has stepped over a threshold, and there's no going back for her," Natalie said.

"Alisha's going to do something extraordinary with her life," Sarah said, "and I want to do everything possible to help her. I realize no one grows up without problems—Lord knows, she's had plenty already—but I feel like I must try to make up for what she lost in the orphanage. I admit it's partly out of selfishness, but I want to be there when my niece learns how it feels to share her music with the world."

"Your *daughter*, Sarah. Alisha is your daughter just as surely as if you had given birth to her, and from what I'm seeing, she not going to disappoint you."

"Well, I'm anxious to hear her play for an audience—and on a better piano than we have. Charlie, God bless him, has been after her to help with the music for the school play, but the way she and Charlie pick at each other, she'll do it, but only after he wears her down and she makes it her own idea."

At times, Sarah nearly told Kate about Alisha's progress, but then she remembered the watch episode. She knew that as long as Kate did not know about the lessons, she could not sabotage her and Natalie's carefully arranged bartering. Natalie told no one. She would tell her husband some day, but, for now, she made Max happy by preparing a new dish for him each week.

Max knew, though. After Charlie accidentally mentioned the lessons, the whispered conversations between Sarah and Natalie made perfect sense. With plans for a new and more modern church music program,

Max decided to keep the information to himself. "I'll just listen and learn," he said to himself and chuckled. "I'd be crazy to ruin the good thing going on in the kitchen."

Max also knew that for the Tawasa Springs First Church, in all of its conservatism, to grow, it must attract youth of the community. He started up a youth program because he recognized that young adults would leave the church if they could not have fun. Max thrived on fun and constant activity and quickly made friends with the Tawasa Springs teens, easily matching their social needs to the youth program. He enlisted a few parents to chaperone and took the teens on trips to the skating rink, where Natalie taught them complex skating routines to the excitement of blaring music and flashing lights. When Max convinced Sarah and other parents that their teenage sons and daughters would benefit by participating in church-sponsored activities, the youth program grew. Then Max decided it was time to update the music program with a new organ to enhance the piano and growing choir.

Max continued to enjoy his wife's cooking and Alisha continued to master fundamentals and theory of piano music. The spring Alisha turned fourteen, Natalie brought to fruition what Mrs. Flowers began—Alisha's flair for classical music. Although she had become a superb cook, Natalie insisted she still needed to improve and asked for more cooking classes. Sarah agreed, knowing the true reason.

Within the next year, Alisha accomplished all the music and techniques from the music Mrs. Flowers sent as she steadily advanced in classical piano. When she realized Natalie overheard that first concerto, she stopped avoiding Mrs. Flowers' books, which still arrived weekly, filled with increasingly difficult music. Her reclusive nature fed her obsession for the piano, and she expanded her boundaries of music to a new level of skill and performance.

One day after Charlie had argued with Alisha about practicing too much, Sarah complained to John, "They argue about everything. I think I will lose my mind if they don't stop soon."

"Lose your mind if you must," John said, "but I doubt that you would faze teenagers with insanity; it's too much like their own behavior. You have only a few years left with them; they'll be gone before you know it."

In a letter to Beatrice, Sarah wrote:

Dear Beatrice,

You were right. Alisha needed to live in a family environment to thrive. Thanks in part to her friend, Charlie, she has almost stopped secluding herself, but she has imposed such a strict self-discipline for practicing that sometimes I think she would sit there forever. Of course, she doesn't, and she seems to be developing a good social balance. I believe she was afraid of something for so long that she could only reconcile her thoughts while she was alone, but now her open and less aggressive friendships are serving her well.

Belinda is becoming Alisha's best friend as well as her critic. She is bossy and tries to manage both their lives. After hours of practice, Lindy drags Alisha away from the piano to visit Caroline or a walk in the neighborhood. I have teenage daughters on my hands, Beatrice, and most of the time, a host of their friends, as well. But John keeps reminding me how soon they'll be gone out into the world to live their own lives, so I'm taking his advice and trying to enjoy them while I can.

Alisha seems happy and well, but as I'm sure you remember, she likes to argue, and Charlie accommodates her well.

Sincerely,
Sarah

Chapter 20

Rushing into the living room, Lindy asked, "How can you sit at that piano so long, Alisha? There's a world out there—look outside. The sun shines! The wind blows! The rain falls! A boy moved in next door! Get up and let's go see what he looks like."

"Oh, hi, Lindy, wait *one* minute … what time is it?"

"It's time to get up off that piano bench. Come on."

Alisha kept playing. "Who's here?"

"Nobody, come on, Alisha, they have a boy!"

"Who?"

"The family next door; aren't you listening?"

"I heard you. I meant, who's the boy? What's his name?"

"How would I know? Come on, let's go to the store for Mom. We'll have to walk right by their house."

Alisha suddenly stopped playing and pulled the cover over the keyboard. "No, we don't," she said and laughed. "You know we always take the shortcut."

The moving van drove away and left Adam Sandburg and Charlie on the front porch, almost hidden among the boxes they were sorting. When Adam noticed two girls walking toward his house, he stumbled over the boxes, trying to get to the front of the porch. "Who's that, Charlie?"

Charlie laughed. "Go on and meet them. I'll finish up here."

"I hope he has a brother, because I do *not* like red hair," Belinda said quietly.

"But look how cute he is, Lindy."

As the girls drew closer, Alisha gasped when the lanky, red-haired boy with his broad, friendly smile came closer. Adam waved, and Alisha giggled and returned his greeting.

Just as Adam reached Alisha and Belinda, his father came out the front door and called, "Adam, hurry back and help Charlie finish moving these boxes inside before it rains."

"Yes sir, be right there," he called over his shoulder and began slowly walking backwards and talking fast. "I'm Adam Sandburg; what's your name?"

"I'm Lindy Devinwood."

Adam looked at Alisha and smiled. "And you're … ?"

Surprised to be so shy in a boy's presence, Alisha finally managed to stumble over her name. "Alisha … Alisha … Alisha Copper. I'm Alisha Copper."

"She's Alisha. Alisha. Alisha Copper," Belinda sing-songed and laughed.

"See you around, Lindy and Alisha, Alisha, Alisha Cooper," Adam shouted over his shoulder as he turned and rushed back to his house.

"*Copper* not *Cooper,*" Alisha yelled back.

Adam turned briefly and gave her an air salute.

"Well, I didn't see a brother; guess he doesn't have one," Belinda said, defeated. "When did you start liking red hair anyway?"

"I didn't think it was *that* red," Alisha said, looking back toward Adam's house.

"Charlie Tumoro's cuter," Belinda teased.

"No, he's not," Alisha snapped.

Alisha watched from her porch for an opportunity to talk to Adam, but he always seemed to be too busy helping his father paint the house or work in the yard to do more than wave to her. She counted the days until the beginning of school.

On the first day of school, Belinda and Alisha arrived early and tried several seats before settling on a side row strategically located for watching students entering the auditorium. To begin the first assembly of the year, the principal, stood on the stage, introduced the teachers, and instructed students to stand as they heard their grades called out. Hearing a booming "Eleventh grade," Belinda stood.

Adam Sandburg also stood—slowly—knowing he would be at least a head taller than anyone in his class. After assembly, Adam turned to see the history/physical education teacher rushing toward him wearing a Wildcats basketball jacket emblazoned with *Coach*.

Most days, Adam joined Belinda and Alisha walking to and from school. Alisha was comfortable with him as a friend, but there was something else about Adam. He was only a year older, but to Alisha it was as if he were somehow more mature than he was supposed to be. She could not decide whether to consider him *friend, brother,* or something beyond what she could identify, especially when he encouraged her to be kinder to Charlie.

One afternoon after school, Alisha lay beside Adam

near the fireplace, watching the rain through the living room window.

"Charlie likes you; can't you see that?" Adam asked.

"I don't care if he likes me. He makes me so mad sometimes," Alisha said.

"Think about it, Alisha, in all his joking and pushiness, don't you think he might have your interest at heart?"

"I guess. I remember how he pushed me into playing that Chopin concerto from the books I wouldn't touch. Then there was the school play. He made me *so* mad that I played but didn't speak to him for..."

Laughing, Adam interrupted her. "Charlie understands how to get things done with you, and he just goes at it differently. He knows you like to argue and—"

"I do not! How can you say that?"

"He's learned to speak your language."

"Adam, are you taking his side? I can't believe you would..." Alisha went on in a feeble attempt to win the point, knowing she would not.

"Easy, Alisha, you know you like to argue. You're arguing with me right now," Adam said, propping up on one elbow and cupping her face in his hand. "Listen to me, sometimes when I walk outside, I hear you play. I'm not a fan of classical music—might never be—but the way you play Chopin... it's beautiful. When you play that music, it stops me in my tracks and makes me want to hear more."

Alisha turned thoughtfully to Adam but said nothing.

Adam smiled and continued. "Okay, answer this

question: Would you be playing the music you're now playing if Charlie hadn't persisted?"

"I think so—eventually. But I guess if he hadn't made me mad, I probably wouldn't have because, when I looked at the books, I remembered the watch Aunt Kate gave me and how it almost stopped me from playing the piano forever. I never understood why she gave the stupid thing to me—never will. Anyway, speaking of playing, that's what I want to do now. See what an inspiration you are." Alisha unwrapped her blanket and stood to leave.

"Go easy on Charlie," Adam said, opening the door and placing his fist on his heart. "Friends?"

"Yes." Alisha returned his signal and ran into the freezing rain toward home to avoid getting soaked, but was not sure if she was running toward the piano or away from Adam.

Chapter 21

Charlie Tumoro was scared. *What if the plan goes wrong?* he thought, sliding down in his seat, hoping Alisha could not see him. Charlie first met Alisha in the second grade when she was afraid and awkward. If she carried more than one book, he could count on her dropping one of them as she made her way to her desk. Everyone laughed when Charlie scurried over to pick up the book, but he was smitten and didn't care.

During elementary school, he could see and hear only this girl. Once, when he showed her he had written *Alisha* on his arm with an ink pen, she only said, "You're going to be in trouble now." As the years went by, he and Alisha competed in whatever they did, but when their debates heated up and she got mad at him, he learned to turn their arguments into a light banter to keep her in his company.

When she realized how gifted Alisha was, Natalie accelerated the lessons in the music books, which still arrived weekly, focusing on strengthening Alisha's technical skills. Recently, Natalie moved the lessons to the church social hall and changed their schedule to

Saturday mornings. Accompanying her student on an old organ, she channeled Alisha's discipline and polished her performance until she was satisfied that the blend of piano and organ music achieved a concert of praise and beauty. She constantly pushed Alisha to reach deeper into her soul for precision, and the result was always dramatic and powerful.

On Saturdays, Max loitered outside the social hall listening to Alisha and Natalie's lesson. When he arrived early on Sunday mornings, he found Alisha alone, replaying the music. He routinely suggested that she play for church services, and she consistently refused. "If you would play out there one time, Alisha, you'd be comfortable and love playing for an audience."

"Oh, no, I wouldn't. I like to play down here," Alisha insisted.

"Alisha, you're much too talented to keep your music to yourself. Everyone who attends this church would enjoy hearing you play."

"No, Max." Alisha kept playing without looking up.

"You're stubborn, but you don't hold that monopoly," Max mumbled and walked away.

Convincing Alisha to play for the Sunday morning service was near hopeless until Max took Alisha's rejection as a challenge and sought Belinda's help. The genius of her plan was including Charlie, "Because," she assured Max, "he knows more tricks than anyone where Alisha's concerned."

Belinda's role was to get Alisha to arrive early. "Let's go by the choir loft, Alisha," she said on Sunday morning. "I left my book on the table by the baptistery."

Max instructed the choir to gather at the front of the church and enter the sanctuary after his introductory song. When Alisha and Belinda arrived, Max looked up from thumbing through a book. "Oh hello, girls; Alisha, I'm glad you're early. Natalie's late, and I need to warm up my voice on something familiar. Would you play for me just a min—?"

Alisha interrupted, "No, Max, you know I…"

"Just until she gets here," he pleaded.

Unexpectedly, Belinda shocked them both. "Alisha, you're being ridiculous. For Pete's sake, go play the piano."

Surprised by Belinda's reaction and Max's defeated expression, Alisha grudgingly agreed. When she opened the door slightly to check out the gathering congregation, her heart raced and her eyes gaped. "No, I can't do this," Alisha said, closing the door. "I'm nervous. There are too many people out there." She looked at the clock and went back to the door to peek out. *Why is everyone here so early anyway? There's Adam—and Ellie.*

"I can't do this, Max," she pleaded and closed the door again. "It's not time."

Adam watched Alisha open and close the door and realized she was considering Max's request, finally. She had said once she would be the first one to know when it was time to play for an audience—*must be now,* he thought and whispered to Ellie, "She's scared; I have to talk to her."

"I'll bet *she's* already talking, more likely, she's arguing," Ellie replied, annoyed at Adam for getting involved.

Adam stood just inside the door listening to Max

and Belinda pleading with Alisha. The more Belinda and Max tried to persuade her, the more agitated Alisha became. They were all talking at the same time when Charlie bolted through the door.

Charlie walked straight to Alisha and into his role. "I knew you were back here. Come on, Alisha, I'm sorry I helped with this. You don't have to play if you don't want to—let's go."

Adam sighed with relief. Already frustrated, with fire in her eyes, Alisha sprang to her own defense. "What do you mean, you helped? Get out, Charlie!" She turned to Belinda. "Lindy, I'll get you for this."

Alisha steadied herself to deal with Charlie but sensed that the decision she was about to make was not about him. She stormed toward the door, saying, "Okay, Max, I'll play *one* song." Adam opened the door, and Alisha walked by, her eyes silently pleading, *what am I going to do?* Adam took a long, deep breath, reminding her to do the same.

"That's a start," Max said, walking so close behind that he pushed her through the door.

The piano seemed a mile away. Alisha reached the bench and sat down, inhaling deeply, knowing there was no turning back. She hated feeling naked before the world, but there was no one to clothe her now. Alisha sat for a moment, until she felt the familiarity of the keyboard and began to breathe more evenly. She consciously guided her thoughts to that inner place Natalie talked about— her source of music and energy, where she could play anything, anywhere, any time.

Forcing one breath after another, Alisha heard a whisper and knew she was no longer alone. *Stay calm and abide the storm. I'm beside you, just as I've been all along. Your life is different now, and being afraid is no longer good enough. Only you can direct your path now. The door is open and it's safe to walk through. You must do this yourself... because it's time.*

Alisha relaxed and glanced up from the piano. Shaken at seeing a full church, she rose slightly from her seat, trying to give in to the old desire and run away. *How quickly fear comes back... was it ever really gone?* Alisha turned her attention toward the stage. There was Natalie sitting at the organ, smiling.

She's not late! Is there anyone here not involved with this trick? But Alisha relaxed at the comfort of having Natalie close and returned her smile. Natalie began Schubert's *Ava Maria* and the Sunday morning service began. Alisha adjusted her music and knew beyond doubt that she was exactly where she wanted to be. The desire to run away had passed.

As Natalie began fading out the prelude, Max looked toward the piano and nodded. Alisha blended her music into the end of the prelude and into Max's chosen song, "Amazing Grace," just as she and Natalie had practiced. Max's rich tenor voice filled the church as the piano yielded to Alisha's touch. She suddenly realized why Mrs. Flowers allowed her to play one piece of music freely outside the boundaries of the written note. Alisha had kept *Amazing Grace* as that one piece of music from which to learn creativity and style, and from that hymn she learned to infuse a unique and personal style into all her music. As never before, Alisha felt the presence of her first teacher.

Belinda, sitting in the front row near the piano, chilled at the sound of the music, remembering Alisha's first attempts at learning music, and recognized the importance of this day. Sarah and John watched the choir fill the choir loft, softly humming along with Max. As the parishioners witnessed Alisha's performance, Sarah knew that she would remember every sight, every sound, and cherish this church service forever. She breathed a sigh of relief. *I knew this day would come.*

When the service ended, Alisha stood, bowed slightly, and whispered, "I did it." As if to validate her success, Sarah walked to where Alisha stood and for the first time in their relationship, embraced the daughter she had come to love as her own. "It's the songbird, Alisha; it knows you and it is singing."

Chapter 22

When the Huntington Ridge School of Agriculture became a state university, Joe Miller was appointed dean of the new West Ridge Research Laboratory. He and Bess traveled much more and left the three Copper brothers with Lester, knowing he was devoted to their care.

In the summer of 1950, the brothers were at the farm for the first time in three years. They had come home to visit Lester and to see the Millers off on their long-anticipated African safari. Robert's business was in its third year and already booming. James was eager to finish his last year of college and take his place as the second partner with the Copper Brothers Architectural Design and Building Company. Martin was home on leave after completing three of his four years in the Air Force.

After a weeklong reunion, Lester and the boys waved goodbye to Joe and Bess as they boarded a train to New York where they would then board a ship for Africa. For almost a month, Bess sent postcards daily, describing their adventures at sea and their arrival in Africa. After they left their hotel on the safari, postcards arrived less frequently, "for lack of a nearby post," Bess had written, but still they came. Then, near the end of the second month when the boys were packing to leave, Lester realized the postcards had stopped altogether.

In her last postcard two weeks earlier, Bess had written, "The trip is exciting, and Joe is awed by the variety of plants and wildlife. He talks endlessly about importing rare plants from Africa, but I'm homesick and miss my boys—you too, Lester." The card was signed, *Bess and Papa Joe.* Afterwards, Lester watched James become increasingly restless, sleeping only a few hours each night. Speculating he might simply be anxious to get back to school, Lester made little connection between the lack of news from Bess and James not sleeping, until James was not sleeping at all. Lester knew something was wrong.

Early on the morning the boys planned to leave, Lester walked into the Bing Café just in time to hear CBS reporter Edward R. Murrow report in his clipped and deliberate radio voice, "Four Americans were brutally killed in the African jungle—just horrible...." Then Lester knew. He also understood that James had somehow sensed the impending danger all along.

Without listening further, Lester left the café to intercept the messengers before they arrived at the farm. As he approached the university, he watched the sheriff and the assistant dean drive away in the direction of the farm, confirming his worst fears.

Lester arrived home behind the sheriff's car and saw suitcases on the steps and the boys dressed and ready to leave. They stood in the front yard and listened as the assistant dean delivered the tragic news: The Millers were traveling through an African jungle when they became trapped in the middle of a tribal war. Everyone in the safari was viciously hacked to death in the massacre. James slept through the night and the following day.

The Millers would never be coming home. Lester mourned their violent deaths. Robert, Martin, and James grieved for the parents who gave them a second chance in life. For the memorial service, Lester placed a granite marker in the center of the rose garden where he and Bess began their friendship. With tears streaming down his face, he kneeled and stroked the two roses engraved in granite. The spirits of Joe and Bess would rest forever on the farm they loved.

When the Millers talked to their adopted sons about their education and future, they never mentioned a will. In an attorney's office a week after the Millers' memorial, Robert, Martin, and James were surprised to learn they were now property owners. They listened to the attorney explain how they would equally divide the Miller property and other assets with Lester. The estate would continue to fund the farm and all of their lives. Lester would receive his share immediately, and each of the sons would receive his full inheritance as he graduated from college, a provision Joe insisted be included in the will. The farm now belonged to Lester and the Copper brothers.

Robert returned to his company, James left for his last year at school, and Martin returned to Korea. All somber, the three brothers were each considering how to assimilate the new changes into their lives.

After returning to duty, Martin graduated from fighter pilot training. In that same year, the North Korean army attacked South Korea and changed the world. Lieutenant

Martin Copper went directly into a raging war. Martin wrote often to his brothers and to Lester. He proclaimed his love of flying and thanked Lester for introducing him to military life. He also informed them he had decided on a military career and would stay in Korea until the North Koreans were defeated.

Lester found the farm, normally filled with people and activity, a lonely place with the Millers and the boys gone. Pain from his war wounds returned, and he found it more difficult to bear responsibility for the farm. He admitted his problems to Robert in a letter and was thankful when Robert and James began visiting him again on alternating weekends. Lester made a gallant effort to be cheerful but now found it impossible to hide his physical pain.

James was the first to detect the severity of Lester's worsening health and suggested that he find someone to move to the farm to help with the work. Because George lived alone and rarely went to the Bing Café anymore,

Lester invited him to live on the farm with him so the two could help each other. Soon, Lester and George found a peaceful coexistence as helpmates and companions.

Chapter 23

Sarah was exasperated with Belinda for "flitting away her summer," as she described her daily jaunts to the lake, but Belinda was celebrating her friends' graduation and didn't notice Sarah's concern that a nursing career for her daughter might never materialize.

"Lindy, we used most of our money paying for this house and may not be able to send you to nursing school. You need to help me find a way to get you into school or consider choosing another career," Sarah suggested.

"I don't know what I can I do that you haven't already done, Mom. Anyway, I'm not graduating until next year; you'll figure out something."

"Well, I know this. You're not accomplishing anything at the lake every day."

Not realizing the extent of her mother's distress, Belinda said, "At least I have fun and don't worry all the time like you do," Belinda said and went out the door.

"Somebody around here has to worry," Sarah said, rushing to her room and closing the door behind her.

John came in through the back door during the exchange and followed his wife to their room. Sarah stood at the window. "John," she said, "it's so hard to accept that we can't send Lindy to college. She has been dreaming for so long about being a nurse."

"I'm sorry too, Sarah," John said and embraced his wife, "but I'm too old to do much of anything to earn that much money."

"I know," Sarah said.

"I wish Asyah and Angeni could see Alisha now," John said quietly. "She looks like them both."

Sarah relaxed against John's embrace. "I believe they *can* see her, John. I remember when Asyah was a little boy he sat under the apple tree, playing his music and singing so loud. When we yelled at him to quiet down, he said, 'I'm playing loud so the songbirds can hear me.' Our mother convinced him that loud music would only drive songbirds away. Sure enough, one day we heard the screen door slam and Asyah yelling, 'Guess what, there's a cardinal in the apple tree!' I believe Asyah is sending a songbird to Alisha now."

When her senior year began, Belinda realized that her mother had become increasingly anxious, but chose to ignored her nursing school problem in favor of spending time with friends. She and Alisha tried various ways to cheer up their mother and their latest was a musical ploy.

Sarah had a long-standing habit of waiting on the porch after dark for her children to come home. She enjoyed a respite when her older children married and moved away, but when Alisha and Belinda began going out at night, she resumed her vigil. Sarah knew the girls were embarrassed when their friends saw her waiting, but when it came to protecting her daughters' virtue,

Sarah did not consider embarrassment an impediment. When the girls were out alone, she and John often waited together. They enjoyed listening to their chitchat and new ghost stories, but recently John had begun to retire soon after dinner and Sarah waited alone.

Sarah was dressed in her warmest robe, and her hair flowed in the night breeze, free from its daytime chignon. The night was moonless and cold. She rocked while she waited and soon became bored without her husband's companionship. To force her thoughts away from the time when John would be gone and the girls wouldn't need her anymore, Sarah walked from one end of the porch to the other, then down the steps and across the driveway into the soft grass. As she started retracing her steps back to the porch, she heard Belinda's laughter.

Most of the time, the girls rolled their eyes and took Sarah's ritual in stride. Belinda teased her mother, calling her the *Ghost of Devinwood*. To conceal their embarrassment from their friends, Alisha told ghost stories and as an ending, Belinda called, "Look, there she is, the Ghost of Devinwood."

Alisha and Belinda played Monopoly with Adam most of the evening. Belinda looked at her watch. "It's time to go home, Alisha. Let's go see the Ghost of Devinwood. She'll be *wwaaiittiinngg.*"

Adam smiled at Belinda. "Better not poke fun at your mother; it'll come back to haunt you some day."

"Oh, I get it; Mother Ghost will haunt us. Ha. Ha. Ha. Adam, she already does—every time we come home," Belinda said.

When the girls reached their driveway and saw Sarah on the front porch, they were still laughing at Adam's admonishment.

"Let's sing it," Belinda said.

Alisha nodded. "This is as good a time as any; Adam can't hear us now."

They hooked arms and sang a verse they had made up about *Mother Ghost* to a tune that seemed to fit "When Johnny Comes Marching Home." When they knew Sarah could see, they began waving their arms like wings and gliding along like ghosts on the same path they knew Sarah took during her vigil.

When the girls come walking home at night
Hurrah. Hurrah
They know a ghost is on the porch
Hurrah. Hurrah
To welcome home her darling girls and protect them from all warriors' hearts
The ghost is on the porch.
When the girls come walking home at night,
Hurrah. Hurrah
Tawasa Springs' girls are safe once more,
Hurrah. Hurrah
When the girls come walking home!

As a finale, Alisha and Belinda bowed before their mother, who was roaring with laughter.

"I needed that," Sarah said between laughs. "It's a nice departure from you girls falling in and out of love."

"We're not in love, Mom," Alisha said.

"Speak for yourself," Belinda said and went inside for the night.

Adam watched from his front porch until Alisha and Belinda were safely home. He heard their laughter, shook his head, and went inside.

Belinda met a new boy at the first basketball game of the season, and she was in love again. Alisha warned her, "He's too old for you; Mom will never let you go out with him."

"Yes, she will."

"Betcha."

Mark Howard caught Belinda's eye as soon as he walked into the auditorium and scanned the bleachers. He had played basketball in college, and when he graduated and joined the Army, he followed regular season competition of local teams to stay near the sport. He traveled with a team from near the Army Camp Grenadier to his first Tawasa Springs Wildcats game where he fell for Belinda at first sight.

Belinda tried to tell her mother about Mark, but before she could finish, Sarah said, "He's too old for you. You can't go out with him—might as well not ask."

"I'll soon be eighteen, and I'll be out of high school next year, Mom. Anyway, he's only twenty-three. When you were my age, you—"

"That's *exactly* why you can't go out with him," Sarah retorted. "I don't want you to get married as young as I did and have children before you have a chance to live your life."

"But, Mom, he just asked me to go to a movie. He

didn't ask me to marry him … yet," she mumbled under her breath.

Sarah stood firm. "No. And don't ask again."

"I told you," Alisha said.

"Don't rub it in. Besides, I'm still working on it. Mark's coming to church Sunday morning, and by then I'll have Mom talked into letting him have dinner with us. The poor boy never has a decent meal at that Army camp."

"He didn't look that hungry to me," Alisha said.

The following Sunday, Mark joined Belinda at church. When Mark asked if Sarah said yes to their date, Belinda rolled her eyes and shook her head. "But you are invited to have dinner with us."

"Thank you; then never mind the date," Mark said. "I can handle your mother."

Sarah politely greeted Mark as he arrived and presented her with flowers. She found his conversation straightforward and the ease in which he moved around in her kitchen, comfortable as a friend. A month later, Sarah opened the front door and there stood Mark with his mother, Isabel. Gradually, Sarah's doubts about Mark's age began to change into an appreciation of his maturity. She now felt at ease with the possibility that he and Belinda might marry.

Sarah watched her daughter's new romance blossom throughout the basketball season. In early 1952, when Sarah thought she had lost the battle of an early marriage, Mark completed pilot training and the Army sent him to demonstrate his skills in the Korean War.

Chapter 24

The rain made the cold, February day seem endless and the end of the school year a lifetime away. Belinda and Alisha sat with Sarah at the kitchen table, talking and waiting for the cookies to bake and laughing at Caroline and Ellie practicing a cheerleader routine for that night's basketball game. The cheerleaders stopped, and the four girls sat at the table with Sarah, their moods matching the day, each in her own thoughts.

Alisha noticed Ellie watching her with a far-away look and wondered if Adam was as happy with Ellie as she was with him. The last time she and Adam had a long conversation, they were at his house wrapped in blankets near the fireplace. She thought he had seemed a bit too indifferent, brushing off Ellie's plans for marriage and their future, as if he were closing off reality. She would miss Adam, her friend and confidante, when he went away to school, but Alisha also felt a gnawing jealousy— Adam could also be going to a wife.

Just as Sarah jiggled the cookies off the baking tin and onto a cooling rack, John came in from working in his tool shed, joined the rush to take a warm cookie, hurried back out, and then immediately returned, announcing, "Quick, look outside; the rain is turning to snow!"

Sarah and the girls rushed to the window to watch while the silent, gleaming flakes floated to earth and magically covered roofs and mailboxes with a white powdery snow. Adam's car turned into the driveway and Ellie's mood lightened. "Good, we can go to practice now."

Alisha watched Adam hurry to the door. To her surprise, she wished he was coming for her. To escape Ellie's watchful eye, she fled to her arc of safety. She was lost in new music for a while, but the smell of cookies fresh out of the oven filled the entire house and competed for her attention. Just when she was about to give up and return to the kitchen, Adam stuck his arm through the door, swirled a cookie into the room, and said, "Come and get 'em, Mozart."

"You're a bad person, Adam," Alisha playfully scolded. She and Adam joined the others at the kitchen table and soon the cookies were gone.

Snow had completely covered the ground and rooftops, leaving the roads barely distinguishable. Alisha stood at the window and flinched as Adam opened the car door open for Ellie. In contrast with Ellie's brightened mood, he had been uncharacteristically quiet. Adam closed the car door, hesitated for an instant, then walked back toward the house. Alisha hurried to the living room, sat on the sofa, and thumbed through a magazine.

Alisha looked up from the magazine but kept silent while Adam walked through the kitchen, calling her name. With a short rap on the door, he eased into the living room. "Hi again," he said. "I'm coming in," and Adam walked into Alisha's life.

Adam sat close, took the magazine from her, and laid it on the table. With a searching look, he opened his mouth, but no words came. He took Alisha's hand, held it in a fist over his heart, and looked into her eyes. Then his words rushed out. "Alisha, you know we're no longer just friends; I've known it for a long time. There's a picnic at the lake before the end of school, and I want to take you."

Alisha's silent, wide-eyed reaction was, *yes*. "But, what about Ellie?" she asked aloud.

Adam squeezed her hand and slowly placed it back on her leg. "Ellie doesn't know it yet, but when basketball season's over, we're breaking up. She's making plans that I can't agree with. I've been trying to tell her, but she's not hearing me."

When Alisha thought about Caroline, she stood and paced around the room. *Caroline is my best friend, but she's also Ellie's sister.* "Caroline will be mad at me ... I know she will," she said in an urgent whisper, as if she might be overheard.

Adam walked to Alisha and took her hand again. "Probably, but she would—," he said, releasing Alisha's hand.

Ellie walked in and closed the door behind her. "What's going on in here?" she asked, sounding more like a mother who had caught her children misbehaving than a jealous girlfriend. She looked back and forth from Adam to Alisha and her eyes filled with tears.

Adam backed away from Alisha and took Ellie's arm. "Let's go, I've been trying to tell you, but you won't listen."

Ellie jerked away and rushed out the door with Adam following, neither speaking another word to Alisha. Alisha knew her earlier wish would soon come true. Adam would come for her instead of Ellie. She returned to the piano and played softly. She barely heard the door slam, the car engine start up, and the tires screech as Adam spun on the snow-covered street.

The next thing Alisha knew was Belinda calling her to help set the dinner table. She ignored her sister and kept playing, all her thoughts blending into one—one that dominated—the one that had just walked out the door. For as long as Alisha could remember, her life had revolved around music. From this day forward, her music would compete with another love—and she wanted both.

Belinda flung open the living room door. "Can't you hear…what's wrong with you…why did Adam come back? Oh, no, don't say it! Don't even think about it. Ellie will kill you. You know Adam is her boyfriend."

Alisha sat spellbound. "I don't care," she said and then realized she and Lindy had never talked about Adam outside the context of friendship. She eased the cover over the piano keys and quietly asked, "How did you know, Lindy?"

Belinda, frustrated, replied, "You'll care all right when Ellie gets you. Anyone could tell something's different by the way you two look at each other, especially you. You know she'll find a way to keep Adam as long as she wants him. Come help me in the kitchen and let's finish dinner and get out of here. And find your boots; we're walking to the game. Charlie's in the kitchen with Mom."

"Good," Alisha said, "Tell *him* to help you set the table," and Belinda stormed out of the living room.

While she dressed for the game, Alisha struggled to stay calm and make some sense of what just happened. She had always felt defined by choices other people made for her—until today. She could not imagine how her life could be better—until today. So today, she concluded, she would make her own decisions about her life with Adam.

As Alisha, Belinda, and Charlie were pulling on boots, hats and gloves, Sarah, with John at her side, gave them her customary instructions to be careful and stay out of trouble. John instructed Charlie to take care of the girls and added, "Alisha, please try to go for one night without arguing with anybody."

"Even Charlie?"

"Especially Charlie," Charlie said, laughing.

"How could anything exciting ever happen to us, if we sit, watch each other, stay away from fights, and not talk to strangers?" Lindy asked her mother.

"Just do it, and have a good time anyway," Sarah said as she and John ushered the teenagers out the door.

"Put on your hat and coat, Sarah," John said, watching Charlie and the girls wade through the snow. "Let's go for a walk too."

When they reached the gymnasium, Belinda sat with her friends, and Charlie followed Alisha to sit with their classmates.

"Charlie, go sit with your friends," Alisha said.

"You heard your mother. I have to make sure you don't talk to strange people."

"I'm talking to a strange person now; anyway, she said 'stran*gers*.'"

Charlie left and returned with a group of boys to claim seats around the girls. The boys hovered around the girls, and Charlie was not fazed when Alisha ignored him.

Alisha thought of Charlie as a brother; after all, they had practically grown up together. As she watched Adam on the basketball court, she glanced at Charlie and wondered, *what will I do with Charlie—what would I do without him?*

At halftime, with the score tied, the players vanished into the locker rooms. Cheerleaders from both teams screamed their routines, trying to out-shout the fans for the opposing team, and then took their break. Charlie went with the boys to get food, and the girls headed toward the restroom to check makeup and hair and exchange gossip.

Alisha was standing against the wall talking with Caroline when she heard Ellie say loud and clear, "You'd better leave him alone. I don't care what he's telling you."

Caroline tried to steer Ellie in the opposite direction, pleading with her sister, "Leave her alone; she doesn't want him for a boyfriend."

With piercing eyes, Ellie spat at Alisha, "I'll just bet. You'd just better stick to your music, because you're not getting Adam."

"Maybe I'll have both, Ellie," Alisha said calmly and with more confidence than she felt.

Belinda came in just in time to hear the last of the exchange and walked between Ellie and Alisha. "Ellie, get away from her." She turned to say, "I told you so, Alisha. Come on, we're going back to our seats. Didn't you hear Dad tell you not to argue?"

"I'm not arguing. I'm calmly stating a fact."

Belinda and Alisha returned to the gymnasium. Alisha refused to sit with Belinda or, "to be chaperoned," she said and walked toward her seat.

Adam caught up with Alisha. He had already heard about the incident in the restroom. "Are you okay?" he asked.

"I'm okay. Ellie's mad, Lindy's bossy, and Charlie's hovering...why does Charlie always act like he's my bodyguard?"

"Charlie likes to take care of you—a lot of people do, but I don't think you'll need a bodyguard, Alisha," Adam said, smiling. "I'll fix this thing with Ellie once and for all—I promise—just give me a little time." Adam turned away at mid-court to join the team.

Charlie almost bumped into Alisha coming from the other direction. "Here's your Coke," he said. "Come on; let's hurry while we still have seats."

"Thanks, Charlie." Alisha took the Coke, suddenly grateful for Charlie's friendship.

"What's going on? You're not arguing with me," Charlie said, smiling as they scrambled to their seats. But Alisha ignored his question.

The coach saw the glow on Adam's face and understood why he had lost momentum. "Adam, learn this. Women will make you forget who you are, what you're doing, and why you're even on the basketball court." Then he yelled, "Go sit on the bench until you can think about playing basketball again!" He walked away muttering, "Women, always women."

Adam sat on the bench with the others, but alone. Out of the game, his mind would not focus on anything but his changed relationship with Alisha and the inevitable fight that lay ahead with Ellie. Deep in thought, he was deaf to the *tat-tat-tat* of the bouncing basketball and the squeaking of tennis shoes on the hardwood court. He could hear his father's standard advice, *make a decision, boy; make a decision,* and his coach's answer to everything, *play ball, or sit on the bench until you can play ball.*

Adam had been dating Ellie since he moved to Tawasa Springs. He was approaching adulthood and had in his mind a vivid finality to his high school life. To complicate the vision, his affection for Ellie had faded as he realized his true feelings for Alisha. His relationship with Ellie had been as an immature teenager, and she had interpreted their recent intimacy to mean they would always be together. *I'm not being fair, Ellie. Life's not fair. I've changed and didn't realize it … it was almost overnight, you see.* Adam decided what he wanted to do—would do.

The buzzer sounded. The players separated and rushed to the sidelines. Adam's attention was fully back on the game. The coach looked at Adam and knew. "Get over here," he yelled.

The team was losing and the coach was angry. "Adam, are you ready to play ball?"

"Yes sir!"

Adam glanced toward the bleachers and saw Alisha.

He couldn't resist her smile and briefly touched his fist to his heart, smiling as she returned the signal.

Charlie's smile instantly faded when he saw Adam and Alisha do that stupid fist-over-heart signal. Dejected, Charlie mumbled, "Don't count me out sport, not yet." Until tonight, he had not considered the possibility of losing Alisha, but after watching her and Adam, he knew she was slipping away.

Ellie was not smiling either. She saw Adam talking to Alisha at halftime, and he had blatantly ignored her since they arrived. She pondered the possibilities: Angry? Oh, yes. End of Adam's feelings for her … probably. Their relationship was no doubt in trouble. Accept the inevitable … *not that easy, Adam.*

Caroline calmed her sister, but now she was disturbed. Because she lost most battles with Ellie and arguing made Ellie more determined, Caroline was happy to stay out of this one, but would place bets on her sister anytime.

The Tawasa Springs Wildcats lost the game, and Adam blamed himself. He was angry, and Ellie standing at the car intensified his anger. "Where's Caroline?" he barked.

"She has a ride, Adam. Just take me home," Ellie replied without emotion.

Adam opened the car door, and Ellie slumped down in the front seat. Adam was unprepared for Ellie's response and took his time walking around the car to get in. Before he opened his door, he turned and saw Charlie, Alisha, and Belinda walking home. He watched Charlie put his arm around Alisha's shoulder, directing her attention the other way. Anxious to end his and Ellie's relationship with the least possible trouble, Adam sped to Ellie's house, stopped in the driveway, and turned off the ignition. Instead of getting out of the car to walk her to the door as usual, Adam stiffened his arms, pushed on the steering wheel, and laid his head back on the seat. "You know I won't be back."

Ellie turned her head slightly toward Adam. "Yes, you will," she said and quickly slipped out, closed the car door, and ran inside her house.

Adam was stunned and made no move to go after her. He watched the porch light go off and sat motionless until he saw her bedroom light come on, then drove slowly away with her promise replaying in his head and chilling his heart.

"Lindy, how does this woman find out everything so fast?" Alisha asked

Belinda looked at Alisha sarcastically. "She has a network of spies, and they meet in the woods before daylight every morning... *I*... don't... know."

When Sarah heard about the confrontation in the restroom, she declared the girls grounded, "until you two can behave yourselves," she had said. Sarah was angry, and to make sure they understood, she added, "Alisha, John told you not to argue, and Lindy I don't really care what happened. The basketball season will soon be over, and they can finish without any more trouble from at least two girls I know."

In the past, Alisha and Belinda had tried various strategies to get through Sarah's anger but had only recently discovered the most successful one yet.

After breakfast, Belinda said, "Okay, Alisha. You know what to do. Let's get busy and don't argue for a change."

Alisha said, "I will but you *could* stop being so bossy, you know."

Belinda went the kitchen to find her mother's favorite recipe. Alisha gathered cleaning supplies and began cleaning at the opposite end of the house while she fantasized about her new relationship with Adam. Soon, dinner was on the table and the house was spotless.

Sarah, aware of their motive, sauntered through the house admiring Alisha's work and praising Belinda for the appetizing dinner. "Good practice, girls. You're getting really good at this," Sarah said with a wicked grin.

"She tricked us, Lindy," Alisha said under her breath.

"Shut up. She's happy," Belinda replied through clenched teeth.

Driving his new car through the countryside and enjoying his freedom, Adam imagined his future now that he was free of Ellie. He was relieved that the relationship ended without the arguments and tears he expected. But there was still that lingering doubt. Had Ellie really gone down without the fight she promised? Charlie had reported to Adam Ellie's vow to get him back. "Oh well, it won't be today. School's almost over and I'm free," Adam said.

Adam was in high spirits. He would graduate from high school in a few days. Saturday afternoon was here, and after his long drive trying out his new car, he was on his way to pick up Alisha for the picnic.

Alisha was dressed and anxiously waiting for Adam. Apprehension set in only when Belinda cautioned her to watch out for Ellie.

John watched Adam driving up in a 1952 blue and white Chevrolet Bel Air convertible and thought Adam already looked like a college student. John met Adam at the car—a graduation gift from his parents—and looked it over with approval. "Congratulations, son; I hear you're going off to college soon."

"That's my plan, sir."

"Don't let anything change your plans. Education's very important."

Anxious about any serious conversation with John, Adam asked, "Is Alisha ready?"

Alisha stood at the window as Adam arrived. She overheard his and John's conversation. Sarah stood, watching with her hand on Alisha's shoulder. "He is the handsomest boy around here; you'll make a cute couple."

"I know, Mom, but go close in on Dad before he scares him off."

Sarah hurried to the front porch and casually sat in the swing, calling to John to join her.

When Alisha and Adam arrived at the lake, their classmates had gathered. Charlie rushed to greet Alisha and Adam, but when he saw their hands entwined, he stopped short and his smile vanished. He turned away to join another group, struggling to recover his sense of humor.

Exciting voices, laughter, and sounds of summer activities permeated the air. Juniors and graduating seniors ate from a large variety of food laid out on a long table, listened to music, played volleyball, and swam in the lake. For most, the picnic was a celebration of the approaching summer, and for seniors, it signaled the beginning of a new life.

When Alisha caught Charlie looking her way, she started toward him, but he moved away before she could reach him. Alisha detoured and talked to Caroline instead. "Ellie and I are going to Chicago to visit our aunt this summer," Caroline said.

"For how long?" Alisha asked, surprised.

"We won't be back until school starts in the fall."

"Why all summer, Caroline? You'll be bored, and I won't have anyone to talk to."

"You seem to have worked that out," Caroline said, glancing toward Adam, who was headed their way. Alisha felt dejected but knew Caroline was only being loyal to her sister and left the conversation unfinished.

The summer party ended. Charlie ducked out, unseen. Belinda and the other graduates left for other parties, and soon everyone was gone except Adam and Alisha. They sat inside a picture booth, depositing coin after coin, making funny pictures, each silly expression bringing on a new fit of laughter. Just as one flash went off, the camera captured their spontaneous glance, reflecting a love born out of their friendship. The photo was Alisha's favorite.

Late afternoon turned to dusk, and a full moon made a dramatic appearance over the horizon. When darkness came, the moon glowed in the sky like a huge silvery light. The moon always brought back memories to Alisha. She told Adam about the front porch at the orphanage, snuggling in a blanket and warm pajamas and making up *man-in-the -moon* stories.

"Those stories seem like a lifetime away until a great moon fills the sky, like tonight," Alisha said. "I wouldn't have chosen to live there, but I'll always remember Miss Beatrice and how she took care of me."

"I don't understand why your Aunt Kate didn't keep you," Adam said.

"I don't either, but I brought it up once, and she got so upset I never mentioned it again."

"You're the one who should be upset," Adam said and hugged her shoulder. When she did not reply, he hugged tighter, then released her, and they walked on.

When their walk around the lake ended at the pier, Adam spotted a rowboat. With a quick glance at each other, they jumped into the boat and paddled out to the small island in the center of the lake. Alisha asked Adam to explore the island with her, and so they strolled on the winding trail.

Pine trees dotted the island, and their shiny black needles subtly contrasted the moonlit sky. Alisha relaxed as they crossed the island, gazing at the moonlight through the trees and listening to the soft lap of waves against the shore. Tonight, her world seemed bounded by the serenity of the island, and she felt her life was in perfect harmony.

Alisha and Adam held hands as they walked, then spontaneously stopped and embraced in the stillness and silence. Their embrace turned into a kiss, their kiss communicated passion, and secret whispers ordained their love.

Chapter 25

Four years after leaving home, James graduated from college, received his inheritance, and moved to Minneapolis as the second partner in the Copper Brothers Architectural Design and Building Company.

Robert thought James worried unnecessarily about Martin. James thought Robert should be *more* concerned.

"I *wouldn't* worry so much," James said, "except for the dreams … almost every night … I see his face so clearly. Even his freckle is more prominent; then, I hear his voice calling me and I can't find him. When I'm awake, he's on my mind all the time."

Robert and James worked well together and were content to be together again. Robert constantly tried new ways of averting James's attention from Martin, but nothing worked. Finally, just as they both agreed it was time to look for their sister, their search was tragically diverted.

As they opened the door to leave for work one morning, a military officer was about to ring the bell to deliver a message to Robert and James Copper. On May 18, 1952, one month after his twenty-third birthday, Captain Martin Copper was killed. His squadron had been guarding a narrow pass from a Chinese ambush when they took the full force and firepower of Chinese and North Korean troops pushing south, inflicting heavy casualties on United States forces. Martin, shot down while supporting ground forces, was among thousands of American forces that had died in Korea since the war began in 1950.

Robert and James heard the major's words but could not comprehend the reality that Martin was dead. They drove home, talking about how Martin's death would surely affect Lester and sinking into their own sorrow. Through their disjointed conversation, they surprised themselves with the decision they knew would have offended the Millers. They resolved that whatever time it took, whatever the cost, they would put their lives on hold, locate their original home, and lay Martin to rest next to their parents, and in this process, they *would* find their sister.

In the early morning fog, George walked to the barn with a cup of coffee to join Lester and watch the horses as the sun rose. When the horses whinnied, the two men turned to see Robert's car slowly pulling into the driveway.

"Lester, I didn't know the boys were coming home, did you?" George asked.

"No, I didn't," Lester said, and the two men walked toward the approaching car.

Robert parked near the rose garden and waited for

Lester and George. As soon as greetings were exchanged, Robert told them, "We have terrible news." He paused. "It's Martin. He was killed in Korea."

Lester became numb and speechless, his eyes wide with shock. He could not have been more devastated if Martin had been his own flesh and blood. In his mind, the boys were his sons from the time they left the Boys Home and began to reclaim their lives with the powerful force of love—the Millers' love and his own. The Copper brothers learned to love Lester as a father long ago, and today, Robert and James felt his loving embrace and realized the crucial role this man had played in their lives.

In the following days, friends and neighbors visited, understanding that although this family had experienced a severe loss only a few years earlier, this time their pain was as undying as their love and would change their lives forever. Robert and James honored Lester's wishes for a memorial service at the rose garden but held fast to their decision to find their birthplace and only then would they bury their brother. When sadness inevitably turned to anger, their resolve to locate their original home was galvanized. They felt that only by locating their sister could they face the reality of never seeing Martin again and begin to heal.

When Lester left the boys in the barn loft the day they first talked to him about their family, he promised to look for their sister. But the Millers had discouraged him from trying to reunite the siblings until they were adults, and Lester never began his search. Early on the morning after the news about Martin, Lester drove to the Holy Cross Boys Home while Robert and James were still sleeping.

Father O'Kelly's dream of cleaning out the Boys Home had faded when he began receiving young boys into the home faster than he could find homes in a community that would not take them in. He left Father Joseph Murphy in charge, an emaciated man hardly as tall as the boys for whom he cared. Lester explained the circumstances to Father Murphy and pleaded with him to hand over any information about the Copper boys' family. Father Murphy disappeared into the office and to Lester's amazement, returned with a letter from Sarah Devinwood, dated almost two years ago.

Handing Lester the letter, Father Murphy said, "I found this letter from a woman who claims to have the Copper boys' sister in her home."

"What? Why have you kept this letter to yourself? You should have forwarded it to those boys when it first arrived—they were grown men then."

Father Murphy saw a desperation that Lester rarely displayed. "Lester, Father O'Kelly had a large box of unopened correspondence. As you know, for a few years before he retired, he focused on finding homes for the boys and just tossed all the mail into boxes. I'm afraid he neglected the administrative part of the job. I agree, it was tragic to keep this letter from the Copper boys, but it's taken me a long time to sort the contents and determine to whom each letter should go. I assure you, my next step was to locate the recipients, so I'm glad you're here."

Lester returned home and cooked breakfast. Over

coffee, he laid the open letter in front of Robert and James and explained the delay.

"Do you mean this letter has been at the boys' home for two years?" Robert asked after reading the letter.

"It appears so."

"Martin could have known her," James said sadly.

"And Sis could have known Martin," Robert said. She doesn't know about any of us." Reading the letter again, he said, "Alisha was taken to an orphanage soon after we were and she stayed there for five years. How could that be?"

James shook his head in disbelief. "How could anyone give away a six-month-old baby?"

"Well, it seemed to be really easy for Uncle Hank and Aunt Kate," Robert said.

At last, they could again think of Alisha as a real person. At the time of Sarah's letter, Alisha was fifteen and beginning her freshman year in high school. They read and reread what Sarah had written—Alisha was tall and pretty, and she had an exceptional talent for music, even played piano at church, but they still could not put a face to their sister. Although pleased to finally know where Alisha lived, for the following few days, Robert, James, and Lester struggled with an all-consuming grief mixed with joyous anticipation.

The next day, Robert wrote a long letter to Sarah, telling her about their lives, about Joe and Bess Miller, and of course, their lives with Lester. He explained how Martin's young life had ended, and that it would take six weeks to get his body shipped back from Korea. He asked her to arrange to have Martin buried next to their parents and sent the letter special delivery. When he contacted the military official to finalize their plans, he shivered at the finality of learning an officer would escort Robert and James taking Martin's body to its final resting place.

On an early morning in June as a gentle breeze blew through the rose garden, Robert, James, and George stood silent among friends, neighbors, and Veterans of Foreign Wars, both young and old, as Lester memorialized Martin. Lester recalled the morning he awoke to find the flag-covered truck, a gift from the VFW, how the sun rose over the mountain and melted the fog. "That scene," he said, "eventually dimmed bad memories of my last battle and was also the genesis of Martin becoming a soldier."

"Martin ran to the flag-covered truck and asked where it came from. I told him it came from friends—very good VFW friends. Later, I showed him how to fold the American flag. 'Why don't you just hang it up?' he asked. I explained each fold, and Martin asked a corresponding 'why.'

"Because Martin was so curious, I talked on and on about the war and military life in general. Then I brought out all that war memorabilia I came home with and pictures I hadn't looked at in years. We continued to talk and look through my military history most of that morning.

"From then on, I think, in his own mind, he was a soldier. Then, at an air show, he became enamored with airplanes. I've been so proud of him all these years as I watched him become a soldier and then a strong military officer. Now, he has given his life for his country and I'm still proud. But if I take any pride in making him that military officer, I must also take equal responsibility for his death."

They watched as Lester fell to his knees, weeping and sobbing uncontrollably, and felt his pain and loss, and they all grieved with him.

Robert and James placed a second granite stone, engraved with the United States flag, next to the memorial for Joe and Bess. They knew that soon the rose buds would burst into bloom, embracing three loved souls at rest.

Chapter 26

"Alisha's brothers are coming home," Sarah repeated aloud, as though speaking the words would make Robert's letter more of a reality. She read the letter to John while he drove her to their neighbors with a telephone so she could call Kate. At first, Kate was pleased, but she also dreaded the day she would have to confront her nephews.

"I know it's time to acknowledge what my sister did, Sarah. More importantly, it's time for me to face what I failed to do."

"We all make mistakes, Kate. Let's hope it's not as bad as you imagine."

"Oh Sarah, I wish I had your hope. I think I've gained some measure of acceptance from Alisha—but, oh I dread facing those grown boys. I remember how sweet they were the last day I saw them. They thought they were only going for a ride with Hank."

"Kate, let's just get through this one step at a time. Come early tomorrow afternoon. This is something you need to tell Alisha yourself—as soon as possible. She needs some time to adjust and prepare herself for her brothers' arrival, and she must hear this story from you."

After telephoning Kate, Sarah and John drove to the church and discussed Martin's funeral with Max. Back home, Sarah brewed coffee and sat with John in the porch swing, talking about the letter. "Robert wrote extensively about Alisha as a baby," she said sadly "and how they always wanted to locate her. But now only two brothers are left to get their wish." She stopped the swing, breaking into tears. "John, after seventeen years, this family will be together again—at least what's left of it."

John said, "You should be *happy* for that part of it, woman. Why are you crying?"

"Oh, John, my heart is broken for Alisha—and for Robert and James, for Martin's awful death—for the reason the children will finally see each other again. I'm sorry for all they've been through. I even feel sorry for Kate, now that the wait is over. She's probably suffered much more than we know."

John shook his head. "Kate's the only one I don't feel sorry for, but you—you'd better cheer up and give yourself some credit. You're the one who got those kids back. You're their hero, Sarah, and by the way, you're my hero today too." John moved closer to his wife and started swinging. "Do you know what today is?" he asked and pulled her close.

Sarah wiped her tears. "Not really."

"Even with all the excitement going on, I'll bet if you think about it, you'll remember that we were married forty-six years ago today. Remember that little church?"

Sarah laid her head on John's shoulder and smiled as she thought about their wedding day. "Oh, yes, I do, John. What a day. Remember the buggy?"

John laughed. "Do I remember! I borrowed that old

buggy from the preacher, but I forgot it didn't have a top and then your friends stuck flowers in every nook and cranny; it looked like a circus."

Sarah laughed along with John and they drifted into the past for a time. "And the rain started pouring down just before we arrived at the church. We had to run to keep from getting soaked, and I slipped and almost fell running into the church."

"And the horse whinnied all during the ceremony," John said.

"Because it was raining on him all through the wedding," Sarah said, "and that poor horse had to stand out there attached to the buggy with flowers all over it...and...Martha, remember Martha? She was so nervous she forgot the words to—what was the name of that song, John?"

"I don't know; I didn't know it then, and I don't think Martha knew it either," John said in their cleansing laughter.

Belinda walked up the driveway from school and heard her parents' laughter. "Just what goes on here when we aren't here to watch you two; what's so funny?"

"Today's our forty-sixth wedding anniversary," John said and wiped tears from his face.

"Being married forty-six years sounds boring, not funny," Belinda said. "Dad, how could you make Mom laugh about her wedding day?"

"Lindy, life either gets funny or depressing as you go along—I like funny," John said, hugging his daughter and leaving for the tool shed.

Sarah's laughter subsided, and she beckoned her daughter. "Oh, sweetheart, you would have to have been there to appreciate the humor in that day. Come sit with me and let me tell you something wonderful that's about to happen. Alisha's brothers are coming home." Sarah handed Robert's letter to Belinda and she read it quickly.

"I'm so happy for them, Mom—and you too. It's too bad it had to be the war that helped you find them. Why didn't you tell Alisha about her family a long time ago?"

"I probably should have, but I believed her life had been hard enough without adding a frustration we could not help her with. Kate will be here tomorrow after school, and I'm leaving this revelation to her, so please keep this information to yourself."

"Don't worry. I don't want to be the one to tell her. By the way, Mom, any news—remember, I'm graduating from high school in a couple of weeks … scholarship … nursing school … Nurse Belinda?"

"I'm really having a hard time telling you this, Lindy, but I've searched everywhere, and getting you into nursing school without working is the one thing I wanted to give you, and I can't. There are just no scholarships available." Sarah hugged her daughter.

Belinda hugged her mother in return, feeling a keen disappointment. "I don't know what to do with my life if I can't be a nurse; there's nothing else I want to do." Seeing her mother's pain, Belinda took her hand. "I know it's hard for you, Mom. I'll try to help you more. Maybe I can get a job at the hospital until I can get into school."

"I so want you girls to do something different with

your lives—something meaningful and something you love to do," Sarah said. "You just have to break the mold of an early marriage and large family. I don't want you to have to live your lives through others."

"Mom, my chances of getting into nursing school might be better in a couple years. One way or the other though, I'm going. You'll find a way—you always have."

𝄞

Walking home on the last day of school, Alisha caught up with Charlie. "Hi, Charlie, what are you doing this summer?"

"Might go work with my un—" he began, but as they neared the driveway, Alisha noticed Kate's car and interrupted.

"I wonder why Aunt Kate is here? It's not time for me to go to her house, and I'm not sure I want to go this summer anyway."

"Good, maybe we can go to the movies or—"

"I'll see you tomorrow, Charlie," Alisha said and rushed home, leaving Charlie standing by the mailbox. As she reached the porch, Adam's words rang in her ears. *You should be nicer to Charlie. He likes you.* She turned back toward the mailbox, but just as she raised her arm to wave goodbye, he turned and walked away.

Kate watched Alisha hurry up the driveway. *So much time has passed,* she thought; *how can I explain to her how her life began the way it did; no, how can I justify to her what I did?*

Kate attempted to explain, stumbled twice, started

over, and then abruptly said, "Alisha, I want to ask you something very important."

Alisha was sure she had done something wrong but could not think of what it could be—except the watch. "I didn't lose that watch, Aunt Kate, it's still in the drawer. You can have it back—I don't want it, anyway."

"No, no, it's not about the watch, Alisha, although I understand why you never wore it. This is important, Alisha, so listen. What would you say if I told you that you have brothers—three brothers; that is, now you only have two brothers."

At first, Alisha thought Kate was talking about Belinda's brothers, but the numbers didn't add up. She stopped the swing and leaned forward. "What do you mean I have brothers? What are you talking about, Aunt Kate?"

"It's a long story, Alisha, a sad story, and I'm not very proud of my part in it."

"What did you do? What happened?" Alisha stood and walked around Kate's chair, impatient to hear what her aunt was struggling to say, but dreading to hear something that might change her life. "I like my life just like it is; please don't change it again, Aunt Kate."

Kate slowly found the words to tell Alisha about her family. She talked most about Angeni and the legend of the spirit angel surrounding her mother's name, of their lives growing up, that her father, Asyah, married Angeni at age sixteen, how the birth of each child weakened Angeni's health, and how her father and mother had died. Kate left the most difficult part for last: that she and Hank had placed the children in orphanages, how

Martin had died, and that because of her, Alisha would never see one of her brothers at all.

Alisha walked from one end of the porch to the other in stunned silence, listening to Kate and feeling angrier by the moment. With no words to express her frustration Alisha said, "Remember me asking you, Aunt Kate, about my mother and father, and you told me they got sick and died soon after I was born? Why didn't you tell me the truth then?"

"Alisha, I thought I was doing the right thing to protect you from something you could never do anything about. I wanted you to have a chance in life."

"By dumping me in an orphanage for five years? Come on, Aunt Kate, you got rid of us as soon as you could because you—maybe just Uncle Hank—didn't want to be bothered with kids and you didn't want to change your life either. Admit it. You didn't care that you were destroying our lives. That's my truth now, Aunt Kate."

Alisha was horrified. She had brothers—a family— all these years and had missed the chance to know them. She stormed into the house, slamming the screen door as hard as she could, hating everyone.

Sarah was shocked from the severity of Alisha's reaction. Then she heard a car engine start and realized Kate was driving away, leaving her alone with the consequences of a very bad situation, as she had done before.

Belinda waited in the living room, relieved. Until Belinda read Robert's letter, she had known nothing about Alisha's family. She had discussed the possibilities with Alisha—and Adam once when he brought it up.

Now Alisha knew the whole story. She had told no one, except Adam, for she knew Alisha would turn to him first. Belinda heard the door slam and steadied herself for the storm. "Alisha, I didn't know until yesterday," Belinda said as Alisha rushed in slamming the door.

Alisha flopped down on the sofa, crossed her arms, and sat very still, staring into space and trying to grasp the strangeness and heaviness of Kate's confession and the difference meeting her brothers would make in her life. After a while, she asked, "Does Adam know?"

"Yes, but he's the only one," Belinda said.

"All of a sudden, I feel different. Even this room looks different."

"You life is different," Belinda said and took her hand.

"It sure is."

The cloud of anger and sadness reshaped itself as a sense of loss, but with it, a new curiosity. Alisha had never even seen a picture of her parents or her brothers and tried to visualize her family so she could imagine what life would be like if they were together.

Belinda knew Alisha well enough to leave her alone with her thoughts. She stretched out on the sofa and closed her eyes. Her mother would be getting ready for Robert, James, and Lester's arrival and it seemed no one remembered her problem. Alisha sat silently and Belinda sank into her depression. *No scholarship... I almost wish Mom hadn't told me. What can I do? Nothing. If there's no scholarship, there's no nursing school. There just has to be some way.*

John came into the room, quietly closing the door and pulling up a chair close to his daughters.

Alisha looked up as if he'd been there all along. "I've never known anyone who died, Dad. I've never even been to a funeral."

"Me either," Belinda said with her eyes still closed. "You wouldn't let me go to grandfather's funeral, remember?"

"You were just six years old, Lindy," her father said.

"Are you going to my brother's funeral?" Alisha asked.

"Yes, of course. We're all going," John said.

"James. Robert. Martin, but now it's only Robert and James," Alisha said. "I'll have to get used to their names. I wonder what they're like, where we lived, where they grew up."

"You lived in Koasati Springs," John said, "a small town a couple of hours from here. The letter Sarah received said the boys lived in West Virginia with a family named Miller and Lester Green, a man who managed their farm. Robert and James are in their twenties, graduated from college, and have their own business. I would bet my bottom dollar they're a lot like you."

"I hope so. How long did *they* live in a stupid orphanage?"

"Sarah said they were there only a short time, in a place called the Holy Cross Boys Home, but you'll have plenty of time to get to know them and hear all about their lives."

"I'll bet they're still mad at Uncle Hank," Alisha said.

"If they're still mad at their dead uncle, I'll bet they'll really be mad at their live aunt," Belinda added.

Alisha's anger subsided as John talked, and she became more curious about her brothers. She was surprised to feel a pleasant sense of belonging that she had never recognized before today. *Now I know why this room feels strange—it's never been my room—not really. I've never belonged to the Devinwoods—not really—and they've never belonged to me.*

"Lindy, how does it feel to have a real family—real brothers?"

"Good, I guess," Lindy said. "But I've always had my real family and brothers, so I can't make a comparison."

John left the girls talking and went to his tool shed. He unwrapped pictures of the Copper family hidden away in a trunk for years, untied the yellowed string, and removed the photographs. He cleaned the frames and glass, reassembled the pictures, and returned to the house to do what he was now free to do. "Alisha, I've always wanted to help make your situation as right as I can," he said. "I've not been able to do much, but I hope in some small way, these pictures will help."

Alisha took the pictures from John, studied the small photograph, and easily recognized a young Aunt Kate but saw only a glimpse of familiarity in the other girl she assumed was her mother. "My mother looks like she was about my age."

John shook his head. "She was a year younger than you in that picture. She and Asyah were married when Angeni was just sixteen."

"Wow," Alisha said, looking at the picture of her parents and three young brothers. Staring at three little boys, a father and a mother, she grasped the truth intellectually but was unable to feel the connection she sought. She laid the family of strangers aside. "I can't love a mother and father that I don't even remember," Alisha said, shaking her head wistfully. "I hope it will be different with Robert and James, but I can't imagine the three of us ever loving each other as if we had grown up together. But then, Aunt Kate made sure we missed that, didn't she?"

"Believe me, Alisha," John said. "I've never given Kate much of a break, but I'm sure she has paid more than any of us; in fact, sometimes I think she might be paying for all of us. In the letter, Robert said they called you Sis. I'll bet they're going to remember you, and at the age they were when you were born—nine and six—they would've been crazy about you."

"You're probably right, Dad. I just hope they remember that."

They heard a soft knock on the door. "That would be Adam," John said. "I'll leave you girls to visit with him."

As he opened the door to admit Adam, John turned and said, "Alisha, try to remember you're looking at your family as they were before you were born. That's a long time ago.

You can't be expected to love them, but still I think you might be surprised some day when you do."
Adam hugged Alisha for a long time and asked, "What do you think about having brothers, Alisha?" At the same time, he noticed the pictures. "Hey, look at that—your family. Do you want me to hang these in your room?"

Pulling away from Adam, Alisha said, "I don't know what I want to do with those pictures and I don't know what to think about having brothers right now."

Chapter 27

As thunder and lightning tore through the sky on an early morning in July, Robert, James, and Lester arrived in Tawasa Springs. A military honor guard from Fort Monroe waited in the bus for the hearse bearing Martin's body. When the thunderstorm subsided, the group moved the casket inside the funeral home where it would remain until the procession to Koasati Springs.

Adam, and Charlie were there too, to show Robert and James the way to the Devinwood home. Max and Natalie met the Copper brothers and took Lester to their home, next door to the church.

The storm awakened Sarah early. She joined John with a cup of coffee at the front window and they watched lightening streak across the sky while they waited for the Copper brothers to arrive.

Thunder awakened Alisha, and she crept into Belinda's bed, snuggling close and pulling covers over her head. "Lindy, do you hear the thunder?"

"Not 'til you woke me up," Belinda said drowsily

"How can you sleep with all that noise?"

"Be quiet, and I'll show you."

"I'm too nervous to be quiet. Remember, today's the day Robert and James will be here."

"Oh, yeah, I almost forgot." Belinda rolled over, eyes still closed. "Are you scared to meet them?"

"Not really, I just want to get it over with. So far, they're strangers. I'm more scared for Aunt Kate. When we talked on the phone yesterday, she said she's sure Robert and James are mad at her for not letting us live with her and Uncle Hank, and she's probably right."

"Aren't you mad at her?"

"Not anymore. I was for a long time, but it wore me out. After all that's happened, I just feel sorry for her now," Alisha said, and for the first time in her life, she cried. *What's different about this time,* she wondered. She had no answer, but neither could she stop crying.

"I feel sorry for her too, in a way; but she shouldn't have dumped those three little boys like she did—or you either," Belinda said. "Stop crying, so you can hear me."

"I can't. She didn't actually do all the *dumping*," Alisha said through bouts of crying. "Uncle Hank dumped the boys—she dumped me."

"Other than the alligator tears, you seem to be all right with everything now, at least on the outside," Belinda said.

"I am," Alisha sniffed, "but after being here with you, I don't think I would've liked living with Uncle Hank anyway. He probably would have drowned the boys in Lake Vista before they had a chance to grow up."

"Well, at least all of you could've stayed

out of orphanages."

"Yes, that's true, but I like my life now," Alisha said and cried more.

"Stop crying so much," Belinda said and turned over.

"It feels good to cry, but I'm not sure why, except maybe this is the first time I've ever felt like I belonged to someone."

"Get up, lazy bones, and get dressed. We have company," were the next words the girls heard.

Alisha jumped off the bed and rushed to her room before Sarah could see her swollen eyes.

"Mom, you're louder than thunder. I'm still sleepy," Belinda said and pulled covers over her head.

Alisha splashed cold water on her face, slipped into her bedroom shoes, and threw on a blouse and pedal pushers. She headed toward the kitchen but stopped short outside the door to listen. She was surprised to feel a sudden familiarity just hearing her brothers' voices. Cups and saucers clinked and their conversation with John sounded like any Saturday morning in this house.

Alisha moved into the doorway and stopped again. Robert and James saw their sister and abruptly stopped talking. With their mouths open, they stared back at her. Except for gender and hair color, Alisha saw a mirror image of herself. As Alisha moved into the kitchen, Robert and James rose from their chairs and with a rush of emotions, the siblings knew that, somehow, their spirits had remained united throughout their separation. All the years melted away.

"I don't know what to say," Alisha cried. "I didn't know it would be like th—"

In an instant, Robert embraced Alisha in a bear hug before she finished, rocking her back and forth. "It's been this way all along, Sis. We've never stopped loving you and thinking about you—not for one day."

James rushed into the embrace, and the Copper siblings stood encircled, hugging and crying until they were dizzy from the experience. Alisha immediately felt a union with her brothers that she could never have imagined, a bond that had little to do with their similar appearance. Only their hair color was different, and James had a birthmark on the right side of his face.

Belinda finally walked in, poured a cup of coffee, and stood aside waiting for the emotional exchange to subside. Robert glanced toward Belinda and with his arm still around Alisha, did a double take. "Whoa, who's this? Where did that beautiful girl come from?"

"Shhh … calm down," Alisha said, sniffling and relaxing from the embrace. "If you tell her she's beautiful, she'll really get bossy."

James rushed to take Belinda's hand. "Pay no attention to him, Lindy, I'm here."

"No, you don't, brother, I saw her first." Robert released Alisha to greet Belinda.

"Welcome to our house," Belinda said, shaking their hands. "I'm so sorry about Martin. I wish this reunion could've been sooner so we could've known him too."

"We wish that too," Robert said as they all found their places at the breakfast table.

Sarah listened as she prepared her traditional mountain breakfast of smoked ham and blueberry pancakes. Robert and James told their story, beginning with the single memory of Hank: how he left them standing on the front porch of the Holy Cross Boys Home, shivering and watching his car drive away.

"We rode all night and were starving," Robert said. "Uncle Hank stopped just long enough for us to go to the bathroom. We ate snacks in the car until we fell asleep again. When Uncle Hank stopped at this huge house and yelled, 'Wake up sleepyheads; we're here,' we had no idea where *here* was and how far away Uncle Hank had taken us."

"Then he was gone," James said. "It was just that fast, but he did stay long enough to give us ugly red jackets."

Robert laughed. "It was so cold, it didn't matter how ugly they were; we put them on as fast as we could."

"We know what *not* to get you for Christmas," Belinda said, and everyone laughed.

Robert was suddenly somber. "You know, I've always wondered if Aunt Kate was in on it or if it was just Uncle Hank's idea to do what they did with us...and you too, Alisha."

Alisha felt compelled to defend Kate. "I've never heard Aunt Kate blame just Uncle Hank, but when you talk to her now, you just know she didn't always agree with him. He died nine or ten years ago, so we may never know unless Aunt Kate tells us. Anyway, what difference would it make after all this time?"

"Maybe none," Robert said. "But I'm not sure I'll ever be able to close the subject without knowing more. It has been like an ugly scar that never goes away."

"Lester rescued us though," James said. "He was

working behind the house and saw what was happening. He got to us just as Uncle Hank drove away. We were huddled on a bench trying to get warm, and Lester took us inside for breakfast. He came by every few days, asking what we wanted for Christmas. Then, about a week before Christmas, the Millers and Lester came for Christmas dinner and took us home to the farm."

"In the letter, it sounded like Lester took care of you more than the Millers," Belinda said.

"In the beginning, the Millers were there most of the time," Robert said. "Then they started traveling, and we spent more and more time with Lester. His wife had died after he came home from the war, so he just built a house on the farm and lived there with us."

"Lester didn't *just* take care of us," James said. "Lester was always there, and he was more like a father to us than Papa Joe."

"Lester's getting old," Robert said. "He was wounded in World War I and has recently slowed down—a lot. After the Millers died and we left for college, George, Lester's fishing buddy and old friend, moved to the farm. I don't know what they'd do without each other."

"What happened to the Millers?" Alisha asked. "Mom said they died a few years ago."

Robert explained the African safari tragedy and ended the account by telling about the memorial they and Lester built in the rose garden for the Millers and for Martin. "The Millers were always good to us and to Lester as well."

Sarah began breakfast in the dining room. Alisha and

Belinda pushed back their chairs to help, but James was up in a flash and helping Sarah serve food before they could get out of their chairs, and then after breakfast, he cleared the table before the others could move to help.

Robert smiled at Alisha and Belinda staring at James in wonder. "You might as well let him help or else he'll go mad," Robert said. "Alisha, I hear you're quite the pianist. Come play for us and let James work."

Belinda introduced Robert to the family photographs in the living room while Alisha selected music. When they reached the photo that John had saved of the Copper family, Robert took a sudden deep breath. "That picture ... that's the only family picture we had. I've thought of it so often."

"Alisha's only had it for a few days," Belinda said. "No one told her the truth about her family until you wrote to Mom. She didn't even know she had brothers."

"The Millers protected us the same way. We wanted to find Alisha, and I always thought Lester could if the Millers had agreed. If only Lester and your mother had made the connection sooner, we—"

"But look what you have now," Belinda interrupted, as Alisha arranged her music just so and began to play. She took Robert's hand and led him to the piano.

James came into the room and silently walked from one side of the piano to the other, watching Alisha's hands and noticing her facial expression as she lost herself in the music. "Does she know we're in the room?" James whispered to Belinda.

"Not really," Belinda replied. "She learned to play by

shutting out everything else, and she still practices that way. She explains that when she plays the piano at church, she is aware of other music but *feels* her own music."

"I guess the result is all that matters," Robert said.

Belinda served coffee as Alisha played her last sonata. They lingered in the living room, sharing memories and becoming acquainted.

"I don't remember much about my life at the orphanage until I was three or four years old," Alisha said. "My first memories are of hiding when Miss Beatrice yelled at me, and for some reason, I wouldn't talk to anybody; I whispered to myself, but only when I hid. Naturally, everyone thought I couldn't talk, so we made up a sign language, which was fun, I remember, so I kept everybody fooled. Then, Miss Beatrice caught on. She sat me in a high chair at the kitchen table every day while she cooked and said nursery rhymes. I still wouldn't respond to her until one day when she was out of the kitchen, a pot of soup boiled over and scared me. I yelled for Miss Beatrice and my secret was out."

"That sounds like something James would do—you two must be related," Robert said as he and James laughed.

Belinda was resting her head on the sofa back, staring at the ceiling, and listening to their conversation. Without moving, she said to more laughter, "And Mom boils the soup over every now and then to check her out."

"Miss Beatrice was always interviewing families for me, and I'd always run to the storeroom and hide," Alisha admitted. "But Belinda's family was the first I didn't run from. You should've seen Lindy. She was sitting across the room talking as fast as she could. I was hooked, and she hasn't stopped talking since, have you, Lindy?"

"When I stop, you argue," Belinda said inattentively.

James had noticed Belinda staring into space. He stood up, stretched, and walked around the room looking at family pictures grouped on every wall. He stopped when he reached Belinda's senior class picture.

"You just graduated, Lindy; where are you going to school? Is there a college nearby?" James asked in rapid succession.

Belinda became anxious at the mention of school but fired back, "Yes, nowhere, and no."

"Mom said there are no scholarships for Lindy this year," Alisha said.

"Alisha, sometimes you talk too much."

"Don't be mad, Lindy, and you shouldn't give up on Mom. She works miracles all the time, just look who's here."

"Forget it, she won't work one this time. Anyway, Mom had a little help getting your brothers here." Belinda stood and walked to the window. "I think the rain has stopped; let's go for a walk."

Alisha followed Belinda to the window, "Uh-oh, Robert and James, get ready. Aunt Kate just drove up."

Robert and James looked at each other and stiffened.

Alisha walked outside to meet Kate, who said, "Hello, dear, where are my nephews?"

"They're in the living room. We were just going for a walk."

"Well, I want to see them before you go." Kate went directly to the living room. "I'm your Aunt Kate," she chirped, hugged Robert and James, and then extended her sympathies for Martin. Neither of the young men returned her hug and barely mumbled a thank-you. As their hostility registered, Kate's smile faded, and she focused on Robert. "Oh I see, you're not happy to see me, are you?"

"You're right, Aunt Kate. We're also not very happy right now for another reason too," Robert said.

James remained silent until Kate turned to him and then he said, "I don't know what to say, either, Aunt Kate."

Kate briefly hung her head before looking at her nephews. "We have things to talk about. I want you to come to my home for a visit while you're here. Will you please?"

Robert was blunt. "Aunt Kate, there's not much left to talk about. You and Uncle Hank said it all a long time ago."

"As awful as that was, Robert, I still believe we can at least talk. There are reasons for all of this that I want you to know, but I see now is not the time. I can wait until you're ready."

The storm had blown over by mid-day, revealing a bright sun breaking through the clouds and turning the dark morning into a bright, sunny day. Lester finished breakfast and read the morning paper before stepping out on the Maxwell's front porch. He looked up the road and saw the Devinwood home, a colonial two-story white house set on a hilltop between two huge gnarled oak trees. Summer had turned the lawn into the greenest grass imaginable. He was walking toward the Devinwood home when he saw Robert and James walk out of the house with two young girls.

The tall one, Martin, that's Alisha. Ah, son, you should be here. You wanted this as much as anyone.

On the drive to Tawasa Springs, Lester had listened to Robert and James discuss visiting the farm where they were born, and this seemed like a good day to go. He walked the short distance to greet the group walking toward him.

"Don't tell me … I know already, you're Alisha. I read Sarah's letter too," Lester said as he took her hand and then he turned and took Belinda's hand as well. "It's good to meet you too, Lindy. Could we go inside for a few minutes? I'd like to meet Sarah and John."

"Aunt Kate's here too," Alisha said. "So far, her visit has not gone well."

"I can imagine," Lester replied. "Let's go in anyway; I want to meet her. She and these boys have a lot of talking to do."

"Not me," Robert said.

"Nor me," James said.

In a tense atmosphere, Robert introduced Sarah and John, and then, without making eye contact, introduced Kate. Lester greeted each of them and said to Sarah and John, "I was just thinking, this is a good day to go out to the farm. John, will you show us the way to Koasati Springs?"

"We will," John said, "but we'll need to leave soon." Sarah looked at Lester's clothes and added, "I hope you have some old clothes. We haven't been out there this year, and I'm sure the weeds and bushes are taking over."

"We've been repairing a few things out there every year, and the buildings are holding up well to be almost a century old, but the place still needs major work," John said.

"Somebody needs to live out there to keep up the place, but the property belongs to the children," Sarah said. "They'll have to make that decision."

"But, Sarah, if somebody lives up there, where would we spend our vacation?" John asked with a laugh.

Sarah poked John and laughed too. "Really though, we did want to keep the house presentable. Even though our youngest brother and both our parents died when Asyah and I were teenagers, I still feel their presence in the house; their spirits are still around. Asyah once said he could feel that too."

"Why don't we all ride out there?" Lester suggested. "You and John can show us the way, and we can visit while we're driving."

Kate quickly picked up her purse. "Well, I have things to do; I must get home. Alisha, will you walk me to the car please?"

Lester rushed to offer his arm. "Let me walk you to the car, Kate. I'm almost as helpful as James," he said winking at the girls.

"You can't be," Alisha said.

As they walked to the car, Lester said, "Kate, I hope you'll give Robert and James a chance to come around. They're harboring some very bad memories about being abandoned, and that's now compounded by Martin's death."

"I know, but they wouldn't even let me explain about what really happened back then."

"They will, but first they have to work through a lot of grief. They were very close to Martin, you know. Be patient, give them time, they'll get to you. Who knows—you might even become a family again," Lester said, opening the car door.

"If it's the last thing I do, I will discuss how all that happened, and I *will* seek their forgiveness." Kate slipped behind the wheel of her car and drove away.

Lester watched her disappear down the hill. *She has a big heart behind all that show.*

Alisha and James rode to the farm with Adam, and John sat in the front giving directions. Lester, Belinda, and Sarah followed with Robert.

Sarah and John led the way into the old Copper house, entering through the rear door. The others followed close behind on a tour through all the rooms. Sarah's great-grandfather had built the oak-timber log house over one hundred years ago. Extensive changes had been made over the years, expanding the rear of the house to add a new kitchen and dining area on one end and a family gathering place and a fireplace on the other. A long, wide hallway, separating the living room and bedrooms, ended in the newer section of the house.

"Asyah started the porch after Robert was born," Sarah explained, "and by the time the twins were born, he had wrapped the porch around the front, east, and back, interconnecting the house making it seem to flow into itself."

The beds were bare, but otherwise the furnishings were the same as when the Copper family gave life to their home. When they reached the front hallway, Robert saw his father's banjo case and his heart almost stopped. He caressed the case but forced himself to move on.

John caught Robert's reaction and led them toward the front door. "Adam, why don't you take everyone outside to look around while Sarah and I open up the house?"

They walked onto the front porch, and Robert swung the door back and forth a couple of times. "This old door feels like it has gotten heavier with time."

James stopped to trace the marks and scratches left by time. "Robert, why did you scratch it up so much? By the way, do you still have that pocketknife Daddy gave you?"

"Yes, I do, and I'll have to claim some of the marks; after all, I had to practice carving somewhere."

"Until Mama caught you."

"How did they keep this house warm?" Belinda wanted to know. "Look at that crack under the door."

"It *was* warm. I remember that much," Robert said.

John pointed toward the meadow. "Adam, take them down that trail. The weeds are taking over but you can still find your way." *They might as well go to the meadow, see the river, and feel the pain where their mother died, and get it over with.*

"Lester, make yourself at home," Sarah said. "The house is clean. All we have to do is remove the dustcovers, open the windows, and start a pot of coffee, and the house will be ready."

Lester smiled and nodded. "I'd like to walk around outside for a while, Sarah. Being here is a lot to take in, in such a short time." Lester walked around the house and true to his nature, began to assess the buildings, easily identifying the ones in disrepair from lack of use and the ones that needed to be torn down.

Alisha, Adam, Belinda, Robert, and James walked down the weedy path that John had pointed out. James, the first to come out of the woods and into the meadow, stopped short and said, "There's something here; I feel it," he said, gazing around the tree line surrounding the meadow.

Robert, accustomed to James' *feelings*, ignored him. "Martin would've loved this place. I wish he was here."

"He is," James said. "Robert, I want you to feel him too. It's such a warm, soft feeling, like a warm sun on a cold winter day."

"I can't," Robert said, unable to shake his terrible memories of that tragic day and make room for the feelings of which James spoke.

"Let's go down to the river," Alisha suggested.

Adam traced a mile-long path, marked by yellowing strings tied to trees, until they reached a small white cross, it too faded by age, which someone had nailed to a tree close to the riverbank. Alisha found an opening sloping down to the river. She stopped at the decaying cross, shivering.

"Just think—this is where our mother just walked into

the river. It looks so *cold*." Gazing into the rapid current, she said, "I don't ever want to see this river again."

Adam and Belinda stood silently by while Robert pulled his sister and brother together and slowly led them away from the place where their mother had died. They walked back through the meadow where they had picnicked with their mother seventeen years earlier. Robert and James recounted to Alisha a few things they remembered from that fateful day. While they were talking, Alisha imagined herself as a six-month-old baby, lying on a blanket with her brothers, and a mother in such an unfathomable state of mind that she exchanged her children for death.

"What kind of mother would leave her children in the middle of the woods?" Alisha finally asked.

James, looking toward the mountainside, said angrily, "The same kind of mother that could kill herself."

"A very sick one could do both," Robert said. "Apparently, she and Aunt Kate were both capable of doing what she did. I'd bet neither knew they had a disease; the difference is, Aunt Kate has medicine—our mother did not."

As they walked away, high above the riverbank, an eerie glow again bubbled from the cave's entrance, and the branches of the ancient oak tree façade shimmered. James caught a glimpse of light and looked toward the mountainside. "Someday, Robert, I'm going to find that cave Daddy talked about."

Alisha felt sorrow in the air, trying to seep into her bones. Shaking her head, she sped up to join Adam and Belinda.

Lester leaned against the fence and looked over

appraisingly at the family cemetery. Someone had weeded and raked around the graves and placed fresh flowers in vases stuck in the ground next to each headstone. The cemetery was still and had a peaceful feeling, except for a newly dug grave that glared at him like a cruel open wound.

When Belinda, Adam, and Alisha walked up behind Lester and looked around, Alisha said quietly, "I'll bet Max is responsible for all this work ... to get things ready for the ... uh ... *funeral.*"

"You're right," Lester said. "Max said an old Indian man they call the gravedigger just showed up after Sunday services at the church here in Koasati Springs, somehow knowing a grave was needed. He had done it enough times before that the congregation trusted his instinct, so they did the rest."

Robert and James walked up in time to hear Lester say, "Maybe after this is all over, we could arrange for someone to keep up the place, including the cemetery."

James drifted over to the empty grave and stared at the open hole, feeling a profound sadness. Then he abruptly shivered and turned away from the gravesite, shaking away the heaviness he felt. "Hire someone," he said incredulously. "Robert, we can do that work in an hour. Anyway, we might like this place someday. After all, Martin will be here too."

"I'll come out here to visit but I don't think I'll ever *like* it," Alisha said. "Hey, maybe we could stay here for a couple of days over the Christmas holidays."

"*If* you put in a bathroom," Belinda added. "Did any

of you notice there's no bathroom in the house? That outhouse, it has to go."

"*First,*" Alisha confirmed.

Robert looked over the house. "Okay, first. It's also time for a new roof and porch, don't you think, Lester?"

"Yes, there's plenty of work to do, but if we're coming back for Christmas, let's have the major work done soon while the weather's still good. I'll bet they have serious snow in these mountains."

"I'm sure," Robert said. "Lester, let's arrange for all the work to be done. We can't come back this Christmas because James and I have to get the business back on track. But the following Christmas we can come back and stay in our house."

"Don't forget about the outhouse," Belinda mumbled.

On Friday morning, Sarah walked into the kitchen, surprised to see breakfast already in full swing. James stood and pulled out a chair and set a cup of coffee in front of her. When Belinda came into the kitchen, Sarah pointed toward James. They both exclaimed, "He's staying with us."

"Where's Alisha?" Sarah asked.

Belinda rolled her eyes. "She went to get Adam to take her to the church. She woke up in one of her moods and wanted to practice."

"Why not practice here?" James asked.

"She loves the new piano, and she says she feels a sacred atmosphere there," Sarah explained.

Robert pushed back his chair, sipping the last of his coffee, "I'll be back in a while; I want to go listen to Alisha play."

Lester walked out of the Maxwell's front door, stretched, and saw Robert hurrying toward the church. He waited and they slipped into the church together and sat next to Adam. Soon James arrived with breakfast. They listened for a while before Alisha noticed they were there.

"I smell food," Alisha said, looking up to see her audience of four in the back row. "What are you doing here? Who has that food? I'm starving!"

Adam and Robert looked at James, who reached underneath the seat, pulled out a covered plate, and retrieved a fork from his pocket. Alisha joined them and devoured her breakfast. When James and Alisha left with Adam, Robert stayed to talk with Lester and Max.

"Max, I need your help in the strictest of confidence," Robert said. "Sarah needs help. Belinda wants to go to nursing school, and I want to make sure she does. I want you to surprise them but somehow maintain Sarah's reputation for performing miracles.

"Lester, I know you're good at this kind of thing because I've seen you in action. I need you to look into nursing schools near Minneapolis and send whatever it takes to Max here at the church." The three men nodded in satisfied agreement.

Martin's casket sat positioned on a frame over his grave surrounded by flowers. A military honor guard stood by. On Saturday afternoon, family and friends had gathered to lay to rest a fourth generation of Copper men in the cemetery behind the farmhouse where they all were born.

As Lester eulogized Martin's life, memories came flooding back to Robert. All his sorrow swelled in his chest, and he felt their spirits—his mother, his father, and his brother—surrounding him as if he were in a cocoon. After seventeen years of clinging to despair, he now mourned for the abrupt loss of his parents, his traumatic childhood, and that of his brothers and sister. Above all, on this day, he was overwhelmed by the loss of Martin.

James took his brother in his arms, whispering, "Let me take care of you now, brother," and felt Robert surrender to his embrace.

Although Alisha did not experience the same emotion as Robert and James felt for their parents and for the brother she would never know, she did feel the past slip away, making her feel whole, as if she had never been apart from Robert and James.

On Monday Lester visited Kate at the hospital where she had voluntarily admitted herself when she left the Devinwood house. He understood Robert and James' long-held bitterness toward her and saw the wounds deepen when Kate did not attend Martin's funeral, but after the visit, he had a glimpse of what Kate had also suffered.

Early on Wednesday, Lester awoke early. The Copper siblings were together, at last, and Lester knew they would find it difficult to separate again, but it was time for him to go home to see about George. His job here was done.

Chapter 28

Something feels wrong about this letter, Alisha thought as she took Caroline's letter out of the mailbox and held it away as if it were poison. "Nonsense," she said aloud, "it's just a letter."

Alisha had recently told Belinda that having brothers felt great. "I'm tired of resenting Aunt Kate too," she had said, "and wrong as it was, I *think* I understand how her fragile state of mind affected her actions." Alisha's life seemed perfect—maybe too perfect. Alisha knew too well the foreboding feeling of a storm cloud gathering.

With Ellie gone, Adam relaxed and enjoyed the summer, spending time with Alisha and preparing for school in the fall. When Ellie's letters arrived, he threw them in a shoebox unopened, partly because he was disinterested, but mostly he didn't want to deal with the possibility that his intuition was right. Adam's affection for Alisha intensified and he believed he had found the girl he wanted to be with for the rest of his life. *What a difference,* he thought, *being with someone who makes you want to plan the future instead of dreading it.*

Over the summer, Alisha and Adam's relationship grew from a childhood friendship to a love she now counted on to last a lifetime. Alisha feared only that she might have to choose between her love for Adam and her love for music, a fear that seemed unrealistic.

For a while, Caroline wrote often from her aunt's house in Chicago and seemed to be making up for all the weeks they had not seen each other. Alisha enjoyed Caroline's flair for describing the big city and wrote newsy items back about their friends, her brothers, her music, and of course, Adam, but in the past few weeks, Caroline had not responded to any of Alisha's letters. Then, when summer was almost over, Alisha stood at the mailbox with a foreboding so strong, the envelope felt alien in her hand. Now she knew why Caroline had stopped writing to her.

> *Dear Alisha,*
>
> *Things are not going well. I don't know how to tell you this but Ellie is pregnant—with Adam's baby. That's why we're at our aunt's house for the summer. Ellie planned to have the baby here and give it up for adoption. She's six months pregnant and now insists on returning home and keeping the baby instead, and Mom has agreed.*
>
> *Ellie thought if she wrote to Adam about the baby, he would come to Chicago and marry her. I can tell from your letters that either Adam ignored what Ellie wrote to him or he is not reading her letters. You should have already known about the baby— from him.*
>
> *I hope this doesn't upset you too—*

Alisha could not finish reading. Trembling, she walked

in a daze to Belinda's room and handed her the letter. Alisha stood by in shock while Belinda read the letter, then she rushed out and fled to the piano.

Adam was outside shooting baskets when he saw Belinda running toward his house. Seeing she was upset, he sprinted down the road to meet her.

"You'd better read this, Adam; this has gone too far to ignore. How could you keep something like this from Alisha?"

Adam, puzzled, took the letter Belinda thrust at him.

When Adam saw the word *pregnant,* he could read no further and knew in that instant, his life had changed.

"Lindy, I swear I didn't know. Let's go to my house."

They walked slowly; Adam reading the letter through, and Belinda knowing he was telling the truth. Adam left Belinda on the porch while he retrieved the shoebox of unopened letters, sat beside her on the porch swing, and displayed its contents. He could feel life draining from his body.

"Oh my God," Belinda said, "you really *didn't* know, did you?" Adam could only shake his head.

"Well, you know it now and you'd better do something. You could start by reading these letters because Ellie will be home next week."

Belinda left and Adam went back inside his house with the box of letters, knowing how disappointed his parents would be and that he would do exactly what they expected and what he knew to be the honorable thing. He made his way to his room, lay on the bed, and opened all the letters. Reading each one, he relived the doom he felt when he last saw Ellie.

Adam's father had observed Belinda and Adam's porch scene. After Adam disappeared into his room, his father came to the open door. "What's the matter, son?"

Adam stood when his father entered the room and nodded toward the letters, emotionally frozen, unable to verbalize his feelings.

His father summed it up. "Seeing Belinda running toward our house, I imagined it would be something serious."

"Almost the worst news I could imagine..." Adam began, stumbling over his words.

Adam's father picked up one of the envelopes, saw the return address, and said, "I knew it was important, but I had one detail wrong—the name of my future daughter-in-law."

"Yes, sir," Adam said, verifying what his father had concluded.

"You realize your mother's going to be very upset, don't you?"

"Right now, I can't name anyone who won't be upset. I'll go talk to her."

"Wait a while. Let me talk to her first."

Belinda calmly walked home from Adam's house, pulling the scholarship information from her pocket and reading it again to make sure she wasn't dreaming. Sarah had just handed Belinda the envelope moments before Alisha came in with the letter from Caroline.

Max had delivered the envelope to Sarah and John late the day before, explaining that an anonymous donor felt compelled to fund nursing scholarships around the country after his wife died from poor nursing care. Belinda was so relieved that she was going to nursing school that even in the midst of Alisha's trouble, she was impossibly happy.

Belinda heard Alisha playing the piano as she neared the house. The music sounded vicious, loud, and full of pain. Belinda found Sarah standing in the hallway in tears. "What's the matter, Lindy?" Sarah asked.

Belinda told her mother about the letter and they clung to each other. They waited at the kitchen table until Alisha emerged from the living room, emotionally spent. Alisha leaned against the doorframe, staring into space. When Sarah realized the extent of Alisha's distress, she said softly, "We'll get through this, Alisha."

Alisha shook her head.

"Do you want to go visit Robert for a while?" Sarah asked. "He's already invited you stay with him and complete your senior year in Minneapolis. If you don't like it there, you can come back and finish school here."

Sarah waited for a response, but Alisha gave no indication that she had heard her speak. She tried another, more hopeful tack. "Alisha, yesterday Lindy received a scholarship to a nursing school near Robert's home, and she'll be starting classes in another month."

"Think about it, Alisha," Belinda added. "We'll be

together and we could ride the bus back home for visits whenever you want."

Sarah left the two girls to find her husband. When she returned with John, Belinda said, "Dad, see if you can talk some sense into her."

"Leave her alone; this is a big problem," John said. "We can't solve this one for her, and she can't solve it either until she stops drowning in her pain." John turned to Alisha and hugged her to him. "Alisha, all you have to do now is think about what you might like to do—not decide—just think. We can talk later when you feel better."

Exhaling a sigh, Alisha finally spoke. "Dad, I'm not sure I'll ever feel better."

"You will," John said, "but probably not soon," and he walked out.

For the better part of three days, Alisha stayed in bed and cried. She ate when Sarah brought her food and woke when Belinda lay on the bed with her and talked or when Sarah or John sat beside her.

The first day Alisha was in bed, Sarah accepted Robert's invitation for the girls to visit. In a letter, she told him about the recent events and his sister's broken heart. Then Sarah and Belinda arranged bus travel to Minneapolis. Sarah did not call Kate. She did not want or need interference, or another patient, at this time.

On the morning of the fourth day, Alisha woke up when Belinda rushed into her room and demanded, "Alisha, get out of the bed and finish packing. We're going on a trip, and we're leaving tomorrow. You can stay with Robert and finish high school in Minneapolis or you can come back to your miserable life here, but you *are* going with me."

Alisha knew Lindy was right. Considering how she felt, it didn't matter what she did. She asked, "Is Charlie back?"

"No. I haven't seen him all summer," Belinda said. "I wish I knew how to reach him."

"I wish I knew, too."

Adam dreaded Ellie's return. He knew his fate, but wanted to see Alisha anyway. He had no hope for their relationship and knew he had nothing to offer Alisha now, but he sought some relief from his pain. He stopped by the Devinwood house once a day to try to speak with her, but John or Sarah met him at the door and said that Alisha was asleep and could not see him. Adam realized he would not be welcome in the Devinwood home for a long time, but still he tried. The last time he went by the house, Belinda answered the door and said that she and Alisha were going to visit Robert. When Adam could not persuade Belinda to give him any more information, he realized he might never see Alisha again. He was determined to say goodbye and appeared at the bus station for every scheduled departure. Finally, the Devinwoods arrived.

Adam walked toward Alisha, and John walked toward Adam, but not as fast as Sarah did. Sarah stood in front of Adam. "John, leave him alone and let him say goodbye to Alisha. He's going through a lot too." As soon as John paused, Sarah hugged both girls and motioned to her husband. John hugged them too and said goodbye, but as they walked toward the bus with the luggage, Sarah saw John give Adam a hard warning glare.

As the bus driver was placing the last suitcase in the storage compartment, Adam saw Alisha turn pale and caught her in his arms. They clung to each other until Belinda nudged Adam. "It's time to get on the bus," she said and led the way for Adam to walk Alisha to the door, where he kissed her forehead and whispered a final goodbye.

Belinda guided her sister to their seats. As the bus pulled away, Alisha stared through the window at the love of her life until he faded from view.

Adam left the bus station thinking he was not strong enough to watch Alisha go away and doubted if he could stay sane in a marriage he did not want. The single star that shone through the dark clouds was his unborn child. Adam, in tears, went directly from the bus station to see Max.

Max stayed with the soon-to-be-father and much-too-young-husband until Adam's grief was spent. In the early morning hours, Adam went back to the same bus station where he had said goodbye to Alisha to meet his future wife.

After Adam left, Max joined Natalie in the kitchen. She had made a fresh pot of coffee, and they talked about the good and bad changes in the lives of three families they loved. Belinda would realize her dream of being a nurse. Their church pianist was gone, as was Alisha's dream life with Adam. On the other hand, they admired Adam for the husband and father they expected him to become.

The day after Ellie arrived home, she and Adam were married in the office of the Justice of the Peace with Max and Natalie as witnesses. Two months later their son, Jacob, was born.

Alisha did not have to choose between Adam and her music.

Chapter 29

Although it was early September, there was an early snowstorm awaiting Alisha and Belinda when they arrived in Minneapolis. They had never seen that much snow back in Tawasa Springs and stepped off the bus into glistening knee-deep white powder. Robert saw them from a distance, and when he called their names, they looked up, saw him, and eagerly rushed to get the hats, dangling coats, and gloves as he pulled each one from a shopping bag.

"Better not be red," Belinda said.

"Never!" Robert exclaimed and hugged them.

Surprisingly, the cold air swept away much of Alisha's gloom. If the snow had not cheered her up, Belinda would have, as they walked a short distance through the snow to Robert's house.

The house was huge and was the first of Robert's architectural accomplishments. Alisha, shocked, said, "What a big house! Why do you need so much space?"

"Why, for you of course."

Alisha turned to Belinda. "Lindy, this house reminds me of the castles we used to build in the woods."

Belinda laughed. "We had vivid imaginations back then, didn't we?"

The inside of the house was as beautiful as the outside. When Alisha walked through the home Robert had created, touched his furnishings, and admired his artwork, she began to know her brother.

𝄞

With Alisha and Belinda out of the house, it seemed to Sarah that her life had changed overnight. The past year had been filled with a monotony she had never known. She dug down to the in the letterbox and began reading, starting with the note Robert mailed to her the day Alisha and Belinda arrived. She read all their letters and reminisced about the past year.

Dear Sarah,

The girls arrived today in good spirits, thanks to the early snow welcoming them to Minneapolis. Other than being constantly cold, they are fine—they just thought the weather was cold in Tawasa Springs. Tomorrow, Lindy plans to look over the campus and her dorm room while Alisha and I go out to look at pianos. I am optimistic that she will play again, as I believe she will not die from her broken heart, after all. If you have ideas to reignite her interest, let me know.

Alisha will miss having her sister in the house when Lindy starts school, and I will certainly miss your daughter's bright personality. Lindy is

*committed to the nursing profession, and when she
learns that she does not have to hide her compassion
for others, I believe she'll be very successful.*

> *Sincerely,*
> *Robert*

Sarah was relieved but lonely without the girls around.
She read the short letter to Robert that she included with
all the music books from Mrs. Flowers.

Dear Robert,

*Thank you for taking care of the girls. Don't
worry about Alisha's interest in music; her gift is
so much a part of her, she can't ignore it very long.
As sure as songbirds sing their song again, she will
return to music. With a piano in the house, she'll find
her way back home to her passion, as she has done
on a few occasions already ... and when she begins to
play again, help her locate a good music school.*

*Those girls gave me reason to worry at times, but
at least life was more interesting with them around.
I look forward to next Christmas, and I hope you'll
help the girls plan their trip home. Of course, you and
James must also come for the holidays.*

*Give my love to Alisha and Lindy. I'll write
them each a letter soon.*

> *Fondly,*
> *Sarah*

Sarah finished the last letter she had just received from Belinda, then slowly made her way to John's room. Her steps were heavy, realizing she must face the more serious difficulty that had worsened in the past year. It was almost noon, and John was still in bed. He had been uncharacteristically idle, but remained adamant that he too missed the girls and that he felt just fine. Sarah knew better.

Belinda enjoyed her life in the dormitory and Alisha felt more and more at home with Robert, and he with her. "I'm happy you're here and I want you to stay," he had said while watching her unpack suitcases on the day she arrived.

Alisha graduated from high school knowing she *wanted* to attend Ross Music School, but she felt immobilized by unfinished business.

At dinner one night, on an impulse, Alisha said, "I need to talk to Adam, Robert. I feel like I'm a walking open wound."

"Tell you what, Sis," Robert said, "why don't you tell Adam everything you feel in a letter, hold on to it for a few days, and then mail it to Max. You could ask him to make sure Adam gets your letter. He'll understand; in fact, there's a good possibility that Adam's feeling the same way. It's past time to close this hurt as soon as you can so you both can move on with your new lives."

Alisha wrote and rewrote the letter, exhausting her emotions, and at last came up with the version that expressed her feelings without anger.

Dear Adam,

I'm writing this letter from my brother's house in Minneapolis, and I'm dealing with a sense of loss that, at times, is almost overwhelming.

Loving you is so wonderful in ways that now I'll never know. Separating from you was painful beyond words—but you already know that. Here I am, writing, against my better judgment, about the advantage of being marked, because you will always be the love of my life. However, I believe that loving you as I do then losing you far outweighs the void of never loving. The best comparison I can make is loving music, a platform from which I now plan to launch my life.

We've made choices: First, about beginning the relationship, then yes, the way the relationship had to end, but they were our decisions to make and they are now our responsibilities to live with . . . and live them we must . . . I am doing that, here and now.

I hope to find someone I might love as I love you— someone safe, someone who knows and understands me as you do, someone with whom I can share my life as I so wanted to share it with you. Turns out that love might be music.

I hope we stay in touch as we walk through this life, but for now, let's just love each other as best we can. I wish you happiness in your commitment to the woman you've chosen, by circumstances, to share your

life. Love her the most, but keep me in the proper place in your life, but keep me … in your heart.
I'll always love you and honor you,
Alisha.

Alisha sealed the letter and placed it on her dresser and went for a walk on the same route she had walked to school the past year. She came to a tall, white building tucked between two other buildings set further off the street, conveying a unique setting. The building had two rows of windows adorned with pale blue shutters, giving it an inviting look. She went closer to admire the entrance then impulsively walked straight into the *Ross School of Music* and enrolled before she could change her mind.

The next day, Alisha took the city bus to visit Belinda, who would soon earn her R.N. credentials. They had lunch at their favorite café, a local trendy place filled with medical students.

"Lindy, why don't you want to be a doctor?"

"I do, but it's next to impossible to get into medical school, Alisha. Anyway, I've always dreamed of being a nurse, so I'm happy."

"You should know by now, all you have to do is call in Mom, the miracle worker, if you want to be a doctor."

"It's not a matter of money—I'm a woman, and women rarely get in, but I think I've figured out how Mom pulled off this miracle."

"Me too, but don't let her know," Alisha said. "She and Robert make good partners, although they don't tell each other everything.

"You know, Sis, you're going to help save a lot of lives from here on, but you've already saved one—mine, during that awful time with Adam. Remember getting me out of the house and dragging me to the bus station to come here? You saved me back there."

Belinda leaned closer to Alisha. "Yeah, I remember."

"I love you for plenty of reasons, but I don't remember even saying thank you for that—by the way," Alisha said, "I've enrolled in the Ross Music School."

Belinda squeezed Alisha's outstretched hand. "I knew you would."

The rain kept James awake most of the night, and he was making a second pot of coffee when Robert came into the kitchen. Soon, Alisha heard the morning paper hit the front porch, retrieved it, and joined her brothers. Without noticing what loomed on the headlines, she casually tossed the paper on the table in front of Robert and turned to get a cup of coffee.

Robert took one look at the headlines and threw the July 27, 1953, *Minneapolis Star* across the room. One year and two months after Martin's death, the United States President had declared a cease-fire, setting the border between North and South Korea at the 38th parallel, exactly where it had been when the war began.

Robert and Alisha had shopped for the piano together. All he asked in return was for her to play again someday, when she felt ready, but Alisha had ignored the piano month after month, leaving it lifeless and untouched. One morning after she began studying at Ross Music School, she stood at the window behind the piano, watching the cars cross the Third Avenue Bridge and go into downtown Minneapolis; then she abruptly turned and sat down at the piano. She touched the finish of the sleek black baby grand and slowly pushed back the cover of the keyboard.

"Where do I go from here?" she said aloud.

Play. Play the music you hunger for, and the answer will come.

Remembering Mrs. Flowers' explanation of the guardian angel, Alisha cried, "You're back. Where were you when I needed you so badly?"

I was there. That's how you came to be where you are now.

"But I was so happy with Adam, and I miss him more than you'll ever know," Alisha said, tears flowing, cleansing her soul.

You would have missed what's before you even more.

"That's what you think, but I hope you're right."

Alisha welcomed the release she felt washing over her, and with the release, a new surge of energy rushed in, flooding the void where pain was no longer welcome.

Old favorites coursed through her, and she *had* to play her music or her heart would burst.

When Robert arrived home hours later, Alisha was still playing. The following day Robert retrieved the package from the closet, unpacked Mrs. Flowers' books from Sarah's careful wrapping, and stacked them on a table beside the piano.

Mom and Robert, Alisha sighed, feeling great pleasure at seeing the books and appreciation for Sarah's determination.

The next day, Alisha walked directly to the post office and mailed her letter to Adam. Soon, she was spending her spare time watching other music students practice. The more aware she became of each student's technique, the more she realized none was as difficult or original as hers. Alisha persisted in perfecting every concerto, every sonata, every movement, drawing interest from the best teachers. To her surprise, she began receiving occasional invitations to play in concerts in Minneapolis.

On days when she began to take life too seriously, she remembered James telling her it was important to have fun, and she simply played the music she loved. His words rang in her ear: *Your music sounds much too violent at times. Stay balanced and express yourself equally from joy as well as sorrow.*

Alisha and Caroline began exchanging letters again. Alisha was eager for news about her friends, and at first, neither mentioned Ellie and Adam. Caroline wrote long letters about her senior year at Tawasa Springs High School, wishing Alisha could have graduated with her class. Caroline changed her mind about going to college, found a job near home, and married her fiancé.

One letter from Caroline was all about Charlie. Alisha was stunned to read that Charlie had a new girlfriend, and they seemed very happy. She laid her head back on the sofa with the letter resting on her chest. *I never pictured him with a girlfriend.*

She raised the letter and reread Caroline's words, *He would never have found her if you had stayed here, Alisha. He said he had been unable to imagine his life with anyone else since he was a little boy and had become blinded to other girls until he met this one. You'll be pleased to know that he claims he is completely happy and he thinks of you as a part of his life, but no longer as his whole life.*

For the first time, Caroline disclosed that when Charlie heard about Ellie and Adam, he came to her house, angry and distraught. *He could not bear to see you so upset, and he almost ended his friendship with Adam. You know Charlie, though. He finally recognized the tragedy for what it was, and he has reconciled with Adam. He values their friendship and, by the way, Charlie loves Jacob—that boy will have two fathers; you wait and see.*

Alisha wrote about her new life at Robert's house, James' travels, and her visits with Belinda, assuring Caroline that she missed living near her but could not honestly say she regretted not graduating from Tawasa Springs High School. Alisha added a postscript in a recent letter: *I missed the holidays at home last year, but we'll be home this Christmas. Robert is teaching Lindy and me to drive on this trip so we won't have to ride the bus around town anymore. I hope you and I can visit while I'm there. I miss you.*

Caroline did not immediately tell Adam about Alisha's plans to come home but soon reasoned that warning him might be a good idea. Anyway, Ellie had confided in Caroline that she and Adam were divorcing and that she knew her marriage had been a sham. The big surprise to Caroline was that Ellie was in love again and happier than ever.

Soon after Jacob was born, Ellie asked Adam for a divorce, but they agreed to delay a separation and causing their parents added grief. Ellie felt nothing but disdain for Adam, trying to mask his relief. "The man finally gets his woman," she said sarcastically

For an instant, Adam wanted desperately to tell her that he knew about her affair, but replied, "You know more than I do, Ellie, where there's life, there's hope."

After working on a job that required nothing but manual labor, Adam realized what a struggle he would face without college. He eagerly agreed to an offer from his parents to advance his inheritance for his and Ellie's education and living expenses. He began planning another future, which would include accelerating his undergraduate work, then law school. He now had the financial freedom to make his life work, and equally important, he and Ellie would be free from the chains of a marriage neither ever really wanted.

Chapter 30

Belinda read her mother's latest letter and winced. Sarah had written that John was staying in bed most of the time, but Belinda wanted nothing to do with the implication that this Christmas might be his last. When she read in the closing line that her mother wanted her and Alisha to come home early to help make the holidays joyful for John, she jumped off the bed, brushed off her mother's concern, and grabbed her coat and scarf. "Mom," she said aloud, "you're the one who needs holiday cheer, not Dad," and she headed for the car.

A week before Christmas, Robert sat behind the wheel, waiting for the car to warm up and for James to finish reorganizing all their luggage and gifts to his liking. Belinda finally said, "Enough, James, Christmas will soon be over," and they left Minneapolis to spend Christmas with Sarah and John. The nearer their journey took them to Tawasa Springs, the more anxious Alisha and Belinda were to see their parents.

Belinda and Alisha took turns driving during the day, then Robert and James drove overnight. A few hours from Tawasa Springs, Robert stopped for the last time for everyone to stretch their tired bodies. When they returned to the car, James stunned the girls. "Lindy, Alisha, listen to me," he said firmly. "I know you don't want to believe it, but you're losing your father."

"No, we're not," Belinda said. "He'll get well. You'll see."

"No—not this time. Sarah has also written to us about John's condition. It has worsened, Belinda, and you need to recognize what you're about to face." James spoke with such conviction that he launched a gloom comparable to the circumstances under which Alisha and Belinda had left Tawasa Springs a year and a half ago.

Back on the road again and no longer denying her father's fate, Belinda's spirits sank. "I know Mom needs help and I should stay home, but I really want to finish this year of school."

"Before you make any decision, Lindy, let's wait and see how things work out. We'll help you reckon with this," Robert promised.

When they arrived, Sarah was doing her best to handle a very serious situation. She had employed a nurse to help care for the seventy-nine-year-old John, who was bed-ridden and needed constant attention. The older sons and daughters came and went daily, helping and crying. With all the caretakers around, John wanted only his wife's presence while he desperately clung to life. Sarah tried to give him comfort, but nothing pleased him as he drifted in and out of consciousness.

When he heard Alisha and Belinda's voices, he struggled to wake up, but his speech was barely audible and he could not focus his once clear blue eyes. Immediately after mumbling a greeting, he asked Belinda, "Now, who are you again?"

Alisha and Belinda slowly left his bedside, knowing that their father had left them already and no longer recognized his own children. The family stayed at John's bedside for the next few days as he clung to the last stages of life, telling Sarah at last, "Stay with me a little longer." Then he died.

John was laid to rest in the Tawasa Springs community cemetery three days before Christmas, casting a pall over the holidays. After the funeral, friends and relatives filled the Devinwood house, bringing food and flowers or just dropping by to visit. Sarah knew the grieving process would eventually run its course, and that, as the sole occupant of an empty house, life would take on a very different hue.

Charlie was among the first to visit. He was the Charlie that Alisha remembered, and he surprised everyone by bringing his new girlfriend, Leah Rubens. Charlie and James resumed their friendship, which helped relieve some of the gloom surrounding the Devinwoods. James teased Alisha about being jealous of Leah, but only after realizing how happy she really was for her friend. When Charlie and Leah were ready to leave, they invited everyone to a Christmas Eve party.

"It's also an engagement party," Charlie said to Alisha, taking her hand. "Leah and I are getting married."

"Charlie, I couldn't be happier for you," Alisha said and covered his hand with hers, "but if this means I'm losing you, it'll hurt."

"If you lost me," Charlie said, gently brushing her hair off her face, "it was when you showed up with Adam at the picnic. If it's our friendship you're talking about, that's forever." They hugged each other and walked on to the car in silence. Before Charlie opened his door, he whispered in her ear, "Everyone will be there."

"Message received," Alisha said.

Sarah's telephone rang four short rings, a pause, and two more rings, meaning someone was calling her on her new, shared telephone line. Not far away, three other families were also counting the number of rings.

"Don't say anything you don't want the world to know," Sarah warned the girls as she answered, greeted Kate, and handed the receiver to Alisha. Kate was inviting Alisha and her brothers to spend the following afternoon with her. Robert watched and frantically shook his head. Alisha nodded pleas of yes to Robert, while saying, "We can't make it tomorrow Aunt Kate, but I think we can make it Christmas Eve afternoon. Will that be okay?"

Robert acquiesced. "Only for you, Sis," he said, squeezing her shoulder

Alisha was surprised at how old Kate looked. Her gestures were shaky as she struggled to find words to explain her actions of almost two decades ago. Over time, Alisha had become numb to the abandonment issue, and although sometimes fragile, her relationship with Kate could no longer be broken. She watched Robert struggle to maintain his composure and then his eyes retreated into a blank stare, isolating himself. *That's how he has survived,* Alisha thought.

James interrupted, "Aunt Kate, there has to be a better reason for chucking us off to an orphanage than these long-winded excuses you're asking us to believe. What exactly are you *not* telling us?"

Robert excused himself but soon returned with his hands full of prescription bottles he found on the bathroom shelf. "Aunt Kate, what are these?"

Kate sighed and slowly explained the manic-depressive disease she and Angeni inherited and why she and Hank did not keep the children. "I know we could've done things differently, and Lord knows if I could turn back the time, I would. I'm exhausted from the guilt, and I've stopped taking the medicine. I don't want to go on this way."

Alisha instantly went to her side and James followed, but Robert was not yet ready to yield. "Aunt Kate, why did you wait this long to tell us, when you knew we needed and deserved an explanation?"

"I didn't know where you were."

"You could have told us when we were here for

Martin's funeral; why not then?" Robert asked with a pained look back on his face.

Kate knew she was defeated. "I don't know. I've never known, and I *don't* have a good answer for you now. I've carried this burden long enough and have one request: If you think you might ever forgive me, do it now."

Late in the afternoon, Alisha and her brothers left Kate asleep and alone in her misery. They had been unable to help, except to telephone her doctor and make her take her medicine. They did not have an answer for her either.

$\oint$

The Christmas Eve party was over. Charlie and Leah's engagement was official. Alisha was delighted with Caroline and her new husband. James helped buffer the tension when Ellie and her fiancé arrived; then Robert, James, and Belinda walked out with them when the party ended. Alisha and Adam lingered after the last guests were gone, reluctant to leave the happiness that filled Charlie's house and to face the uncertainty of their relationship. Near midnight, Leah looked at her watch and asked Charlie to take her home. The two couples walked together to their cars, each couple anticipating their future.

Alisha went driving with Adam, and they ended up at the lake. "This is where it all began," Alisha said, turning away from the warmth she felt looking at Adam.

"Seems like such a short time ago," Adam finished, leaning against the window to increase the distance between them.

"So much has happened," Alisha said.

Adam turned to her. "Yes, I know. Alisha, look at me. I want to be back in your life, and more than ever, and I want you back in mine."

They fell into an almost comfortable discussion about Adam's pending divorce, his living arrangements, and Alisha's growing compulsion to pursue a career in music.

Alisha turned away again. "It's funny, Adam—not *ha ha* funny—but *weird*. I've wanted to be with you and nobody else since that first night here at this lake, but now after all we've been through, just thinking about spending our lives together seems strange. In fact, I'm convinced that *we* are not meant to be."

Adam knew the words he was about to utter were a mistake, but said them anyway. "Okay, Alisha, maybe it *would* be best for you to forget about me and focus on music until I get through law school—"

After all the pain Alisha had gone through, a fury rose inside her. "What do you mean?" she said. "Don't you think it's a little late to prescribe what's best for me? It might come as a surprise to you, but I don't need your permission to do anything, to feel anything, and most of all, although it's what I prefer, your presence is no longer required!"

Adam scrunched down in the seat. *Typical Alisha argument.* "No, I'm not at all surprised," he murmured.

When the silence overcame Alisha's anger, Adam

straightened up, reached for her hand, and softly brushed a strand of hair from her eyes. "Remember, in the beginning I asked for you to be patient and give me a little time to fix things?"

The sweetness of that day came back, bringing her close to tears. "Yes, I remember," Alisha whispered.

"Well, I'm telling you again, some day, somehow, some way, we'll be together again. That's a promise."

Adam drew Alisha close to his chest, and she rested her head on their clasped hands. They sat in the stillness of this curious night until headlights suddenly beamed directly through the rear window. Shocked out of his trance, Adam bolted from the car, shouting, "Lock the car!" and rushed toward the headlights but stopped short when he recognized Robert's car and saw Belinda in the passenger seat.

Robert saw the chance he'd been waiting for. He jumped out of the car and began shouting at Adam, "What do you think you're doing? Don't you think she's been through enough? Do you think I'm going to let you hurt her anymore?"

Adam tried in vain to defend himself, "Look man, I wouldn't do that, I—"

As though Adam had not spoken, Robert said, "Leave her alone—I'm telling you to just *leave her alone.*"

Alisha listened to the exchange between Robert and Adam and knew her brother was right and that Adam had no defense. Disheartened, she slowly picked up her purse and got out of Adam's car and into Robert's.

Belinda moved to the back seat and hugged her sister. "Are you all right?"

"As all right as I'll be for a while," Alisha said. "How did you know where to find me?"

"When we got home, Robert was worried and insisted we look for you. James told us exactly where you would be and that you'd be with Adam."

"I wish we were still at Charlie's party. It was a lot more fun." Alisha slouched back against the seat.

Robert continued his barrage of words and Adam kept trying to defend himself. When it sounded like the battle of words was calming down, Robert suddenly swung his fist and hit Adam square on his jaw, surprising even himself. "That one's for her," he said and got in his car and sped off while Adam was picking himself up.

Neither Alisha nor Belinda said anything to Robert.

"I know he may not have deserved that, Alisha, but I wanted him to understand that he's dealing with both of us now," Robert said unapologetically.

Alisha hid her face in her hands, shutting out the world. *It's okay, Alisha. Let them work it out. They both love you.*

The whisper was unexpected, leaving her warm. Sitting in the back seat of Robert's car on this cold winter night, Alisha hugged Belinda again, a little tighter this time, and understood the different kinds of love from three of the most important people in her life.

𝄞

On Christmas Day, Robert suggested that Alisha and Belinda drive Sarah around town to look at Christmas decorations. He had awakened that morning realizing he could not forsake Kate, no matter her reasons for what she did. A reality about how much power a person has to change lives had shaken him during the night, and by morning, he had divided people into two categories: those who use their power purposefully to help or hurt someone and those who use their power with no thought of consequences, good or bad, to anyone else's life. In Robert's estimation, Kate helplessly fell into the latter, and he knew he would see his aunt as often as necessary to reconcile their relationship.

Robert chuckled when he realized he didn't regret hitting Adam last night, but decided to walk over to see him and apologize anyway. Adam, surprised to see Robert walking toward his house, hurried to the door to meet him. He remembered Robert's anger and had to be sure inviting him in would be safe for Jacob.

"Sorry, I shouldn't have hit you so hard," Robert said, seeing the bruise on Adam's face.

"Don't worry; I probably deserved it. I'll be okay in a year or two," Adam said and shook Robert's hand.

Robert sat on the sofa watching Adam care for his fifteen-month-old son Jacob, and he felt jealous. "I think I've waited much too long to start a family."

"Jacob is what I live for." Adam looked up. "Robert, I

want you to know I would've done things very differently if I could turn back the clock."

Robert laughed. "You and Aunt Kate both! She said those exact words yesterday."

"Well, sometimes, if we're very lucky, some of us get a second chance to fix our mistakes," Adam said and smiled.

"Don't wait as long as Aunt Kate did."

"You can count on that," Adam promised.

Kate came to visit the afternoon before Belinda and the Copper siblings left. Sarah sat with them and listened to Kate give her account of the Millwater family history and Indian heritage, talking most about growing up with Angeni, her spirit-angel sister. At dusk, Robert, James, and Alisha walked Kate to her car. Sarah followed, looking at the perfectly clear sky and the moon just beginning to glow. She missed John.

James opened the car door. Alisha released Kate's hand and asked, "Aunt Kate, why didn't you tell me about our father and the Copper family?"

Kate's smile fell away. "Asyah sang and played the banjo at church," she said and hurriedly got in and grasped the steering wheel. "I have to get home before dark."

"I know," Alisha said kindly. "You didn't like him though, did you, Aunt Kate?"

"I couldn't. He never liked me. If he had, he would have shared my sister with me, but he didn't. He kept her away from me." Kate closed the door, turned the ignition, and lowered the window. "I'm sorry," she said and drove away.

Sarah was speechless—and cold—walking back to the house with Alisha, Robert, and James. Fighting back tears, Sarah marveled at Kate's perception of Asyah and Angeni's marriage. She knew Kate could never take any responsibility for the fractured relationship with her sister. After hearing Kate talk that night, she shuddered at the thought of Angeni never escaping from the confines of living with Kate, of never experiencing her marriage, and of never bearing her beautiful children.

Robert finally broke the silence. "I know this is from a young boy's perspective, but to me, my parents always seemed happy. Do you think they were, Aunt Sarah?"

"Yes, they were," Sarah said, "there's no doubt about that. If Angeni had stayed with Kate, their existence would have been sad indeed. Kate survived her disorder because Angeni married, unintentionally freeing her sister to find a husband and the care she needed. None of us knew about their disease until Angeni died, but Asyah always thought Kate had a problem because of the way she hovered and thought of herself as Angeni's mother. I know he loved Angeni and you children and did everything he could to protect you. Keeping Angeni away from Kate was his way of protecting her from her sister's unnatural control. I know my brother and Angeni were happy—it showed."

When they reached the house, Sarah said, "I loved Asyah's music. Robert, I know you must remember the story about how your father learned to play the cowbells."

"Yes, I do. Grandpa Copper gave Daddy the banjo for his—"

"…sixth birthday," James took over. With a staccato and exaggerated bass voice, he finished the story as a rhythmic oration. "There stood Grandma watchin' Daddy sittin' on the floor makin' noise tappin' a spoon on pots and pans. *How weird*, Grandma thought. When Daddy started walking, he got even weirder. One day, he followed Grandpa to the barnyard and walked straight to the cows because he liked the jangle and tinkle of cowbells. *How weird*, Grandpa thought—he and Grandma thought alike," James explained. "But wait! Daddy went right up to a cow and took off her cowbell. 'Oh, I'm gonna get you boy,' Grandpa said and tried to scare Daddy, but it didn't work. Daddy kept going back, getting him a cowbell, and making noise. Grandpa said, 'I'm gonna fix you, boy' and gave him a banjo. Grandma and Grandpa lived happily ever after—couldn't hear with all that noise, but they were happy."

Reverting to his normal voice, James said, "However, Daddy did have an ear for music, and in a few years, he started playing with local musicians, and when he grew up he had a powerful baritone voice and sang with small bands—and to us." James turned to Robert. "Remember, Robert, the night Alisha was born, how loud Daddy sang on the front porch—the whole world could hear."

"Yes, I remember. He sang *Blue Moon of Kentucky*. I still like that song. You left off my favorite part of the story though. I liked how he ended the story, and I quote: 'As far back as I can remember, music was my life—that is, until you boys came along.'"

"After Daddy died, Robert told that story at least once a week," James said. Sarah smiled and cried at the same time.

𝄞

After Christmas, Alisha continued studying at the Ross Music School. Living with Robert and James felt right—like a family. She enjoyed their close relationship and no longer felt the urge to return to Tawasa Springs. She was home.

In the spring, after graduating from nursing school, Belinda surprised everyone by secretly applying for medical school while her teachers and classmates tried to convince her that being admitted was impossible. Belinda was not deterred; after all, she was the daughter of a woman who had taught her that miracles were not only possible but routine.

Belinda planned to be a doctor *and a wife.* Mark had been discharged from the Army and was coming home. They planned to marry in Tawasa Springs and relocate to Mark's new job on the east coast.

Alisha was very proud of her sister. "Lindy," she said, "I can't wait to get sick so I can go to *Doctor Belinda Howard,* who will make me well again."

Chapter 31

Robert shook Alisha and whispered loudly, "Wake up, wake up."

She roused herself, asking, "What for? Is it over?"

"No," he whispered, helped her stand, and guided her to the aisle.

They had arrived late and were sitting in the back row, and the last thing Alisha remembered was saying to Belinda, "If Robert hadn't insisted on coming to this recital, we could be having dinner and planning your wedding instead of sitting on these hard metal chairs listening to music I've played a million times."

The highlight of the Ross Music School annual recital was awarding scholarships to graduating students. "Alisha Copper. Miss Alisha Copper, please come forward," a male voice intoned.

Robert had known about the award since the director of Ross telephoned to inform him, "I'm submitting an application on Alisha's behalf to the Philadelphia Music Hall. I don't want her to be disappointed if it doesn't work out, so don't tell her. Just make sure she attends the recital."

Convincing Alisha had not been easy. Robert knew she and Belinda were planning the wedding, and as he read the program, he watched her squirm out of the corner of his eye. When Robert mentioned the scholarship awards, Alisha had argued, "That's no reason to go; I'm not getting one. The director is just trying to get everyone to go to the recital."

When Alisha heard the announcer say, "... presented to Miss Alisha Copper," her senses came into focus. She was at the front of the aisle before she remembered that she had not applied for a scholarship, but she walked onto the stage gasping as Mrs. Flowers suddenly appeared beside her. Alisha had not seen her favorite music teacher since she was eight years old, but there was Annie Flowers glowing in her bright red dress. Alisha then noticed what she remembered the most—a flower in her hair the exact color of her dress.

Student and teacher embraced and wept, while the director presented the award to Mrs. Flowers's star student, a full residential scholarship to the Philadelphia Music Hall, the most prestigious school in the country. Robert and Belinda stood with the rest of the audience and applauded their sister.

When Mrs. Flowers left Tawasa Springs ten years earlier, she had moved to Philadelphia to be near her daughter. A well-known music school, also located in Philadelphia, needed an administrator. The Philadelphia Music Hall hired Mrs. Flowers to chair a permanent committee to select future students. A benefactor funded the scholarships and each committee member scoured the country each year, choosing one student to join their elite residential program. Mrs. Flowers had located Alisha at the Ross Music School and kept up with her progress. When she received the application from Ross, Alisha was her clear choice.

Alisha stood before the audience, unsure whether she was more elated about the award or about being with Mrs. Flowers again. Both, she decided.

Chapter 32

The dressing room was ghostly quiet. Solitude surrounded Alisha like an old friend and she sensed the spirits of past performers hovering, melding with her own. They were in costume and excited to recapture their performance along with hers. *When they first performed here in ages past, did they travel willingly or did they resist the gift of their birth and complicate their journey? Did they also fight fearsome monsters, or did they embrace success as a long sought-after lover?*

Alisha stepped into a long ivory satin gown that matched her sun-streaked hair. She and Belinda had spent their summer vacation at the beach, the first time they had been together since Belinda married and they began school again. The dress left Alisha's right shoulder exposed and draped over her body perfectly—*Mom, you're a genius.*

She fastened a gold chain around her neck. The chain supported a heart-shaped locket, holding the picture of her and Adam at the lake. She received the necklace the week after she returned Adam's engagement ring, and wore it every day. *Adam, you are the love of my life.*

Alisha stood before the mirror, admiring her gown and fully appreciating the life Sarah made for her. In fact, Sarah's nurturing and support—even the discipline—and the love she was finally able to show, all served to bring about this night. *Thank you, Mom.*

Suddenly, James rushed in. "Hurry, Alisha, the hall is filling up," he said breathlessly and rushed out again. Robert played his role well as head of the family, but tonight yielded to James's eagerness to run the show.

Alisha sighed. *Martin, somehow I hope you're here, too.*

The first offstage buzzer sounded, and then a voice announced, "Fifteen minutes to curtain." Alone again and feeling isolated—mentally and physically—Alisha thought about the long practice sessions, first to escape fear, then to conquer fear, and then to master the gift providence had handed her. She knew her musical career could rise or fall on this performance. She thought about her family and friends, pushing and prodding her over the years—now it was all up to her.

Alisha sat down at the dressing table. The invitation to perform at Carnegie Hall arrived when Alisha thought her life would be very different. Adam had come to Philadelphia to propose marriage, and she had accepted without hesitation. Then Mrs. Flowers appeared during the final year of the resident program, delivering the invitation from Carnegie that changed her life once more.

Mrs. Flowers had said, "If you perform successfully at Carnegie, Alisha, you'll be invited to travel on a worldwide tour with an elite group of musicians, guaranteeing your success as a concert pianist."

Ten minutes to curtain. Now it was time to steel her nerves, walk onto the stage, bow as the producer instructed, and play that magnificent piano the best that she had ever played.

"I can't do it," Alisha said to her reflection in the mirror and then looked away to escape the fear staring back at her.

Why? Mrs. Flowers still passionately shares her love for music with you, and her faith in you has never wavered.

Alisha straightened herself up and looked in the mirror again, breathed deeply, stood, and placed a pink rose in her hair from the bouquet on the dressing table and felt that familiar calming warmth. *This one's for you, Mrs. Flowers.*

Five minutes. A new tidal wave of fear rose in her chest just as the door swung open and Belinda hurried in along with Robert and James. Kate was holding onto Robert and clutching a small gift. James, even more fidgety, took the gift from Kate, rushed over, bowed, and presented it to Alisha, then snatched it back and ripped off the wrapping.

Kate smiled. "It's the same gift, Alisha, but this time, it's for the right reason."

She's still trying in the only way she knows how to make things right with you while she has time.

Alisha took the open case from James and withdrew a stunning diamond watch. She rushed to Kate and kissed her, unable to hold back her tears.

James removed his handkerchief and patted away Alisha's tears. He fastened her watch to the exact fit, smelled the rose he had displaced, and put it back in her hair. He headed out the door, repositioning his handkerchief and tugging Alisha to the stage entrance.

Belinda and Robert stood motionless for a moment, watching the frenzied activity, and then followed Alisha and James. Kate looked like she might faint at any moment, but she smiled through it all and held onto Belinda and Robert.

James pushed Alisha to the stage entrance. "Alisha, this is the world where you'll always belong."

Alisha kissed his cheek and said, "I know that now." She turned away from her brother and walked onto the stage. She closed her eyes, focusing her mind and soul on her music, letting her imagination guide her fingers through the introductory notes.

The curtain rose and applause filled the Carnegie Lyceum Recital Hall. Alisha bowed and saw Mrs. Flowers, a rose glowing in her hair. Alisha touched her own rose and smiled, then looked upward and closed her eyes. When she opened her eyes and raised her arm, she imagined a white songbird alight on her palm and heard its song, perfect and chilling. Tonight she would release the music of the songbird, as Sarah envisioned.

At intermission, Alisha returned to her dressing room to a fresh bouquet of roses that filled the room with a sweet fragrance. She knew who sent them before she read the card scripted in Adam's handwriting. *I'll be waiting—always.*

Alisha concluded the program with her best ever performance. For two hours, the audience had been captivated by her music and enthusiastic presentation. The concert ended and the applause was deafening.

Alisha backed through the closing curtain and stood by the piano. She watched anxiously as Amos Bandera, the producer, walked toward her with the Tribune reporter. Bandera stood for a moment simply looking at Alisha while her friends and family walked onto the stage. He raised her hand with his to a burst of applause. Bandera suddenly smiled and held up his other hand, quieting her fans. His white hair and beard shimmered as the stagehands narrowed the revolving spotlights to encircle the producer and his performer. The Tribune reporter photographed the scene as Amos bellowed, "Miss Copper, you're my star now!"

The following morning, Alisha laid the open New York Tribune aside and alternately glanced at the print and watched the sun rising over the Hudson River from her rooftop suite in the Hilton Hotel. Below the newspaper article was a photograph of her and Amos Bandera with their arms raised high.

Alisha whispered his declaration, *"Miss Copper, you're my star now."*

|LIVE

listen|imagine|view|experience

AUDIO BOOK DOWNLOAD INCLUDED WITH THIS BOOK!

In your hands you hold a complete digital entertainment package. Besides purchasing the paper version of this book, this book includes a free download of the audio version of this book. Simply use the code listed below when visiting our website. Once downloaded to your computer, you can listen to the book through your computer's speakers, burn it to an audio CD or save the file to your portable music device (such as Apple's popular iPod) and listen on the go!

How to get your free audio book digital download:

1. Visit www.tatepublishing.com and click on the e|LIVE logo on the home page.
2. Enter the following coupon code:
   1995-4945-3725-1003-55d6-900f-57c4-4b93
3. Download the audio book from your e|LIVE digital locker and begin enjoying your new digital entertainment package today!